G000111529

£2.50

MOTHER'S
BOYS

By the same author

Novels
THE GODSEND
SWEETHEART, SWEETHEART
THE REAPING
THE MOORSTONE SICKNESS
THE KINDNESS OF STRANGERS
MADELEINE

Non-fiction
CRUELLY MURDERED:
Constance Kent and the Killing at Road Hill House
PERFECT MURDER:
A Century of Unsolved Homicides (With Stephen Knight)

MOTHER'S BOYS

Bernard Taylor

GRAFTON BOOKS

A Division of the Collins Publishing Group

LONDON GLASGOW
TORONTO SYDNEY AUCKLAND

Grafton Books
A Division of the Collins Publishing Group
8 Grafton Street, London W1X 3LA

Published by Grafton Books 1988

British Library Cataloguing in Publication Data

Taylor, Bernard
  Mother's boys.
  I. Title
  823'.914[F]   PR6070.A884

ISBN 0-246-13253-1

Printed in Great Britain by
Robert Hartnoll (1985) Ltd, Bodmin

for Brian and Ken

ONE

The bridge would soon be ready.

On the little patch of waste ground behind the shed, the two young boys couldn't be seen from the house. As Kester bent forward over the ground the bright sun shone on his light, sandy hair. It touched, too, the back of his suntanned neck and exposed the faint stain that rimmed the inner edge of his shirt collar. His eyes, the colour of the pale blue sky, were narrowed in concentration. His mouth was a tight, thin little line, his brow puckered. He was thirteen-and-a-half.

With one end of the wire firmly attached to an upright stick, he drew it as taut as he could and wound the other end around the stick on the far side of the shallow pit. The pit, about two feet across, had been scooped out of the earth. The loose soil lay beside it in a little pile.

'This'll be okay.'

This was merely an observation. When he had spoken he glanced up, his face coming out of the shadow, the sun catching on his freckled nose. Kneeling opposite him in the dry, dusty earth, his twelve-and-a-half-year-old brother Michael smiled and nodded in agreement. His hair was a little darker in tone than Kester's – a sort of light mouse-brown – but his eyes were the same colour.

The eyes of both boys were now lowered again to concentrate on the structure they had erected. From beside him, Kester took up a narrow piece of plywood and carefully propped it at a shallow angle against one of the uprights. 'Almost there now.' He reached down again, took up some scraps of newspaper, twisted them into small coils and placed them in the bottom of the pit.

'The fuel . . .'

7

He stretched out his hand and Michael put into it a few dry sticks and other bits of wood. Kester placed it all on top of the paper, then sat back on his heels, surveying the results of the work.

'What d'you think?' he asked.

'I think it's ready, don't you?'

'Yes, I reckon.'

'Shall we start, then?'

'Yes. Let's have the prisoners.'

Michael held out an old Maxwell House coffee jar and Kester took it and removed the lid. The writhing green shapes inside were the caterpillars which, a while before, the boys had picked off the cabbages. Their father had come down the garden path as they had been at work, and seeing them plucking the caterpillars from the cabbage leaves he had smiled his approval: 'Good boys – that's what I like to see.'

Tipping the jar over the slanting strip of plywood, Kester shook out some of the caterpillars. Three or four of them fell onto the wood, while a further six or seven fell onto the earth. These Kester quickly picked up and placed on the plywood strip. Like those already there, they uncurled and then began to crawl away, some up and some down. Kester loosely set the lid back on the jar and placed the jar on the ground beside him.

'Here.'

At Michael's voice, Kester took from his younger brother's outstretched hand a long, needle-pointed thorn. He tested the point against his thumb, nodded, then bent towards the writhing caterpillars. He gave his attention first to those that were moving down the plywood slope, towards the earth. After turning them by means of the thorn, he then prodded them, jabbing their tails with the thorn's point, forcing them to move upwards. 'Go on, you little fuckers,' he muttered. Michael, bending forward, eyes fixed on the moving caterpillars, nodded. 'Little fuckers,' he added.

In a little while most of the caterpillars were grouped at the top of the plywood slope, a couple of them were actually on the stick, and another on the wire itself. Kester tipped the jar and more caterpillars fell onto the earth.

When nearly all of them were on the plywood slope, Kester took a box of matches from his pocket. Then, placing a screw of paper at the foot of the slope, he struck a match and lit it.

'Now – look at 'em go.'

With the flame and the smoke below them, the caterpillars had begun to move quickly up the slope, the few that were too low and too slow quickly succumbing to the smoke and heat and falling off. In a very short time many of the caterpillars were strung out along the wire bridge, moving steadily across, away from the torment. When the wire was covered with the moving green shapes Kester lit the paper in the pit.

As the flames leaped up the caterpillars writhed, their heads rearing. Then, before the boys' watching eyes the bodies began to curl, turn brown and fall, one after another, into the furnace below.

When all the caterpillars were dead, the boys sat back on their heels. Kester gave a little sigh, showing his dissatisfaction. It had all taken so little time, and it hadn't been nearly as interesting as he had imagined it would be.

The fire died. Kester got up, yanked apart the construction of the sticks and the wire and, using his feet, began to push the earth back into the hole. Michael helped him. When it was done they stamped down the soft earth with their shoes, flattening it.

Stepping to the side, Kester looked down at the earth, brushed his palms together, rubbing off the dust, then looked around him. 'What shall we do now?' He sighed again. 'I wish it were tomorrow already, and we were going to see Jude.'

The following morning Kester sat in the front passenger seat of the car beside his father. The other children sat in the back, Daisy in between Michael and Ben. The latter sat on the right, his face to the window, gazing out. Like Kester and Michael, he wore a white shirt, blue jeans and trainers – which took him as close to his brothers as any likeness in appearance was

9

possible. His eyes were of a deeper blue than theirs, his hair of a much darker brown and much finer in texture, and whereas their faces seemed, in his eyes, to be formed, his own seemed to him to be soft, plump and shapeless. At two months off his tenth birthday he was, too, a good deal shorter than they, and lacked as well their developing breadth, particularly that of Kester.

Leaning slightly towards Ben, eight-year-old Daisy sat gazing through solemn brown eyes at the scenery that moved by the window. She wore a pale blue ribbon in her dark, shoulder-length hair, and had put on her favourite dress. Trimmed with white piping, it was blue, with small flowers on it. It was getting a little small for her now, a little tight under the arms, added to which it could have done with a longer spell under the iron. She had insisted on wearing it, though, in spite of Robert's suggestions to the contrary. On her lap she held a book of Hans Andersen's stories, which Netta had given her the week before. Robert had told Daisy that she would have no chance to do any reading, but she had insisted.

'Did you put on a clean shirt, Michael?'

At the question, Michael looked up and saw his father's eyes, in the mirror, flick up from the road ahead and catch his own.

'Yes, Dad.'

'Good boy. And you, Kester?'

'Yes, Dad.'

'Good.'

Robert was thirty-seven years old. He was a tall man; sitting in the car its ceiling cleared his head only by an inch or so. His dark hair – darker than Daisy's – was beginning to thin at the crown. Although he hardly noticed the changes – they crept up so gradually – he was nevertheless very much aware of the advancing years. Still, things would be all right now. The children were his, and now he had Netta, too. Everything would be okay now. There had been a time, just over two years ago, when he had no idea what was going to happen, and he had had visions of losing the children to Judith, of being left alone, and remaining alone. And with those visions he had looked further

10

ahead, seeing himself waking one day to realize that he was old, with the children grown up and making lives of their own, independent, after childhoods in which he'd played no real part. That wouldn't happen now. There was nothing else that Judith could do to him.

With Swindon and its surrounding villages behind them, the Citroën moved out onto the motorway. From the seat beside him came Kester's voice: 'Just over an hour and a half and we'll be there.' And then Michael's voice murmuring in agreement: 'Yes, about that.'

It was strange how very close the two elder boys were. Robert had had brothers of his own, but they had not been as close as Kester and Michael. He could recall that, as a child, the differences in age between himself and his elder and younger brothers, though slight, had been enough to separate them. They had each of them chosen friends from outside – which was the way it had been in other families he had known. Only in their maturing had he and his brothers found any mutual closeness. With Kester and Michael, though, it was different. The year between them seemed to count as nothing. Ever since they had been very small they had spent all their time together – not seeking, and presumably not wanting, companionship from elsewhere.

Moving his eyes briefly from the road, Robert glanced up into the mirror and looked at Michael's reflection. How like Judith he was. Like Kester, too – the same pale blue eyes, the same short, blunt nose, the same narrow jaw, the same freckles.

His eyes went back to the road, wary of the weekend drivers, idiots too fast or too slow, too reckless or too cautious for the good of themselves or anyone else. They were always there.

'Will the sun keep shining, Daddy, d'you think?' Daisy asked.

He glanced up into the mirror and saw her slightly anxious expression. She didn't want to be cooped up in Judith's flat. 'Yes,' he said, 'it looks as if it will.'

It was just before eleven-thirty when Robert and the children arrived outside Judith's home in Streatham in south London.

11

She had taken a ground-floor flat in one of twin, purpose-built blocks in a quiet, tree-lined street. She had been there for just a few months now, following periods in a succession of furnished rooms. She was buying the lease of the flat on a mortgage, the deposit having come from the divorce settlement that Robert had made.

Now, with the car pulled up before the neat front garden of the apartment building, the children piled out, first Kester and Michael and then Ben and Daisy. Trooping into the foyer they found Judith – who had been watching for them from the window – standing in her doorway, beaming at them her bright-orange-lipped smile. The two elder boys cried out, 'Jude! Oh, Jude!' and ran to her. At their words Robert inwardly winced. He hated the way they called her by her given name, or its diminutive. Judith had long ago insisted, though.

Now as they reached out to her she bent to them, wrapping her arms around them, smothering their faces with her kisses. Her expression was all happiness. Turning, Robert saw Daisy and Ben hanging back, waiting. And then Judith, almost as an afterthought, released Kester and Michael and held out her arms to the younger pair. They went to her, and she hugged them and kissed them. Then, raising her head, she said with a wide smile, 'Oh, it's so lovely to have all my children with me again!'

Since the divorce Judith had kept up a regular contact with the children, seeing them about once a month, sometimes all four of them, but more often than not just the two elder boys. When all four visited, as on this Saturday, they would remain with their mother just for the day. When Kester and Michael went alone, however, they usually stayed the whole weekend; on occasions, in the summer or at Eastertime, spending a whole week with her. Whoever was going, though, and for whatever period of time, Robert would drive them up and bring them back home again. He hated the journey, but there was nothing else to be done. A few months before, with Judith promising to be at Paddington station to meet them, he had sent Kester and Michael by train. Judith hadn't been at the station, however, and didn't appear there for almost an hour after the boys' arrival. Robert, hearing about it on their return to Swindon, had been furious; not that the boys had minded much about their mother's late appearance; not in the least – to them it had been something of an adventure. Later, when Robert had tackled Judith about the episode, she had made lame excuses and then gone on to talk of it being good for the boys, it having taught them something in the way of initiative and survival. From then on, he determined, he would, as he had done in the past, drive them to London himself.

'Right,' Judith was saying now. 'You children go on inside, will you? I'll be there in a minute.'

Obediently they went on into the flat. Judith watched them go, then turned back to Robert, her smile now a little uncertain. 'Hello, Robert.'

'Hello, Judith.' The constraint, the awkwardness, was like a fog. He doubted now that it would ever be different. 'How are you?'

She nodded. 'Oh, fine. And you?'

'Yes, fine, thanks.' He gave a shrug and took a half-step away. 'Well . . .'

'I suppose you've got to dash off again, have you? You never stay.'

'No, well . . . There's not a lot of point, is there?' Then quickly he added, 'Anyway, there are several things I have to get from the shops.'

She smiled. 'That's convenient for you.'

As they stood there facing one another he realized how his feelings towards her had changed. He had believed, at the time of the divorce and the custody hearings, that he would hate her for ever. But it had gone, that hatred. Now he felt just a mild sympathy. She was what she was; she would never change.

'When d'you think you'll be back?' Judith asked.

'When the children are ready to go, I guess. You tell me.'

'I thought we might – have a little picnic . . .'

'Good idea.' He half turned, glancing at the sunny day

beyond the translucent windows beside the foyer door. 'It looks as if you've got the perfect weather for it.'

'No, I mean – I was hoping you'd join us.'

'Me?'

'Yes, will you?'

'Aw, Judith, you don't want me around. Besides, I thought I might – '

'Please,' she broke in. 'It would be nice. And the children would like it so.'

He hesitated for a few moments, and one moment too many. 'Okay.' He nodded. 'I'll try. What time?'

'You'll try.' A faint smile, all sagacity, accompanied the note of resignation in her voice.

'Yes, I will – really. What time?'

'Well, we're going to have lunch now and – listen, why don't you come in and have lunch too?'

'No, I'm sorry, I can't. I'd better get going.'

'Oh, all right. Well, then, shall we say – about three-thirty?'

'Okay.'

'If you're not here we'll go on down.'

'To the common?'

'Yes. Look for us round by the tennis courts.'

Robert drove from Woodfield Avenue into a nearby street, parked, got out, and walked up to Streatham High Road. There he did some shopping and then went into a pub where he ordered half a pint of lager and some lunch – steak-and-kidney pie, potatoes and beans.

Sitting at a corner table he slowly, mechanically, ate the dull food, making it last. A visit to the pub – it was often part of the pattern when he brought the children up to Judith's for the day. Then, after this scratch lunch he would find something else to fill in the rest of the time before the children had to be picked up again. Often, usually during the cold, winter months he would kill the time by going to the pictures, or perhaps driving on into the West End to visit a gallery. At other times, in the summer, when the weather allowed, he would sit in the park

14

and read, or work on the planning of his lessons for the coming week.

He wondered briefly why, today, Judith wanted him to join her and the children on their picnic. The two of them could have little to say to one another after all that had happened. Still, he had more or less agreed now . . .

On leaving the pub he went back to the car where he put the bags of shopping into the boot and took a paperback from the glove compartment. After locking the car he continued on down the street towards the common. It was still not three o'clock when he arrived and he found himself a quiet spot among the trees on the west side and there, sitting beneath a large oak, opened his book. He read for almost an hour, then got up, left the shelter of the trees and crossed over the road onto the main body of the common.

As he made his way along the asphalt path towards the tennis courts he heard Daisy's voice calling to him: 'Daddy, Daddy, over here!' and looking over to the left he saw her waving to him. As he walked over the grass towards her she ran to him and he swept her up in his arms, briefly holding her against him.

'I thought perhaps you weren't coming,' she said as he set her down. 'I thought you'd be too busy.'

'No, no.' He squeezed her hand. 'I'm never too busy for you, sweetheart.'

Judith, Kester, Michael and Ben were sitting on rugs close to a little group of trees over to one side. When he and Daisy got to them Judith said, 'Daisy thought you weren't coming. I told her you would. I told her you'd promised.'

'I didn't promise,' he said. 'I told you I'd *try*.'

'Did you?' She shrugged. 'Well, anyway, come and sit down. At least you're in time to eat something.'

He sat down on one end of a tartan rug which he recognized as having once belonged to the two of them – like so many of the things that were crammed into Judith's flat. After the divorce and the settlement Judith had taken away her own things and then had gone through the house with a fine-tooth comb, taking whatever else took her eye. The judge had given her fifty per cent of the value of the house and, as she had interpreted it, her choice of its contents, which had turned out to be quite a lot. Robert hadn't cared.

'We've had hamburgers,' Judith said. 'You didn't come, though, so Kester and Mikie ate yours. Still, there's plenty of other stuff.'

Looking at the spread on the cloth before him, Robert could see nothing that took his fancy. There was part of a cheesecake and a cream sponge, while nearby lay a packet of chocolate biscuits. The children were drinking Coke and lemonade.

'Did you get your shopping done?' Judith asked him.

'What? Oh, yes.' He nodded.

She looked at him in silence for a moment, smiled at him, then said, 'Well – have something to eat.'

'No, thanks. I'm not hungry. I had something in a pub.'

'In a pub,' she repeated. 'You'll have some tea, though, won't you?'

'Thank you.'

From a thermos she poured tea into a mug. As he drank he looked at her as she sat flanked by Kester and Michael. She was quite beautiful in a colourful, rather extravagant way. Her long, sandy-coloured hair hung down past her shoulders, thick and heavy. In her ears she wore large, gold, gypsy earrings, on her wrists an assortment of bangles. She had on a long skirt, a sort of wrap-around affair with a fringe going diagonally from the waist to the hem, and a light, magenta sweater over a white peasant blouse. Her legs were bare; on her feet were sandals. Her style of dress had so appealed to him once. But that had been years ago, when she had been younger, an energetic art student. It had suited her then, that kind of studied artiness; in a way helping to make up somewhat for what she lacked in actual talent. It didn't work now, though – not on a woman of almost forty-one.

'Oh, by the way, did you get my letter, Jude?' Kester was saying, and Judith put one arm around his shoulders and briefly hugged him to her.

16

'Yes, my darling, I got your letter.' She turned to Michael. 'And yours, too, Mikie. Thank you so much, both of you. They made me *very happy*.'

'And mine?' Ben's voice. 'And Daisy's?'

'Oh, yes, I got yours, too, thank you.' She paused. 'You need to work at your spelling, Ben, you really do.' Raising a hand she brushed back the hair that had fallen across her cheek. As the bangles on her arm slipped down Robert saw the faint scar on her wrist. Residue of one of her token gestures.

Kester, having finished the piece of cheesecake on his plate, asked for some more. Robert frowned. 'Haven't you had enough? God – all this junk food – all that sugar.'

'Oh, don't be such an old grump,' Judith said. 'It won't hurt him. He's a growing boy. He needs to eat well.' As she finished speaking she took Kester's plate and put onto it another slice of the cake. 'And you, Mikie?'

When the cake, biscuits, Coke and lemonade were gone Judith said, 'Well, now – let's see what else I've got for you all.' She pulled a plastic carrier bag towards her, put in a hand and brought out some chocolate bars. She handed them round. 'There you are – one each.' As the children unwrapped the chocolate she turned to Robert. 'I know what you're thinking. But I can spoil them a little, can't I? For God's sake, I only see them once a month.'

As the children ate the chocolate Judith said, 'What would you like to do now? Go back to the flat or stay outside a while longer?'

'Stay outside,' Kester said.

Daisy, pointing off towards the pond, said, 'Ben and I have saved some of our cake for the ducks. Can we go and feed them?'

'Feed the ducks?' Kester said contemptuously. 'Don't be such a kid.' He turned, looking towards the little thicket where Robert had sat to read his book. 'Let's go over there, into the trees. We'll have some fun there.'

When all the remains of the picnic had been packed away in the plastic carrier bags, Judith, Kester and Michael set off across the grass towards the trees on the other side of the road. 'We'll catch you up,' Robert called after them. Reaching out to Daisy with his free hand, he said, 'Come on, let's you and Ben and me go and feed the ducks.'

Ben, though, was already dashing off after the others. 'Kester, Michael,' he called, 'wait for me.'

They didn't wait. Briefly turning to him, Kester said irritably, 'No, you go on with Dad for a bit.'

'But I want to go with you and Mike,' Ben protested.

'Well, you can't. Not yet. Go on back with Dad.'

After a moment Ben turned and reluctantly made his way back to Robert's side, while Kester, Michael and Judith walked on across the grass. It was like two separate camps, Robert thought: Judith, Kester and Michael on one side, Daisy and himself on the other, and Ben somewhere in between, torn, not knowing quite where he belonged. 'Come on, Ben,' Robert said. 'You come with us. We'll catch them up in a little while.'

As they walked towards the pond Robert glanced down at Daisy as she skipped along at his side. He thought of her as she had sat at the picnic beside Ben. The two of them had said so little. In their mother's company over recent times their spirit often seemed to desert them. It was so sad, the way they appeared to become intimidated by her. Almost, she seemed to be becoming a stranger to them – though it was hardly surprising. Since the divorce two years ago they had seen a good deal less of her than had Kester and Michael – and before that time Judith had grown progressively more distant from them, even when they had lived in the same house. Now, the more it was happening, the more Daisy and Ben seemed to be retreating.

It was not so at all with Kester and Michael, though. Judith had never stinted in her rather extravagant demonstrations of love and affection where they were concerned. And in the same way, Judith had never lacked for *their* love. Where they were concerned it seemed to Robert that their separation from her only served to make their affection grow stronger.

*

18

At the edge of the woods Kester looked back. There was no sign now of his father and the others. He, Michael and his mother moved deeper into the shadow of the trees. One could hardly hear the sounds of the distant traffic; the woods were silent but for the sound of birdsong. This was the first time they had visited the common and the woods since his mother had moved into the flat. On the previous visits the weather had kept them indoors.

'I bet you come here all the time when it's fine, don't you?' Michael said. His mother shook her head. 'You must be joking. I wouldn't come to a lonely place like this. Not on my own, anyway.'

'Lonely places are the best,' Kester said.

She smiled down at him. 'I'm not so sure about that.'

'I wouldn't be afraid of being here on my own,' Michael said.

'I don't suppose you would,' Judith said. 'And nor would I be if I had you two strong boys with me.'

Michael moved on ahead, and a minute or two later Kester and Judith followed him into a little clearing with a huge, fallen oak in its centre. Michael had climbed up and was standing on its trunk. He grinned at them as they drew near. Crossing the clearing, Judith sat on one of the lower branches. Kester sat beside her and they watched as Michael began to climb up the slope of the tree-trunk. 'Be careful, Mikie,' Judith called to him. She turned then and sat with her hands in her lap, pale eyes fixed unseeingly on the trees and the shrubbery ahead. A woodpigeon cooed. Kester tilted his head slightly and looked up into Judith's face. She had a faint smile on her face.

'What's up, Jude? What are you smiling for?'

'Oh – thoughts.' Her smile became a little broader.

'What thoughts? Tell me.'

'Well – I'm thinking about – us.'

'You and me?'

'All of us. You, me, Mikie, your father, Ben, Daisy. All of us.'

'What about us?'

She paused, then: 'How is your father today?'

19

'Dad? He's all right. You saw him yourself.'

She shook her head. 'I'm not so sure about him, these days. He's changed over the years. Sometimes he's a mystery to me.'

With a *whoop* Michael came scrambling down the tree-trunk, reached the leaf-strewn floor and then, with another yell, took off through the trees. Judith and Kester watched him until he disappeared.

'What *about* us?' Kester said.

'Oh, I was thinking what it would be like if we were all together again. If I came home.'

'Oh, *Jude*, could you?' There was excitement in Kester's voice. 'Could you really? Sell your flat and give up your job at the shop?'

'Job!' she said contemptuously. 'What job!' She shook her head. 'Oh, that's all finished with. I'm free again now. Free as the air.'

'Oh, Jude, d'you think you could come home again? Would you?'

'Well, we'll have to see. You mustn't say anything to the others, though. Not yet. It's too early.'

'But Mike would – '

'Oh, you can tell *him*,' she said. 'But not the others. Not until it's all settled.'

'Of course not.' He beamed. 'Oh, Jude, I so hope you do come home again. I want you to – so much. You always tell us that one day you will, but it never happens.'

'Ah, but now I think it might.' She touched a gentle hand to his hair. 'You really would like that, wouldn't you?'

'Oh, yes! We both would. So much. Mike and I.'

'Yes, you and Mikie would, I'm sure.' She paused. 'Is your father still seeing his latest lady friend?'

'Netta?'

'Yes, Netta. I see she gave Daisy a book.'

'Yes. She's always bringing little things for us. Little presents.'

Judith raised one eyebrow. 'Really. And for you and Michael too?'

20

'Yes. We've had books from her. And stamps. That sort of thing.'

Judith nodded. 'How long is it now – that your father's been seeing her?'

'Oh – about three months, I think. Something like that.'

'Three months. Well – that's nothing.'

'She's coming round for lunch tomorrow.'

'For lunch, eh?'

'She's come round every Sunday these past few weeks. She cooks lunch for us.'

'Is she a good cook?'

'Not bad.'

There was a little pause, then Judith said, 'Anyway, I'm not worrying about her. It won't last.'

'No, it won't,' Kester agreed.

'No. She's not the first, is she.' It wasn't a question. 'Since I left, I mean.'

'Oh, no. There was that woman from the bank. That stupid Linda. And somebody else. Margaret. I forget her other name.'

'Oh, yes, Margaret. A secretary or something, wasn't she? I remember you telling me.'

'Yes. She was really stupid. Really pathetic.'

'They didn't last long, did they?'

'No. I think he only went out with them a few times.' Kester paused. 'Mind you, he's been seeing *her* a lot. This one.'

'Even so – she won't last either, this – Netta – whatever her name is.' Judith shook her head. 'No, I'm not concerned about her. I have a feeling about these things, and I have a feeling that everything's going to be all right for us. I can tell. I've got an inner sense.'

'Have you?'

'Yes, oh, yes.' She gazed at him for a moment in silence then wrapped her arms around him, drew him to her and kissed him on the forehead. 'Oh, Kester, my dear, I love you so much. It's kept me going through all these – these difficult times – knowing that I have you.'

'You'll always have me,' he said. 'Always.'

21

There came a noise from among the trees and the next moment Michael was coming towards them across the clearing. Breathlessly he threw himself down at Judith's side. She turned to him. 'And will I always have you, too?' she said.

He gazed at her, not understanding. Kester spoke up. 'Yes, you will,' he said. 'You'll have Mike, too. You'll have us both, whatever happens. And we'll be together – for always.'

She held them both to her. 'Yes,' she said, 'we'll be together, for always.' She grinned from one to the other. 'And, a little bird tells me, perhaps that time isn't too far away.'

TWO

'Ah, here you are,' Robert said.

Judith and the boys looked around as he and Ben and Daisy approached from the shelter of the trees. 'Did you feed the ducks?' Judith asked.

'Yes, we did. And Daisy picked you some flowers.'

At his words Daisy went to her mother and held out a little bunch of wild flowers: yellow pimpernel, ox-eyed daisies. Judith thanked her and lifted them to her nose. 'Thank you, darling, they're lovely.'

Robert looked at his watch.

'Time for them to go, is it?' Judith said.

'Yes, it will be by the time we've taken all the stuff back to your flat.'

When Kester and Michael had gathered up the bags they all set off back through the thicket. As they emerged onto the open ground Judith said eagerly, glancing off to the right, 'Oh, there's something I want to show you boys before you go.'

'What's that?' Michael asked.

'You'll see. Come with me.'

Turning, she led the way over the grass towards the houses and flats that bordered the common's edge. The others followed after her. She stopped before a large, rather baroque-looking Victorian house with sandy-coloured walls. Robert, looking up at its turrets, thought how out of place it looked hemmed in as it was by the ugly redbrick blocks of flats. 'What's so special about it?' he said.

'It's The Priory.'

'The Priory?'

'The Priory. Don't you know your criminal history?'

'Oh, is it the scene of some famous crime?' And then he nodded. 'Oh, yes, The Priory. Of course. Charles Bravo.'

'Right. The Bravo mystery. One of the great classic murders in England's history.'

Robert nodded again. 'Charles Bravo, handsome young barrister, married to a beautiful woman with a past. Isn't that it?'

'That's it.'

Kester said quickly, 'What happened, Jude? Tell us what happened.'

'Oh, very mysterious doings,' she said with a touch of relish. 'He was poisoned one night. It happened about a hundred years ago.'

'Who did it? Who poisoned him?'

'Ah, that was never discovered. It might have been his wife. Someone in the house, certainly. But whoever did poor Charlie in got off scot-free. Terrible thought, isn't it – someone you love and trust creeping into your room at night and putting poison into your drinking water. After he'd taken the poison he opened the window and threw up all over the leads of the roof below. The doctors had to scrape it up, the vomit, and put it into jam jars.'

Robert, growing increasingly irritated throughout her discourse, said sharply, 'For God's sake, Judith, I don't think you need to keep on about such a morbid, sickening happening. Remember your audience.'

Frowning, she whipped her head around, as if she would make some sharp retort, but then her expression changed and she said simply, 'My two boys are sensible boys. It won't give *them* bad dreams.'

'You haven't only got your *two* boys here,' Robert said. 'You've got your *three* boys here – *and* your small daughter – or had you forgotten?'

Judith was silent for a moment, then, stepping closer to him, she said with a tight little smile, 'I've only got one thing to say to you.' She put her mouth close to his ear. 'Fuck you, Robert,' she murmured.

*

When the rugs and the remains of the picnic had been deposited at Judith's flat Robert brought the car around to the front entrance. Judith was saying her goodbyes to the children. On the front path Robert stood watching. First Daisy and Ben, brisk and no-nonsense, and then Michael and Kester, lingering, with many hugs and kisses; the pattern as usual. When the final goodbye had been said Robert ushered the children into the car. He turned then to Judith who had followed them out and now stood on the pavement. 'Well, so long, Judith.'

She said quickly, 'Robbie, I want to talk to you for a second.'

Robbie. She had used to call him that in earlier times. Now it sounded off-key after everything that had happened.

'What about?' He was aware of his frown of irritation. Whatever it was, why couldn't she have brought it up earlier? Why wait till now when he was anxious to get away? He stood waiting.

'Not here,' she said. 'Inside.'

He sighed. 'I've got the children settled and – '

'It won't take a minute. Please.'

He nodded reluctantly, bent to murmur a few words to the children, telling them to stay put, then followed Judith back into the flat.

Entering the crowded living room he at once recalled Daisy's earlier question about whether the sun would shine for the afternoon, the faint anxiousness she had shown to be out in the open. He didn't blame her one bit. He had rarely been in any place that made him feel so claustrophobic. During the years that he and Judith had shared the house in Swindon he had felt much the same sensation at times – though to a lesser degree – and he thought again of the way she would pack the place with the various items she picked up from here and there. He had fought against it at the time, refusing to be buried and suffocated by her accumulated possessions. And he had managed, somehow, to keep a little space, to be able to breathe. Then, after Judith had left him (going off to find herself, as she would have it – like Kramer's wife in the film, but not nearly as romantically or attractively), he had gathered up her bits and pieces from where they were scattered all over the house, packed them up in cardboard boxes and stacked them in the garage. Afterwards the house had seemed, blissfully, almost empty. When the divorce had been granted Judith had eagerly taken everything away.

And here it all was. Here, along with the other things she had taken from the house, were all those possessions of hers that he remembered so well. There were the grandfather chairs, the sofa and the chaise longue (none of them promising anything in the way of relaxation), and the old rolltop desk; there were the pictures crowding the walls – Victorian prints, her own abstract and surreal efforts in oils, and the framed posters and original pages from old newspapers. There were the books (so many of them never read, he was certain), the old phonograph with its rearing horn, the pile of old 78s. There were the pot plants, so many – and, as in earlier times, looking to be in need of care and attention – the Victorian screen covered with little coloured scraps of angels and children; the empty birdcage ('But I *must have* it, Robbie. I can't possibly live without it another *moment*'); the row of Victorian dolls ('No, Daisy, they're not for *playing* with, my dear'); the Russian dolls, the stacks of ancient magazines, and seashells, the bits of rock; the iceskates hanging beside one of the bookshelves, when the closest she had ever got to ice was with a gin-and-tonic. Robert saw it all and wondered how he could ever have lived with half of it.

'Sit down, Robert, please. Don't stand.'

'The children are waiting . . .'

'They'll be all right for a minute or two. Kester will keep an eye on them.'

He removed from a chair a tray holding a half-completed jigsaw puzzle and sat down. 'What did you want to talk about?'

'Nothing if you keep that impatient expression on your face.'

He made an effort to compose himself. 'What did you want to talk about?' he repeated.

'About us.'

'What about us?'

26

She paused, gave a solicitous little smile. 'How have you been getting on, Robert? How've you been managing?'

'I?' He smiled back, wondering where all this was leading to. 'Oh, all right, thanks. Fine.'

She nodded, as if expecting such an answer. Then she said, 'It's no good kidding ourselves, is it? You know as well as I do that it's just not working, is it?'

'I don't understand.'

'I mean with us, and the children. The way things are.'

He said nothing. He didn't want to be drawn into some pointless, depressing discussion. Judith looked at him in silence for a few moments then, turning to the window, gave a deep sigh. 'God, but I hate this place,' she said.

'Your flat?'

'The flat, the area, all of it.'

'I thought you liked it. You were so keen, so enthusiastic at the start. When you found the place you couldn't wait to move in.'

She turned back to face him. 'Yes, well, that was before I got to know it properly. I can't stand the neighbours for a start. Stupid, unimaginative, intolerant pricks. Forever complaining about my records or something or other.'

Robert gave a little shake of his head. It was the same old story. 'But it's so near your work,' he said. 'If you – '

'I've left my job,' Judith interrupted. 'I got sick of it.'

'I see.' He wouldn't ask what had happened. He didn't want to know. And anyway, the reasons wouldn't be new.

'I couldn't work with people like that,' she said. 'Some of those women – they hated me. I know it. Mind you, some of them loved me, very much. But anyway – I'm much better off out of it.'

'Have you got anything else lined up?'

'Oh – well . . .' She pulled a face and flapped a hand, dismissing the subject. 'Forget all that. That's not what I want to talk about.' She studied him for a moment, her expression softening. 'Anyway, Robbie, how are things with you?'

'I told you. I'm fine. We all are.'

27

She gave a faint little smile. 'Oh, come on, now. Don't treat me like a child.'

'I'm not.'

She looked at him for a moment with her head a little on one side, then stepped towards him and gently laid her palms on the backs of his hands as they rested on the chair arms. He didn't move. After a second she stepped back and sat down on the carpet. She had always done that. She would go into a room full of strangers and, no matter how many chairs might be available, she would sit on the carpet. On a girl in her twenties the action might have had an air of freedom, of Bohemianism. It didn't suit Judith now.

'I've been going back over what happened,' she said.

'Oh?'

'With us, I mean.'

He nodded.

She went on: 'When I left you and the children that time I know very well that you didn't truly understand it. My reasons, I mean.'

'Oh – this is all in the past, Judith. What's the point in – '

She broke in, 'I know it's in the past, but it's not *so long* in the past. And anyway, that doesn't mean it's not relevant, does it? You didn't understand, I know you didn't – my going away.'

'I know what you told me.'

'Yes,' she said quickly, 'and it was true. I know it sounds an awful cliché, but truly, I didn't know who I was. I had to have time – on my own. To find myself. To find out what I was all about. What I wanted from life.'

'You've told me all this before, Judith. Besides, what does it matter now?'

'It matters, Robert. It matters. Anyway, what with my – my time away, and the divorce and – well – I've made a few discoveries. I'm *still* making them.'

'Go on . . .'

'Don't you want to know what they are?'

'All right, tell me.'

28

'Oh, Robert, you don't make it easy, do you – and sitting there with that – that unapproachable expression on your face . . .'

'Go on.'

'Yes, well, anyway.' A pause. 'Listen – I'd like it if we could – ' she took a breath, sighed, ' – could make a new start.'

He stared at her. 'You and me?'

'Yes.'

'Oh – Judith . . .'

'Why do you look like that? What's so strange about such an idea? I mean, I've had time to think now.'

'No, Judith. I'm afraid it's impossible. I – '

'Don't use words like that,' she cut in. 'It's *not* impossible. We're two adults. And we have children. And they need us and – '

'Judith, please. Let's not go into all this. Please. There's no chance of it happening. You know very well it wouldn't work.' He shook his head. 'What's made you come up with this all of a sudden?'

'I don't know that it's all that sudden. I've been thinking about it.'

'But – I thought you were settled now. You've got your flat and – you've made new friends. You've got a relationship going with that chap – Simon.'

She waved a dismissing hand, her bangles clinking on her wrist. 'I've told you how I feel about this flat – and as for Simon, forget it. He turned out to be a real prick. That puerile bastard. Don't talk to me about him.'

'What happened?'

'Oh – never mind what happened. But since he went I've – I've had time to take stock. And I really do believe that we'd be much better off if we were together again – you, me and the children.'

Robert gave a sympathetic shake of his head. 'I'm sorry, Judith. I told you, it just wouldn't work.'

'Oh, but Robert – '

'Really, I mean it, and you must believe it and accept it. We've been divorced for two years now. I've rebuilt my life and – '

'So this is the way it has to be, then? Is that what you're saying?'

He shrugged. 'I wish it could be better. But I can't see how it can be – the way things are.'

'So I have to just go on like this – being alone.'

'It was *your choice*, Judith.'

Ignoring his last words she gave a nod. 'So I just have to go on being separated from my children – be grateful to be able to spend a weekend with them once a month.' She paused. 'It's not fair. They're my children as much as they are yours. They're *more* mine than yours. A mother's rights are stronger by the very nature of things.'

'Judith, that's a load of balls, and you know it.'

Her voice grew sharper. 'Well, you can say what you like, but they're *my children*. And I love them, and I *want* them.'

'Well – I'm sorry.' He got up from the chair. Quickly Judith rose from the carpet. They stood facing one another.

'Please, Robert,' Judith said, 'I want my children.' Her eyes filled with tears. 'I want to live with them. But not just the children. I want us *all* to be a family again. You and me as well.'

'It's out of the question, Judith. You must know that. We've all come a long way in the past two years. We can't go back now.'

'It wouldn't be going back; it would be going forward. I want us to be together. It's where we belong – together.'

He couldn't allow himself to be moved. 'Judith,' he said, 'you should have thought of that before you decided to walk out on us. Before you decided that your *finding yourself* was more important than your family's happiness, your children's welfare – their need for their mother.'

'I told you why I did it. You know why.'

'Yes, right. But it doesn't change anything.' He shook his head. 'No, Judith, the children are much better off now. We all are. The situation isn't perfect, but even so, it's better than it was.'

'What are you saying, that I wasn't good for them?'

'It's not only I who believes that.'

'Oh, you mean that fucking moronic judge? That inhuman bastard.'

'Well, that's a matter of which side you're standing on, isn't it?'

'What do you mean? I was a good mother to those children. I *was*. And *you know* I was a good mother.'

'I'm not going to argue with you, Judith. There's no point.'

'You *know* I was a good mother. But you just wanted revenge, didn't you?'

'Revenge?' His tone was incredulous.

'Yes, revenge. Because I left you.'

'Oh, for God's sake. Can't you get it into your head, Judith? It was the best thing you could have done for me, although I didn't realize it at the time.'

'You're just saying that to hurt me.'

'No, Judith. You just don't want to face the truth. When you walked out, for the last and final time, for *good*, I took a look around me and gradually, over the days, I came to realize that it was the best thing that could have happened. We weren't happy together, were we? We hadn't been for a long time. It was only the children that were keeping us together. Without them we'd have split up long before. But then you went and – well, when I'd had time to take stock I knew it was the best thing that could have happened.'

'You are a bastard.' She glared at him for a moment, then: 'I want to be with my children.'

'Why? You never wanted them when you had them.'

'That's a lie. I loved them. I've always loved them. You don't know what it cost me to go off and leave them that time.'

'Judith, the children are waiting.'

'*My* children.'

'Yes, maybe, but – '

'And I want them.'

'Perhaps, but you'll never get them.'

'You bastard.' Lashing out with her hand, she struck him hard across the face. Then again. As the stinging pain flooded his cheek he nodded, forced a smile to his lips. 'You were

31

always very fond of doing that, weren't you? It doesn't hurt so much now – not as it did in those early years. And at least it's in private here, not in public.' He paused. 'Why do you find it so hard to accept the truth? I'll never live with you again. My God, it's a ridiculous idea. Have you forgotten what you were like?' His voice rose in anger. 'My God, when I think of the time you just took off with Kester and Michael that spring. Took them out of school. And for what? To live in some London squat for a few weeks.'

'It was a *commune*.'

'Oh, excuse me.'

'And I took them because I loved them. And they were happy with me. My children love me. And I love them.'

'When you talk of your children who are you talking about? You mean Kester and Michael, don't you? It's a pity you don't show a little more affection for Ben and Daisy.'

'I love them, too.'

'Yes, so much so that you've always practically ignored them. And still do. Kester and Michael – they were the only ones you ever thought about. Showering them with presents all the time. And sometimes quite ridiculous presents. Endless board games that they tired of within hours. Skis! They never even learned to put them on. All those impractical gifts. Never mind what it all cost, either.'

'Oh, I wondered when we'd get around to that. I suppose now you're going to tell me about the debts I ran up.'

'You're the one who's brought it up.' He gazed at her steadily. 'Jesus, I don't know how I stuck it as long as I did.'

'Have you finished?'

'Oh, I could go on and on. Your blackmail attempts when you couldn't get your own way with me just when you felt like it.'

'I don't know what you're talking about.'

'No?' He reached out both hands, snatching at her wrists, holding them to expose the fine scars there. '*That's* what I'm talking about. And the other times with your bloody pills. What d'you think *that* did to the family you loved!' He let her hands

32

fall. 'No, Judith, I told you – we're better off without you. And that's the way it's going to stay.' He turned again, reaching out to open the door, but she ran around him, coming to a stop in front of him, preventing him.

'Please, Robert, just a moment . . .'

'No, Judith, we've said all that we can ever have to say to one another. We did that long ago.'

'But listen, I – I could help you in your work and – '

'That would be something new.'

'Don't, please. I mean it. And I'd get myself a nice little job somewhere.'

'Oh, let's not kid ourselves. You'd get yourself a nice little job. I don't think there's anything left for you to try. My God, the succession of jobs you've had over the past few years. And anyway, I never expected you to go out to work. You were never obliged to.'

'No, I know that, but – oh, listen – I – oh, Robert, I'm sorry I hit you, I – oh, Robert – surely . . .'

Impatient, and curious, Kester had got out of the car and made his way to the front door of the block. It opened quietly. As he entered the foyer he heard his mother's voice.

'. . . Surely there's something left, isn't there? Between us? Why can't we make another start? We could all be together again. And we could be happy. We could, I know we could. For the sake of the children. For *our* sake. I know I didn't always make you happy before, but this time I – '

'Judith, it's a waste of time talking like this. There's no future for you and me – not together, anyway.'

'Don't you feel anything at all for me now?'

He took a deep breath. 'Judith, whatever I feel for you now is not important. What is important is that I – I've started to put my life together.'

'What does that mean?'

He said nothing. Judith looked at him steadily for some moments, then nodded.

33

'You mean this – Netta, I suppose. The children have told me about her.' She paused. 'Is it her?'

'Yes, well, I – I'm very fond of her and – well, we have a good relationship.'

'Oh, I see the way things are going. So this Netta is going to take my place – usurp my place with my children, is she?'

'Of course not.'

'But you *are* thinking of marriage.'

He didn't answer.

'I see,' she said, 'and what does *she* think about it?'

'We haven't discussed it. Listen, I don't want to talk about it.' Suddenly his own anger rose up in him. 'It's *my life*, Judith!' he snapped out. 'It's my life and it has nothing to do with you. Whatever you may think. I know what it is with you – why you've come up with this ludicrous proposal. You've had enough of living on your own, haven't you? That's it, isn't it? It's all so in character. You've tried living on your own, and it hasn't been quite the picnic you expected, has it? You found yourself a nice flat, a decent job; and you even managed to find yourself a decent fellow – so he seemed to be, anyway, going by what you told me about him. And now it's all gone sour. Everything. And suddenly you've become aware of which side your bread was buttered, and you want the security of family life again – living with a husband with a regular job, children to give you some affection; no hassle, no necessity to look around for a job. Forget it, Judith. It's too late.'

Judith burst into tears. As he stepped forward again she reached out, clutching at him. Pushing her hands away, he held her by the upper arms and thrust her aside. As he moved into the hall towards the main door he could hear behind him the sound of her sobbing.

Upstairs in the semi-detached house near the end of Richard Jefferies Avenue Daisy lay in bed beside Ben. It had been after nine by the time they had got back to Swindon. Daisy was tired. Ben was already asleep.

'Now – you go to sleep, sweetheart.'

34

Robert's voice was soft as he bent over the bed. Daisy nodded her head on the pillow, closed her eyes for a moment, then opened them again. 'Daddy?'

'What is it, baby?'

'She didn't take my flowers.' Her voice was a whisper in the silent room.

'Your what? Who?'

'Jude. Mummy. The flowers I gave her. She left them behind. When we left the woods to go back to her flat. She left my flowers behind in the woods.'

On Kester's bedside table in the next room a framed photograph of Judith looked over the two boys as they lay awake in the bed.

'And they didn't know you were listening?' Michael said, his voice very low.

'No,' Kester answered. 'They were just on the other side of the door. Afterwards, when I saw the door opening I ran back outside. She was crying by that time. Dad came out just a few seconds later.'

'But you heard Jude say that she wanted us all to be together.'

'Yes, she said she wanted to make another start. He told her it was no good talking about it, though. He said they had no future together. That's when Jude said that Netta would take her place with us.'

They were silent for a few moments then Kester said: 'D'you like Netta?'

'She's been very nice to us. She brought me all those foreign stamps . . .'

'I know. And me.'

'And Dad likes her.'

'I know.'

'D'you think he *will* marry her, Kes?'

'He hasn't discussed it with her, he said.'

'Perhaps he won't then. Perhaps Netta won't want to marry him.'

'I expect she would.'

'And what if she does.'

'She'll be a usurper.' After a pause Kester went on, 'All I know is, it's not fair of Dad – making Jude cry like that.'

'No, it's not.'

Kester sighed. 'Ah, well, let's hope it'll all be okay.'

'Yes.' A silence, then Michael added, 'Kes?'

'What?'

'What does *usurper* mean?'

'Oh – go to sleep.'

Long after Michael had fallen asleep Kester lay awake, thinking again of the words that had passed between his mother and father. He kept hearing the sound of Jude's crying.

THREE

A native of Bath, Netta was a teacher of history and geography at the comprehensive school in Swindon where Robert taught English. She had arrived there the previous September, though it had taken Robert several months to get around to asking her out.

She was twenty-nine, and small in stature – just over five feet; standing beside Robert at the sink as they washed up the supper dishes she came up to his shoulder. She was not pretty; her mouth was too wide, her jaw was too square and her nose too long. Her hair was attractive, though; thick and dark, added to which her wide hazel eyes and bright smile showed a warmth of personality which had attracted Robert from the moment they had met.

On this Sunday, the day after the trip to London, Netta had driven over to the house to cook lunch for Robert and the children, after which they had spent the day in various pursuits, much of it out in the sunlit garden.

Now, as Robert finished drying the dishes and Netta began to prepare coffee for the two of them she said in a low voice: 'Did anything happen yesterday when you saw Judith?' In her eyes was a faint shadow of concern. 'You sounded a little uptight last night when I phoned.'

He turned at her words, listening to the murmuring sounds of the TV set in the sitting room.

'The boys can't hear,' she said quickly. 'Not with the television on.'

He gave an ironic smile. 'You don't think so? Oh, hearing like an owl's, believe me.' He paused. 'We'll talk about it later.'

When the dishes were put away and the coffee was ready they took their cups into the sitting room. Michael was sitting

37

in an armchair, his eyes on the television screen. Another mindless game show, Robert observed; another panel of celebrities who were not famous for anything but appearing on game shows. On the sofa Kester sat reading, untouched by the banalities. Netta, holding her cup and saucer, sat down beside him. 'Come on, you boys,' Robert said. 'It's gone nine o'clock. Time you were in bed.'

Kester said nothing, but Michael groaned. 'Oh, not yet, Dad.'

'Yes, go on now. And don't wake Ben and Daisy when you go up.'

Neither of the boys moved. Robert said, a little sharply: 'Come on now – up to bed.' With his last words he stepped forward and switched off the set. 'You won't be fit for school in the morning.'

Michael groaned again, reluctantly got up. 'You coming, Kes?'

'Not yet; I'm reading.' Kester didn't look up from his book.

Robert felt a surge of anger. 'Kester,' he said sharply, 'you heard me. Now get on up to bed.'

Kester sighed, slipped a marker into the book and closed it. 'You know something?' he said. 'It's really anathema to me – being treated as a child.'

'Right.' Robert nodded. 'Life is tough, I know.'

'What are you reading?' Netta asked as Kester stood up beside her.

'About Charles Bravo.' Kester's tone was offhand.

'Who?'

'Charles Bravo. He was poisoned.'

'A Victorian murder victim,' Robert said. 'We were looking at his house yesterday where he died, in Balham.' He turned to Kester. 'You've got a book on it? Where did you get that from?'

'Jude gave it to me.'

'Oh . . .' Robert paused. 'Anyway, leave it down here. I don't want you staying up all night reading.'

'Oh, *Dad*.' Kester's protest was almost a wail.

'I mean it. I know what you're like once you get caught up in a book.'

'Oh, *Dad* . . .'

'You heard me, Kester.'

With evident ill-grace Kester put the book down on the coffee table.

'Thank you.' Robert nodded. 'Now go on up.'

The two boys moved to the door, Kester leading. Then in the doorway they turned and said their goodnights.

When the door had closed behind the boys Robert gave a sigh and sat down on the sofa at Netta's side. The sounds of the boys' feet echoed briefly on the stairs and died away.

Netta said with a smile: 'Poor Kester – he really wanted to read his book.'

Robert picked up the book, shook his head, and replaced the book on the table. 'I'm not sure that it's the best thing for him to be reading anyway.' He sighed.

'You're really quite strict with them at times, aren't you?' Netta said.

'You call that being strict?' Robert frowned. 'I have to be a little firm with them – with Kester and Michael – otherwise they'd get away with murder. They're not too bad right now. You should have known them in earlier days – when Judith was on the scene all the time. And the legacy she left when she went.'

'Really?'

'God, she let them run wild. Encouraged them to. They were impossible. And they were like it for ages after we were divorced. It took quite an effort to bring them under control. They *are* settling down, gradually, but it's taken time. It's all very well her indulging them when she sees them once a month. She doesn't have to deal with the consequences. Whenever they've spent time with her they're always difficult afterwards.'

'In what way?'

'In *every* way. Their language and their general behaviour. And when they've spent any *length* of time with her it sometimes takes days to get them back to an even keel.' He chuckled. 'God, listen to me, going on. If I say any more about them you'll

39

be taking off out the door. Oh, but they're all right. They're not bad boys.'

'No, they're fine.' Netta smiled, then: 'Tell me about yesterday,' she said, ' – with Judith.'

'Oh . . .' He shook his head. 'She somehow thinks that we can suddenly forget the past and start all over again. It's ridiculous, of course – but not that surprising – not coming from Judith.'

'Were you expecting it, anything like it?'

'No, not at all.'

After a moment Netta said, 'How was she when you left her?'

'Crying.'

'Oh, dear.'

'Oh, tears never came to her with that much difficulty. She could always turn the taps on. I know I sound hard, but I had to learn to cut myself off from it – all her spurious displays of emotion. She'd have wiped the floor with me otherwise.' He added quickly, 'Anyway, let's not talk about her now.'

She gave an ironic little smile. 'You never want to talk about her.'

'So you've told me,' he said.

'Well, it's true. You make references to her, but you've never really told me anything about her – your lives together. Tell me. Tell me about your marriage.'

'It – it's over now,' he said. 'It's all in the past. Netta, there's not much to tell.'

She said nothing.

He shook his head, then said: 'You know, sometimes, when I look back, I wonder how I could ever have got into such a situation. How I could have come to marry her. I mean – all the danger signs were there. The signs that it would be a disaster. But I didn't read them at all. And I was very young. I guess all the – the excitement of knowing her, of being with her – it was all a part of growing up for me. It wasn't for her, though. She had grown up – as much as she was ever going to. And of course, later I *did* grow up. Christ alive, I had to. One of us had to have some sense of responsibility. I changed. She didn't.

40

She's mellowed over the years, mind you, but she's still the same woman underneath.'

He sat in silence for some moments and then began to speak about the marriage, filling in the blanks between the few fragments that Netta had already gathered from past conversations. Judith was four years older than he, he told her. He had just started teaching in London when they had met. At that time he was twenty-three; Judith was twenty-seven. A student at Goldsmith's School of Art, she was also a few years older than her fellow students, having decided at a comparatively late stage to make a career in painting.

'She being older than I was,' he said, ' – I suppose in a way it made her even more attractive to me, now that I look back. At any rate, I certainly found her to be – quite potent medicine.'

'Were you in love with her?'

'Oh, yes, desperately. She was beautiful, experienced, funny, kooky. She was like no other girl I'd ever been out with before. She had such a – a bright, unexpected, surprising way about her.'

'What d'you mean?'

'Oh – for one thing, the way she'd just act on the spur of the moment. Whatever took her fancy. She was always dashing off to some museum or exhibition or meeting or something or other.' He shook his head, gave a small, rueful laugh. 'Or to see some odd weirdo she'd heard about – some guru or seer or palmist or crystal ball reader or – oh, anyone who claimed anything in the way of a hotline to Truth-and-Understanding or anything like that. In the end I just tried to learn to expect the unexpected.' He grinned. 'So many impetuous decisions. And all those little excursions. And some not so little, either.'

'You mean the commune? You told me she took the boys off to stay in a commune.'

'Oh, that was later. I mean earlier things. She'd just – take off. She did it once soon after we met. Just disappeared in the middle of her term at art school. Then I got a card from her in Turkey. Turkey! God knows what she was doing there. But she never ever seemed to need any great rhyme or reason; the

41

impulse was enough.' He shook his head. 'Would you believe that while she was living in London she bought a horse? I'm not kidding. Living in a small flat in London and she buys a horse. Stabled it in some back street in Hammersmith and spent half her days cycling over there to feed it, water it and shovel up horse shit. She never rode the poor thing after two or three times. Not that I think it was fit for very much – apart from the knacker's yard.'

'What happened to it?'

'Who knows. I suppose she sold it. I don't know. It went, anyway. As did most of her passions.' He was silent for a moment, then he said, 'You probably think I was crazy to get mixed up with her. But it's hard to explain. As I said, she was like no other girl I'd ever known.'

'And in bed?' A faint smile on Netta's lips.

'Oh, in bed she was wild and wonderful, Oh, God, yes. And of course that was no small attraction.' He grinned. 'I can remember whole Sundays spent in bed together. Sex and wine and television – and records and reading poetry. And sometimes some very expensive caviar she'd pinch from Fortnum and Mason. She'd often do that. Steal from the various department stores – though only the best ones, of course. I thought she was buying it. It was only later, after we were married, when I said we couldn't afford such luxuries that she told me how she was getting them.' He shook his head and gave a little laugh of disbelief.

'How long had you known one another when you got married?'

'Only about seven or eight months. She got pregnant with Kester and – we got married.'

'She had to give up her art studies then?'

'Oh, yes.'

'Did she keep up with her painting afterwards? After Kester was born?'

'Not really. As she gradually realized that she didn't have any great talent she more or less lost interest. She'd still have little spurts of creative energy from time to time – when everything

42

else would be put aside to accommodate some sudden desire to prove herself as an artist, but they never lasted long. Like most of her passions.'

He gazed silently into his coffee cup for a moment, then said, 'It was after the birth of Ben that everything really started to fall apart. I suppose I really knew by then that there wasn't much future for us.'

'Yet you still went ahead and had Daisy.'

He shrugged. 'There's no accounting for how these things happen, is there? My darling little Daisy. She certainly wasn't planned – any more than the others had been. I don't know – perhaps, she, like Ben, was the result of one of those endless efforts to keep the marriage going. Another one that didn't work. After Daisy's birth the whole thing very quickly went downhill. And then, one day, as I've told you, Judith walked out – leaving me with the children.'

'What did she do? When she left you, I mean.'

'Several things. She became a Buddhist nun for a while. Sounds crazy, doesn't it? I went to see her at a convent in the Midlands. She'd renounced everything. Children, husband, all material possessions. The lot. It didn't last, though. Of course it didn't. A few months and she'd had enough. She came back demanding the house and also saying she wanted Kester and Michael to live with her.'

'Just Kester and Michael.'

'Oh, yes, it was only ever those two who meant anything to her. She had some plan whereby she'd keep Kester and Michael and I'd hang on to Ben and Daisy. I wasn't having that, though. It would have been the worst thing for them – the boys – to go and be brought up solely by her. And anyway, I always had the feeling – I still do – that her love for them – her great passion – is only on the surface. I'm damn sure that if she really had to care for them twenty-four hours a day again she'd soon get sick of it. She did before, and I'm certain she would again. Anyway, she sued for divorce and I sued for custody of the children.'

'Was it difficult?'

'Difficult? Yes, you could say that. There were numerous

examinations by the Welfare and other bodies – and I had to get psychiatric reports on her. That's another thing she's never forgiven me for. She got her own back, though, for that. In return she demanded psychiatric reports on *me*.' His smile was bitter. 'I must have passed the test because I got custody.' He sighed. 'God, but it was absolute hell, it really was.'

'I'll bet.'

'Oh,' he said quickly, 'that wasn't all.'

'No?' She paused. 'Tell me.'

He was silent, avoiding Netta's eyes. After a moment he said softly: 'Judith – to get the children – she made the most terrible charges against me in court.'

'What kind of charges?'

'She – she said that I – ' He could barely get the words out. 'She said that I – that I had – *interfered* with Daisy. Sexually. Oh, God . . .' He leaned forward, hands lifting to cover his face, the sobs welling up in his throat.

The moments went by. When he was calm again he said: 'But I got my children. In the long run that was all that mattered. I'll never let her or anybody else take them away.'

Moving suddenly, he turned to Netta, wrapped his arms around her and held her to him. 'Marry me, Netta,' he said. 'Please. Marry me.'

She didn't answer at once. Then she said softly, 'It's what I want, Robert, but – '

'But what?'

She pulled back a little out of his embrace, looked into his eyes. 'I have to be sure that it's the right thing. The best thing.'

'Oh, it is. I have no doubt of that.'

'Yes, but – you told me you'd only known Judith for seven or eight months when you got married. You've only really known me for about three.'

'That doesn't matter. I've known you long enough to know that you're one of the best things that has ever happened to me – that you're what I want. I've learned some of my lessons hard, and I know what I want now – what's right for me – and for the children.' He paused. 'Marry me, Netta. Tell me you will.'

'It's what I want,' she murmured again, 'but – oh, please – let's just leave it a little while longer.'

He nodded, sighed. 'Okay . . .' Drawing her to him again, he held her once more. After some moments his sense of disappointment gave way to the pleasure he felt in her nearness. She felt small and vulnerable in his arms; her cheek was soft under the touch of his hand. His hand moved down, cupping her breast, and after a moment he began to undo the buttons of her blouse. And then, into their silence came the sound of footsteps on the stairs. At once he and Netta sat up, Netta quickly buttoning her blouse. A moment later the door opened and Michael came into the room.

'What are you doing down here?' Robert asked.

'I wanted a drink.'

'There's water and a glass in the bathroom. Why d'you have to come down here?'

'I wanted a drink of milk.'

'No,' Robert said impatiently. 'You've had your supper. Now, please, stop making a nuisance of yourself and get back to bed.'

Michael stood there for a moment or two, glancing from one to the other. Then, with no trace of disappointment in his face or his voice, he said, 'Okay, Dad. Goodnight again.'

As the sound of Michael's footsteps faded on the stairs Robert said with a sigh and a rueful grin: 'Ridiculous, isn't it? – never having any bloody privacy in the house.' He turned back to Netta. 'Of course, I haven't needed it for so long. It's only now, with you, that I realize how much it's lacking.'

'What were they doing?' Kester asked in a whisper as Michael entered the bedroom and moved quickly towards the bed.

'They weren't doing anything,' Michael said. 'They were just sitting on the sofa together.'

Kester shook his head. 'God, how puerile.' He paused. 'Did you ask for some milk?'

'Yeh, I didn't get any, though. Dad just told me to get back upstairs.' Michael got into the bed and pulled the sheet up to

45

his chin. At his side Kester lay for some seconds in silence, then said: 'D'you think they'd been *doing* it?'

'I don't know.'

'For Christ's sake, didn't you notice *any*thing? You must have noticed *some*thing.'

'No, I didn't.'

'Weren't they even kissing?'

'No, they weren't.' Michael frowned. 'Look, I didn't want to go down there in the first place. And if you don't like the way I report back then the next time you can go yourself.'

'Oh.' Kester's eyes widened in an exaggerated expression of surprise. 'Very uppity, aren't we? Very uppity.'

FOUR

Soon after lunch on a Friday, early in August, Kester and Michael made their final preparations to go up to London. It was a month since their last visit. Then, along with Ben and Daisy, they had spent only a part of the Saturday. This time their father was to take only the two of them, and they would be going for the whole weekend. They would leave within the next hour and return when their father picked them up on Sunday afternoon.

Kester stood in his bedroom going through his weekend case once more. Like Michael, he had packed it the previous evening, but, as always, he had to go through it again at the last moment and make sure he had everything he would need. Michael had already taken his case downstairs.

'I wish I were going with you.'

Turning, Kester saw Ben standing in the doorway, leaning against the jamb. Kester raised an eyebrow and turned back to his repacking. 'Well, it's no good you wishing, because you're not, and that's it.'

'I never get to stay a whole weekend.'

'There's not enough room for you, you know that. Jude only has two bedrooms.'

'I could sleep on the sofa, couldn't I?'

'Listen, if you came with us you'd only start whining to come home. You know you would.'

'No, I wouldn't.'

'Well, you're not coming, anyway. For one thing, it's Jude's birthday tomorrow.'

'I know that. We sent her a card, Daisy and me.'

'Good. And so you should. Anyway, she's made plans for the

three of us. We can't change all her plans, can we? Besides you're too young. You and Daisy.'

'I'm older than Daisy.'

'I know that. But you're still too young.'

A little silence. Ben said sadly, 'I never get to go anywhere with you and Michael.'

'Well, you don't fit in, do you?'

Ben said nothing for a moment, then: 'I could – if you let me.'

Kester closed the lid of the case, pressed the catches shut, picked the case up and placed it beside the bed. Then he turned back to Ben, raised his hand and crooked a finger. 'Close the door and come here a minute.'

Ben hesitated only briefly then quickly shut the door, turned and walked towards Kester. He came to a stop and stood looking up at him.

'I said you don't fit in, Ben,' Kester said evenly. 'And I mean it. You don't. I don't think you ever will.'

'Oh, but, Kester, I – '

Kester's voice broke in: 'No, you never will. You know why?' His voice was very low.

Ben shook his head, his lower lip giving a slight quiver.

'Because you're fucking useless, that's why.' There was no anger or contempt in Kester's tone. His words were delivered coolly, an observation. Ben continued to gaze at him, though suddenly in his eyes was the shine of unshed tears. 'There you are,' Kester said. 'I say a little thing like that and straight away you're about to start crying.'

'I'm not, Kester. I'm not, really.' Ben only just managed to get the words out.

'Yes, you are. You've got no courage. No guts at all.'

'I have, Kester. I have.'

'And no initiative, either. You can't even think for yourself.' Turning, he glanced from the window to the rear lawn where Daisy was busying herself at the garden seat. 'And you spend too much of your time with Daisy. And what is she? She's only a girl.'

48

'I won't. In future I won't.'

Kester laughed. 'Of course you will. You're just a puerile little shit.' He watched the hurt gathering in Ben's eyes. 'Anyway, why do you want to come with us and stay with Jude? You don't love her.'

'Oh, Kester, I *do*.'

'No, you don't. Not like Mikie and I do.'

'I *do*. And I want to be with you and Mike, but you never let me.' He paused. 'Why won't you?'

Kester shrugged. 'Who knows? Maybe one day we will.'

'When?'

Another shrug. 'When you can prove you're worthy of it. When you can prove that you're not a baby.'

'I'm *not*.'

'Ah, well, that's something you'll have to prove, isn't it?'

'How?'

'That's up to you. For a start you'd have to show that you can be grown up. Like I said, act on your own initiative.' Silence between them. Kester looked at him steadily. 'Do you love Dad?'

Ben answered readily, nodding. 'Yes, of course I do.'

'Yes, I know.' Kester smiled.

'And you do too, don't you?'

'Of course I do. Very much, only – I love Jude, too – and she needs us.' Then casually Kester added, 'I hear you'll be staying with Netta this evening – while Dad takes Mike and me up to London.'

'Yes. She's coming to collect us soon. We're going to sleep in her flat tonight.'

Kester nodded, then put a hand under Ben's chin and raised his head a little. 'Do you like Netta?' He smiled as he spoke; a smile of encouragement.

'Oh, yes!' Ben smiled back. 'Oh, yes, I like her a lot. We both do, Daisy and I.'

Kester continued to smile for another second, then he raised his hand, drew it back, and swung. The blow caught Ben on the cheek, rocking him backwards with such violence that he almost fell. A look of shock, horror and pain flooded his face and he reached up to his swiftly reddening cheek while tears sprang into his eyes. Before the tears could fall, before Ben could cry out, Kester was leaning forward so that his eyes were only inches from Ben's.

'Don't you dare cry,' he said softly.

Ben, in an agony of grief and pain, was almost choking in his efforts not to give way. His eyes swam in tears, and although he fought to keep them back they spilled over and coursed swiftly down his cheeks.

'Look at you,' Kester said, shaking his head. 'One little tap and you're reduced to a fat, quivering lump of tears. Christ. Now do you wonder when I say that you don't fit in.' He bent, picked up the case and walked to the door. With his hand on the doorhandle he turned back to the younger boy. He studied him for a moment, taking in the bent head, the hunched shoulders. 'Are you going to tell Dad what's happened here?' he asked.

Ben shook his head, while a sob escaped from his throat.

'I didn't hear you,' Kester said.

Ben shook his head again, then said softly, chokingly, 'N-no . . .'

'Good. Not, of course, that I'd be concerned for myself even if you did. It's you I'm thinking of.' Kester paused. 'Anyway, you'd better stay here until you've got control of yourself. But don't be too long. Then you can go and play with Daisy again. It's all you're fit for.'

For some time after Kester had gone from the room Ben remained there. He could still feel on his cheek the stinging imprint of Kester's hand; still hear the words he had spoken. After a while he left the room and went downstairs. There was no sign of anyone in the house, and going outside he found Kester and Michael standing beside the Citroën where his father was checking the oil and the tyres in readiness for the journey to London.

Not wishing to face any of them, he turned and made his way into the back garden where, on the lawn, Daisy had turned the

50

garden bench into a shop counter, its surface bearing an assortment of empty bottles, soft-drink cans, a cornflakes box and other sundry items. Standing behind the makeshift counter she saw Ben as he emerged around the side of the house.

'Ben,' she called to him, 'my shop is open now, so you can come and buy something.' She gave a little laugh. 'If you've got some money, of course.'

He came to a halt and remained for a moment looking at her as she stood grinning at him over her display. Then, leaping forward, he ran towards her across the grass. 'I don't want to play your stupid game,' he cried. 'You're just a stupid girl. What do I want to play with you for?' Then, as Daisy's expression changed to one of horror and dismay, he bent to the bench and, lifting up its front, upended it so that the goods were sent flying, scattering over the grass. 'Stupid, stupid girl!' he said. He let the bench fall on its side, then the next moment he was turning and dashing away down the garden path.

At one-thirty Netta arrived in her Mini, and ten minutes later Robert, Kester and Michael were ready to leave. Netta, Ben and Daisy followed them out to the Citroën and stood watching as Robert loaded the cases and the boys climbed in. Michael got in first, followed by Kester. They sat together in the rear seat. As Robert got behind the wheel Kester wound down the window.

'Ben . . . ?' He smiled, beckoning to his younger brother. Hesitantly, Ben left Netta's side and moved to the car. He stopped a yard away from it. Kester beckoned to him and Ben stepped nearer. Putting a hand through the open window, Kester reached up to Ben's cheek. Ben flinched very slightly, but managed to stand still. Kester's hand was so light it was almost a caress. Ben stood there, Kester's fingers like feathers on his cheek.

'Perhaps one day you'll be able to come with us, eh, Ben?' Kester said.

Ben nodded.

51

'Anyway,' Kester added, 'be a good boy and don't give Netta any trouble, will you?'

'No . . .'

'Good boy. Cheerio, then.'

Robert started the car then and, to a straggling chorus of goodbyes, he and the two boys were off. In a very little while the car had turned the corner at the end of the street and was out of sight.

'Right, you two.' Netta took Daisy's hand and, followed by Ben, turned back towards the house. 'We'll pick up your things for the night, lock up, and then go on to my place. Okay?'

'Yes! Okay!' The destruction of Daisy's makeshift little shop was forgotten now in the excitement of the promised treat in store and at Netta's side she gave a little hop and a jump.

It was just after four when Robert, Kester and Michael got to Judith's flat. Almost before Robert had switched off the engine the boys were scrambling out and carrying their cases up to the front door of the block. When Robert got into the foyer the flat door was open and they were already inside. He followed them in. From the stereo was coming some loud, strange-sounding, oriental-like music. In the sitting room Judith was standing with her arms around the boys. She looked around at Robert's entrance, released the boys and gave him a smile. 'Hello, Robert.'

'Hello, Judith.'

'How was the drive?' She moved to turn off the music.

'Oh, fine. About the same.'

'I'm sure you'd like something to drink, wouldn't you?'

'Thanks, I would.' It was a lie, but pretences were kept up in front of the children.

'Right.' Judith started to turn away. 'A good stiff scotch? How would that suit you?'

'Scotch? I've got to drive again in a minute.'

'It won't hurt you.'

'No, thanks. But I'll have some tea if you don't mind.'

'Tea? Fine.'

52

While the boys went into the bedroom to unpack their cases Robert followed Judith into the kitchen.

'I've been drinking rooibosch,' she said. 'You want some?'

'You've been drinking what?'

'It's all right, I'll get you some Indian.'

She put on the kettle and set out cups and saucers for the two of them. 'How have you been?' she asked.

'Oh, okay. And you? You look well.'

'Yes, I'm fine, thanks.' A pause. 'How is Netta?'

'Well. Very well.' The words came out too clipped. Yet he was relieved that she had brought up Netta's name. A brief pause and then he said, 'I have to tell you: I've asked Netta to marry me.'

Judith hardly paused as she poured the milk. There was silence in the kitchen for some moments, then she said, 'So, obviously you didn't give any further thought to what I said to you.'

'You mean, about our – '

'Our getting back together again. Precisely. Obviously whatever I had to say went straight in one ear and out the other.'

He didn't answer. Judith looked at him. 'I did at least think you'd give it some thought. I hoped you would. I know we didn't part on exactly – good terms, but even so I thought – '
She shrugged. 'Oh, well, that'll teach me. Obviously I'm very much out of touch with what's going on these days.' She shook her head. 'I must be living in cloud-cuckoo-land. I really did have the idea that we could truly make a go of it, if we tried.'

Still Robert said nothing.

'I *did*,' she insisted.

'Well – I'm sorry, Judith.'

'So – now it's all set, is it. Your wedding?'

'No, it's not *all set*.'

'Oh, you mean she hasn't accepted your wonderful offer?'

'. . . She's thinking about it.'

Judith stood gazing at him, as if studying him. 'I really don't know what's come over you, Robert. Proposing marriage when you haven't even known the woman five minutes.' She paused then added gravely: 'You do realize, don't you, that in God's eyes you'll always be married to *me*?'

He gave a short laugh. 'Oh, for God's sake! Don't tell me you're suddenly invoking your Catholic teaching. Well, that's novel.'

'Don't you laugh at me!' She glared at him angrily, then: 'Have you given a thought to your children?'

'A great deal.'

'No, I don't think you can have. Here you are trying to foist some stranger on them. And just because it suits you. But there, you always were selfish. You only ever thought of yourself. Always.'

He sighed. 'I don't think this conversation is getting us anywhere.'

'Oh, I see – now that it's getting a little rough you're going to duck out, are you? Or is this the effect that Netta has on you? Yes, maybe that's it. She's blinded you, has she? Is that it? Blinded you to your responsibilities.'

'Oh, for Christ's sake,' he said wearily. 'Judith, please.'

'Oh, for Christ's sake – Judith, please,' she echoed with a little rocking movement of her head.

'Listen,' Robert said, 'whatever you think, I don't think this is the right time to discuss such things. Not with the boys just across the hall, listening to every word.'

'You think they don't already realize what's going on? No, you don't, do you? And that shows just how little you know your own children.'

'Are we going to keep this up?'

'Oh, I'm *sorry*.' Her voice was heavy with mock contrition. 'I'm making it difficult for you. Do forgive me. How could I be so thoughtless as to cause you a moment's uneasiness? It's unforgivable.' She turned back to the gas stove and turned off the flame under the kettle. 'Forget the tea,' she said. 'I think you'd better get on back home. Your darling Netta will be waiting for you.' She flapped a hand at him. 'Go on, go on. Don't keep her waiting.'

He sighed, started to turn away, stopped. After a moment or

54

two he said awkwardly, though with an attempt to sound casual: 'Oh, by the way, the children and I – we're going down to Devonshire.'

'Devonshire?' Judith frowned.

'For our holiday. I told you I'd been trying to find somewhere to take them for a week or two. Well – I'm taking them to Devonshire. I managed to get a house for us on the edge of Dartmoor. I just got confirmation yesterday. They'd had a cancellation. We were lucky.'

'Oh, yes, very lucky. Very nice.'

'The children are looking forward to it.'

'I'm sure they are. It all sounds very nice.' Her voice was cold.

He hesitated then said, 'We'll be going off in a fortnight's time. We'll be staying for two weeks.'

'Two weeks?' She turned and glanced at a calendar that hung beside the refrigerator. 'The boys are supposed to be with me for that last weekend before they go back to school. A long weekend, we agreed. Did you forget about that?'

'No, of course not. And I know we agreed that, but – well, I'm sorry, but it was the only time available. I'd left it very late. We were lucky to get that.'

'We agreed they'd be with me for the last weekend.'

'Yes, Judith, I know,' he said patiently, 'and I'm sorry, but – look, it won't make any real difference to you, will it? It'll just mean that their visit to you will be delayed for a week, that's all. They can come to you the weekend after. And, if you like, perhaps at half-term they can stay with you for a little longer. Maybe the whole week if you like.' He paused. 'Oh, come on, it's not going to make that much difference, is it?'

'Not to you, no.'

'It's not long.' His tone softened. 'Oh, you don't really mind, do you?'

She sighed. 'I don't suppose it matters if I do, does it? *You've* got custody. You've got control of them. *You* call the tunes – always.'

Robert said nothing. After a second Judith added with a sigh: 'So, that'll be you, Kester, Michael, Ben and Daisy, yes?'

'Yes, of course.' He paused. 'And Netta.'

'Oh, of *course, Netta*. How could I have forgotten dear Netta?' She gave a little smile. 'What's this, then – a little practice for her at playing mother. To help her make up her mind whether she wants to take on the job full time?'

'Please, Judith . . .'

'Robert . . .' She gave a little shake of her head. 'Robert, why don't you just turn around and leave? Please. Just go. Leave me alone with my boys. For God's sake, let me have a little time, undisturbed, with a couple of human beings who truly love me.'

In the sitting room of Netta's small flat in Swindon's Rodbourne district Ben and Daisy slept on the sofa-bed. In Netta's room Robert lay on his back at Netta's side, his breathing slowing after the exertion of his orgasm. Against the back of his hand he could feel the rise and fall of her breast. After a while he turned to her again, nestling closer, kissing her ear.

She turned her face to his and gently kissed his lips. He returned the kiss and sighed with contentment. There was no sound but that of their combined breathing. He felt completely relaxed. He became aware of the feeling, and wondered at it, and then realized that it was because he was where he was – and that Kester and Michael were away. It was so very, very rarely that he ever slept in a bed with Netta; and when it happened it was usually only when the two older boys were up in London. It wasn't that he was concerned that if they knew they would be sure to relate such news to Judith – which he felt sure they would – as for the inhibiting effect their near presence could have upon him. Particularly Kester. With Kester's growing sexual awareness there was little that escaped him these days. He was on to everything, his sharp eyes and ears attuned to the slightest nuance. With Ben and Daisy in the next room, it was different. In their innocence they questioned nothing.

'Do you think – ' Netta's voice whispered softly in the

56

stillness of the room, 'do you really think the children will accept me?'

Robert sighed. They had been over the same ground so many times: her doubts about her ability to take on a ready-made family. He himself had no qualms, but nevertheless it was clear that they remained very much in her mind.

Now, before he could frame an answer, she added, 'I can't help thinking about it.'

'It'll be all right, Netta. It will. I'm sure of it.'

'I wish I were as sure as you are.'

'I mean – well, look at Daisy and Ben. They're so fond of you. There's nothing they wouldn't do for you. You should have heard Daisy when I told her that she'd be spending the night here in your flat. She was so excited about it.'

Netta gave a rueful little chuckle. 'My God, how can anybody get excited about coming to sleep in *this* flat!' Then, in a different tone, she added, 'It's not Daisy and Ben I'm talking about. It's Kester – and Michael.'

He sighed. 'They *are* at a – a more difficult age, I know. But they'll be all right, you'll see. They've had far more in the way of – upheaval in their lives. Much more than the younger ones. They're still going through a period of adjustment – if you want to put it like that. But they'll settle down. They will.'

'I suppose so.'

'Give them time.'

'I sometimes wonder – just recently – whether they actually *like* me that much.'

'Why do you say that?'

'Oh, I don't know. It's nothing I can actually put my finger on. Maybe just an odd look here or there. A tone of voice. Just recently, over the last three or four weeks. I don't know.' She paused. 'It's mostly where Kester's concerned.'

'I think you're imagining it. They like you very much. Of course they do.'

'No, not *of course*, Rob. There's no *of course* about it.'

'No, but they do. They're fond of you.'

'Yes – and also they're *very* attached to their mother. Which

57

is a good thing, of course. It's just that – I'm just so afraid they'll – resent me.'

'Oh, Netta . . .' He put his arm around her. 'I know it's a hell of a job to ask you to take on – to be a mother to my children – and sometimes I've wondered at my nerve in asking you. But it'll work out. It will. I love you so much. And if you love me, then – '

'I do. You know I do.'

'Then it'll be all right.'

'It's just that – sometimes I have thoughts that – well, one hears about families where things end up so unhappily. I couldn't bear it if we finished up like that, you and me.'

'We won't. Believe me, we won't.'

'No?'

'I promise you.'

She smiled, closed her eyes. After a while Robert realized that she had fallen asleep. He eased his arm from beneath her neck and lay there listening to the sound of her even breathing. After a time he too drifted off to sleep.

He came awake with Daisy standing at the bedside, her hand on his arm. He looked at her sleepily.

'Hello, Daisy,' he whispered, 'what are you doing out of bed?'

'I woke up. I couldn't think for a minute where I was. I came to see if you were here.'

He smiled at her. 'Yes, of course I'm here.' Carefully, so as not to wake Netta, he sat up in bed, reached for his dressing-gown and slipped it on. 'Come on.' He took Daisy's hand and led her from the room.

In the sitting room he saw her into bed and tucked the covers up under her chin. 'All right now?'

'Yes.' She drew towards her the doll that Netta had given her.

'Goodnight, then.' He bent and kissed her.

'Goodnight, Daddy.'

He stood there for another few moments then crept back to the bedroom and the warmth of Netta's body.

*

58

'Are you tired?'

Judith sat on the edge of the boys' bed, looking down at them.

'No, not really,' Kester said.

'You should be. It's way after one.'

'I love it when we stay up really late,' Michael said with a yawn. 'At home we have to go to bed so early.'

'Well, you'd better go to sleep now. We have a busy day in front of us tomorrow.'

'Your birthday,' Kester said.

'Right, my birthday.'

'We ought to do something really nice.' Kester gazed at her for a moment in silence, then said, 'Are you all right, Jude?'

'Why do you ask?'

'You look – unhappy.'

She gave a sad little smile. 'Oh, I suppose I'm a little *triste*. A little blue.'

Suddenly as the boys looked at her the tears were running down her cheeks.

'Oh, Jude, don't!' Michael quickly sat up and threw his arms around her. 'Don't, please. I can't stand to see you cry.'

Judith's tears continued to fall while Michael held her and Kester kept his troubled eyes fixed on her anguished face. After a while she grew calmer, and Michael released her and lay back on the pillow.

'I'm sorry,' Judith said, sniffing and dabbing at her eyes. She reached out to Michael and smoothed his hair. 'I'll be all right now.'

'Why were you crying?' Kester asked. 'Tell us.'

She shrugged. 'I suppose – because of what your father told me today.'

'About his asking Netta to marry him?'

'You heard?'

'We couldn't help it.'

She nodded. 'Yes, that was it. I guess I expected it, but – it was still a bit of a shock. You know how it is – you go along

59

thinking there's a chance that everything will be all right, and then something like that happens and . . .' She shook her head.

'But she hasn't said she'll marry him, has she?' Michael said.

'No, I suppose not.'

'Well, perhaps she won't. I don't think she will.'

Judith smiled. 'Don't you? Or are you saying that just to cheer me up?'

'No, truly,' Michael said, 'I don't believe she will.'

'No,' Kester agreed, 'I don't think so either.' He pressed Judith's hand. They remained in silence for some minutes. Judith said, 'Your father told me he's taking you all to Devonshire for your holiday.'

'Yes.' Kester nodded.

'Are you looking forward to it?'

'Not really.'

'Why not?'

'We're going to some little house on the edge of the moors.'

'It sounds nice.'

'Nice?' Kester frowned. 'Stuck out there in the wilds with nowhere to go and fuck-all to do. Yes, very nice. No, I'd much rather be here with you, in London. I don't want to spend my time walking over miles of soggy moorland. The whole idea is anathema. Still, I don't think we'll have much choice.'

'You wait, you'll probably enjoy it when you get there.'

'No, it's going to be pathetically boring. I wish you were coming with us. You'd liven it up a bit.'

She smiled. 'Would I?'

'Yes.' Kester sighed. 'No, I don't want to go. For one thing it means we're going to miss our long weekend with you.'

'Never mind, there'll be other times.' After Judith had spoken, she looked down at Michael and put a finger to her lips. Michael lay with his eyes closed, breathing deeply. 'Mikie's asleep,' she said.

Kester half-turned his head on the pillow and glanced at his brother. 'He hasn't the stamina,' he smiled. Looking back at Judith, he added in a whisper, 'Now it's just you and me.'

'Yes.'

60

Silence fell in the room again, broken only by the sound of Michael's gentle, even breathing.

Judith said: 'I suppose Ben and Daisy stayed with her – your father's lady friend Netta – while he brought you here.'

'Yes, they're spending the night with her. They usually do.'

'He will too, I suppose.'

'I suppose so.'

'Does she have a nice flat?'

'No, it's a horrible, nasty little flat. Just one bedroom, one sitting room, and a pokey little kitchen and bathroom. It's not hers; she rents it. She wants to move, she said.'

Judith gave a melancholy nod. 'It's so sad – that it had to come to this. My snatching the odd weekend with my children. Your father sleeping in some strange woman's bed.' She sighed. 'We were so happy once – all of us. Now I don't know where it's all going. Where it will end.'

'You said the last time we were here that you thought we would all be together again. Don't you think that will happen now?'

She didn't answer for a moment, then she said: 'I don't see that there's much chance. Not now. Not now that he wants to marry his Netta.' She clicked her tongue. 'What a silly name.'

'It's short for Annetta.'

'Even sillier.'

'I agree.'

'I'm afraid his Netta's the pretty fly in the ointment.'

'I don't think she's pretty.'

'Don't you?'

'No, I certainly don't. I think she's ugly.'

'Well, obviously your father thinks she's pretty.'

'He can't do. How can he? She's got quite nice hair, I suppose, but her face is like the back of a fucking bus.'

Judith snorted in unconcealed delight at his words, then said, 'Oh, Kester, you shouldn't say such things.'

'It's true. She's got a long nose, and her jaw is big, much too big.' He squeezed Judith's hand. 'Oh, don't worry, Jude, he'll get tired of her. I'm sure he will.'

61

Judith became serious again. 'I thought so too at the beginning.'

'He will. Or she might just get fed up with him, and go off.' He shook his head. 'I can't stand her. She's really pathetic.'

'How do the others like her? Ben and Daisy.'

'Oh, they like her all right. But they're so young. What do they know about anything? And she's kind to them, and she brings them presents, so of course they think the sun shines out of her arse.'

Judith sighed and shook her head. 'Oh, let's not think about her – Netta,' she said. 'Let's just think about us, the three of us. What d'you think we should do this weekend?'

'Oh, something really nice. What do *you* think we should do?'

'What would you *like* to do? I thought we might go to Portobello Road in the morning. Does that appeal to you?'

'Oh, yes! Mike and I want to buy you something for your birthday.'

'Do you really?' Judith was smiling now.

'Yes, of course. What would you like?'

Judith sat in silence for a moment or two, her face lit by the soft-shaded lamp beside the bed. 'Do you really want to know what I'd like?'

'Tell me.'

'I'd like a bird.'

'A bird?'

'A bird. A bird to put in my beautiful birdcage.'

Kester nodded. 'We shall get you a bird, then. What kind of bird?'

'I don't know. A pretty bird.'

FIVE

They set off the next morning just after nine-thirty, driving towards Notting Hill in Judith's small white Renault. They hadn't bothered with breakfast; they would find something when they got there, Judith said.

Judith parked the car in a side street and they made their way to Portobello Road, joining it towards the lower end. 'By far the most interesting part,' Judith said, 'where all the junk starts. At the other end it's all jewellery and vegetables.'

Joining the crowds, and looking up and down the noisy, colourful street, as far as Kester could see there was nothing but long, endless lines of barrows and stalls, and the milling throng that jostled about them. At a corner stand Judith bought them Cokes and rather greasy hotdogs and they ate and drank as they walked along, every now and again stopping to peer at the goods on display. Michael bought a secondhand book on stamp collecting, and Judith bought chocolate for each of them. When they got to the end of the market they turned at the last stall and began to make their way back, this time covering the stalls on the other side of the street. Halfway along, Judith stopped to admire some bright orange beads. After a little deliberation she bought them and looped them around her neck. 'It's my birthday,' she said with a grin. 'And I'm out with the two handsomest men in town. I'm entitled to indulge myself.'

A little further on they found a pet shop. As they stopped before the window a litter of puppies looked appealingly out at them. A little further away a monkey sat disconsolately in a cage. There was no sign of any birds. 'Let's go inside,' Kester said, and they trooped into the dark, strange-smelling interior.

'Look!' said Michael, pointing. 'A bird!'

There at one end of the cluttered counter stood a cage with a bird inside. The bird was slim and parrot-like, mostly grey in colour, but with a garish red patch on each cheek. 'Oh, but you said you wanted a *pretty* bird,' Kester said. 'It's not very pretty, is it?'

Judith quickly disagreed. 'Oh, I love her!' she said. 'With those badly rouged cheeks she looks like some sad little tart. I *adore* her.'

The shopkeeper, a middle-aged man with an unshaven face and a paunch hanging over his belt, told them that the bird was a cockateel. With patience, he told them, it would learn to speak. Kester studied the bird, leaning forward and putting his face close to the bars of the shoddy little cage. 'Are you sure you like it, Jude?' he asked.

'Oh, yes, I'm sure, I'm sure.'

Kester smiled and put his finger in between the front bars. 'You want to come home with us, birdie? You want to come and be with Judith and have a nice, big, beautiful cage to live in?'

The bird froze on its perch. Kester moved his hand to the side, putting his finger through the bars again, making to stroke the bird's neck. And suddenly, in a little flurry of ruffled feathers, the bird whipped its head to one side and sank its curved beak into Kester's forefinger. Leaping back, Kester cried out. As he put his finger to his mouth and sucked the blood from it Judith frowned. 'Touchy little bastard, isn't he?'

The shopkeeper looked concerned. 'I'm sorry about that. I'm afraid 'e's a bit nervous. 'E'll be okay once 'e settles down.' He turned to Kester. 'You all right, son?'

'Yes, I'm fine.' Kester didn't appear to be much disturbed by the incident. 'I'm okay.' He sucked on his finger for a few seconds longer then asked, 'How much is the bird?'

When the man told them the price, Kester and Michael went into a huddle and quietly conferred for a few moments. Their father had given them money to buy Judith a present, but they quickly realized that this, even added to their own money which they had saved up, still wouldn't be enough. Disappointed, they turned back to the shopowner. They didn't have enough, Kester

64

said. After a moment's hesitation the man responded by dropping the price a little – but it was still above the sum they had
available. Judith solved the problem then by saying that she
would make up the difference, and five minutes later they were
moving out onto the street, Judith holding the birdcage while
Kester and Michael walked beside her carrying bags of birdseed
and other necessities. No longer interested in looking around
the market, they headed straight for the car.

When they returned to the flat in Streatham Judith at once
cleared a space for the cage on a small table by the wall. 'What
d'you think I should call her?' she said as she set the cage in
place.

'Now you're saying, "her",' Michael said. 'How do you know
it's a girl?'

'I don't. I just have the feeling. I suppose we can find out
later. Examine her.' She laughed. 'If you know what to look for
in a bird.' She put her head a little on one side, studying the
creature. Then she turned with a sidelong glance to Kester.
'What about – "Netta"?'

'*No!*' Kester's outburst was sharp. Judith smiled and put an
arm around his shoulder. 'No, darling, of course not. I was only
joking.' She drew him close and kissed his cheek. 'No, we'll
think of something.' She bent to the cage. 'We'll think of
something, won't we, birdie?'

'It's a crappy old cage, isn't it?' Michael said, and Judith
nodded. 'Yes, crappy in every way. Awful, cheap old thing. It
doesn't matter, though.' She turned to the large, ornate, empty
cage that stood nearby. 'When we have a little time this evening
or tomorrow we'll clean this one up. She'll be much happier
then.'

After a late lunch they got in the car again and drove into the
West End, to Baker Street, where they visited the Planetarium.
There the two boys sat back in their seats gazing wide-eyed up
at the domed, starlit ceiling. Afterwards they went next door to
Madame Tussaud's and looked at the waxworks. The boys had
little interest in the staring-eyed effigies of film stars, rock stars,

65

politicians and members of the royal family, but lingered for a long time in the Chamber of Horrors and before the more lurid, dramatic, historical tableaux. Standing before the scene depicting the death of Mary Queen of Scots, Judith murmured into Kester's ear, 'I never before had such a groom of the chamber.'

'You never what?' Kester turned to her, puzzled.

'Mary Stuart's last words,' Judith said. '"I never before had such a groom of the chamber." She spoke them when the executioner helped her to take off her frock. She went to her end very bravely.'

They left the building and set off along the street. They would find a nice restaurant and have an early dinner, Judith said. As they turned the corner at the lights, she went on, reverting to the earlier conversation: 'Famous last words – they can be so fascinating.' She turned to Michael who walked on her left. 'Do you know what Marie Antoinette's last words were?'

'No. Tell me.'

'"I'm sorry, Monsieur, I didn't do it on purpose."'

'How come?' Michael said.

'According to eyewitnesses,' Judith answered, 'she climbed the ladder up to the scaffold almost – eagerly, and then walked across the platform so quickly that she stepped on the executioner's foot. That's when she spoke *her* last words. "I'm sorry, Monsieur – I didn't do it on purpose." But in French, of course.' She shook her head. 'Very courageous. Not like that ninny Madame DuBarry.'

'What did *she* do?' asked Kester.

'DuBarry? Oh, she ran around on the scaffold like a headless chicken. "Don't hurt me! Oh, please don't hurt me!"' A minute later she *was* a headless chicken. No dignity at all. Pathetic creature. Don't you learn any of this in school?'

'Not interesting stuff like that.'

'Shame. It's the interesting bits that make history interesting.' She paused. 'The manner of a person's death is so significant, don't you think? The way they die, the way they face it, it can

66

so often give to their whole past life quite a different meaning. You'll find, right throughout history, that a person can be quite redeemed by the manner of his death.' She smiled. 'I know that when it's my turn I'd much rather go as a Marie Antoinette or Mary Stuart than Madame DuBarry.'

They stopped at a small restaurant in the next street, went inside and were shown to a table in a corner. They had hardly picked up the menus when the waitress, a mid-thirties, tired-looking blonde, came to the table and stood there, pad and pencil poised. Michael, after changing his mind a couple of times, said he would like some eggs. Judith looked at him in surprise. 'Eggs? You really want eggs?'

'Yes, I do.'

'How do you want your eggs?' the waitress asked.

'Ummmmm . . .' Michael screwed up his forehead while the waitress moved the weight from her left foot to her right.

'How do you want your eggs?' Judith said. 'Do you want them strangled or foiled?'

The waitress sighed. Judith glanced up at her then turned back to Michael. 'Tell the nice lady,' she said. 'Would you like them strangled or foiled?'

'Strangled.' Michael laughed. 'On toast.'

Judith looked up at the waitress. 'Two strangled eggs on toast,' she said, smiling sweetly. The waitress sighed again. 'Two scrambled eggs,' she said, avoiding Judith's eyes. She turned then to Kester. 'And for you?'

Kester ordered a cheeseburger and French fries. And at once Michael changed his mind. 'I'll have a cheeseburger too,' he said, adding with a laugh: 'Forget the strangled eggs.'

Judith turned to him. 'Careful, darling.' She sang the words. 'I think someone around here is a little short on humour.'

Tight-lipped, ignoring the remark, the waitress sighed again and looked at Judith. 'And for you?' she asked.

Judith order a steak, baked potato and salad. Then turning to the boys, she asked, 'Do you boys want anything to start with?'

No, they told her. 'Fine.' She nodded; then to the waitress: 'I think I'll start with the chilled consommé.'

To drink, the boys ordered Cokes, and when the waitress returned with them and the consommé some minutes later, Judith said, '*And* I think I'll have some wine, as well.' She grinned at the boys. 'After all, it *is* my birthday.'

'Oh, can we have wine too?' Michael asked.

'Darling, wait till you get home,' Judith said. 'You shall have some wine then if you want it. I don't think they'd allow it here.' She turned with a smile to the waitress who was now holding out the wine list to her. The waitress didn't return Judith's smile but said coldly, while showing, with another sigh, her swiftly growing irritation: 'What wine would you like?'

'Uh oh.' Judith raised her eyebrows and pulled a face at the boys as she took the wine list from the waitress's hand. 'I think soneone's very quickly running out of patience here. Now . . .' Under the waitress's cold eye she consulted the wine list. 'Yes,' she said, 'I'll have a half-bottle of Riesling.'

'Half-bottle of Riesling,' the waitress said, making marks on her pad. She pronounced the word *rise-ling*, slightly stressing the first syllable.

Judith said at once: 'No, I don't want *rise*-ling; I want *rees*-ling. Don't correct me.' Her voice was sweet ice. 'First of all because I'm a customer. Secondly because you should have better manners. And thirdly, because my pronunciation is *correct*. Now,' she smiled, her voice rising a little, 'I'm getting a little fatigued listening to your long-suffering sighs, so kindly get me a half-bottle of *rees*ling and stop being such a pain in the fucking arse.'

As the boys laughed, the waitress's mouth fell open and she gazed at Judith wide-eyed while the blood reddened her cheeks. Pursing her lips, drawing herself up, she had just started to turn and flounce away when Kester stood up from his seat.

'No,' he said quietly, all his humour gone, 'let her keep her fucking *rise*ling.' He glared at the waitress, his head on a level with her own, his eyes boring into hers. 'How dare you correct my mother's pronunciation?' His voice rose. 'How dare you?'

He glanced down, snatched up the wine list and tossed it at her. 'We don't want your wine,' he said, ' – how*ever* you care to pronounce it in your stupid pig-ignorance.' He leaned forward across the table. 'You can forget the whole lot. We're not staying. We're not staying to be waited on by some moronic, long-suffering idiot like you.' His eyes flicked back to the table, and his hand flashed out and drew Judith's bowl of consommé towards him. Then, his hand plunging into the brown, jelly-like mass, he scooped up a handful, drew back his arm and threw it. It caught the waitress on the chin, her neck and the top of her blouse. Without pausing a further instant, Kester moved around the table. He was white with anger. 'Come on,' he said to Judith and Michael, 'we'll go somewhere else.'

Two streets away they stopped at another restaurant. There they ate pizzas and salad, followed by thick, ice-cream shakes.

They spent the rest of the evening at the flat, watching television and talking. At ten-thirty Judith opened some wine and they drank it with sandwiches and cake. At last Michael yawned and, saying that he was tired, added that he would go on to bed. 'Will you be long?' he asked Kester as he got up from the sofa.

'No, not long. I'll be there soon.'

'Okay.' Michael went to Judith where she sat in her chair. He put his arms around her. 'Goodnight, Jude.'

'Goodnight, dearest boy.' Warmly she kissed him. 'Sleep well. And thank you for my lovely bird and my lovely birthday.'

When Michael had finished in the bathroom and disappeared into the bedroom Judith and Kester sat in silence. The television was off now and Kester had taken up a book.

'What are you reading?' Judith asked him.

'One of your books. The one on Constance Kent.'

'Oh, yes. What a little madam she was, wasn't she? Imagine, killing her little brother and stuffing him down the loo.' She chuckled. 'Hardly a sisterly thing to do.'

Kester laughed and she got up, stepped to his side and laid her hand gently on his thick, untidy hair.

'Aren't you tired too?' she asked.

'Not really. Are you?'

'Well – I think perhaps I had a little too much wine.'

'I think perhaps I did too.'

'Don't tell your father you had all that wine, will you? He won't approve, you know.'

'No, of course I won't tell him.'

Judith stretched. 'I think I'll have a bath and go on to bed.'

With the bath water running Judith came back to the sitting room in her dressing-gown. In the open doorway she stood looking at Kester. Feeling her eyes upon him he looked up from his book and turned to her.

'What's up?'

'Nothing. I was just looking. A cat can look at a king, can't she?'

He smiled at her. 'I suppose so.'

'If you must know, I was thinking what a handsome young man you are. Yes.' She nodded. 'And I can't help thinking that it won't be long before you've found yourself a nice young girl. You'll be moving in with her. Making her happy.' She smiled. 'Do you have a nice young girl? Someone you haven't told me about?'

'No. Not yet.' He gave a little laugh.

'Ah, but you will have, soon,' Judith said. 'Oh, I envy her already. How can I ever love her? Tell me that. How can I ever love someone who'd take my Kester away from me?'

He gazed at her for a moment or two in silence, then he said softly, 'No one will take me away from you. Ever.'

After a few seconds, she said, 'I'd better go before the bath overflows,' and turned away. Kester continued to sit there, the open book forgotten in his lap, listening to the sounds as Judith got into the bath. She was bathing with the door open, he realized.

After a few minutes he put the book aside and got up. Going out into the little hall he stood there, looking past the open door at Judith's naked back as she sat in the tub. He remained there for long moments and then Judith's voice came to him, her

70

voice low: 'Kester, darling, hand me my nail brush, will you?' She had known he was there.

He went into the room where he followed her gesturing hand to the shelf below the mirror. He picked up the small brush, turned and, eyes lowered, held it out.

'Closer, please. I can't reach it.' A pause. 'Don't be shy.'

He raised his eyes as he took another step forward and she reached out and took the brush from him. Her other arm, he saw, was across her round, full breasts, which were just above the waterline. Her breasts weren't completely hidden. She smiled at him, thanked him, then casually began to brush her fingernails. On the wall beside the tub was a long, rectangular mirror. His gaze moved back and forth, shifting alternately from her to her reflection. Now as she worked on her nails her breasts were fully exposed to his sight. He gazed, mesmerized. After a few seconds she lifted her eyes to his. 'Have you never seen a woman naked before, Kester?'

'What . . . ?' He shook his head. His throat felt dry.

'Ah, well, there's time.' She paused. 'How's your finger where my little birdie pecked you?'

'Oh – all right.'

She beckoned to him and after a moment's hesitation he went to her. Putting the nail brush aside she took his hand and peered closely at his finger. 'Does it hurt?'

'No, not now.'

'You were so brave. You didn't make a fuss at all. You didn't even show any anger towards it.'

He shrugged. 'Why should I have? The bird was a little nervous, that's all, poor thing. It was afraid. That's the only reason it went for me. You can't blame it for that – standing up for itself.'

She nodded, drew his hand nearer, kissed the little wound and then took his finger into her mouth. As she sucked on it he could feel the warm wetness of her tongue. Her eyes looked up at him over his captive hand. After a moment she released him. 'There, all better now.'

He gave an awkward little laugh and she reached up and put

71

both hands up to his face, one on either side. Her touch was very gentle. 'Oh, God . . .' She gazed into his eyes. 'I don't know what I'd do if you weren't there.'

'I'll always be there, Jude. Whenever you want me I'll be there.'

She leaned forward, at the same time drawing him towards her. She kissed him on the lips, soft, just a whisper of a touch. He closed his eyes. He could smell more strongly the scent of her soap. And then he felt the touch of her lips again, this time lingering, more insistent, moist. He felt her lips part against his own, felt the touch of her tongue. His own mouth opened and he felt her tongue move over his eager lips, touching his teeth, his own tongue. At his loins he felt the rising of his member.

When the kiss had ended she drew a little away from him and gazed into his eyes. She shook her head in a brief gesture of wonder. 'My boy. My boy.' Then, withdrawing her hands from his face, she said, 'Do you want a bath afterwards?'

'. . . Yes.'

'I'll run the water for you when I'm finished.'

He straightened, then turned and went from the bathroom. In the sitting room he sat down again on the sofa, his erection tightening the crutch of his jeans. He sat very still, his damp palms pressed together.

Later, when Judith was out of the bathtub and had run the water for him, he threw off his sweater, trainers, socks and shirt and went towards the bathroom. As he entered he found Judith standing in front of the mirror, wiping the steam off the glass. Her hair was wet and she was wearing a blue towelling robe. He tested the water, found it was just right, and turned off the taps. He stood then for some moments at a loss, uncertain of how to proceed. Judith, standing towelling her hair, showed no sign of moving out. As he still hesitated she said, without looking at him: 'I'm your mother and I'm your friend. You don't need to be bashful in front of me.'

She went on drying her hair and Kester undid his belt, pulled down his jeans and stepped out of them. Then his underpants. Quickly he stepped into the tub. Judith had put some kind of

72

foaming softener into it and the water's surface was high with a soft, thick layer of cloud-like foam. As he lowered himself into the water the white, foaming suds came up to his lower ribs. Judith, still rubbing her hair and facing her reflection, said casually, 'Oh, I feel so much better now. It's been quite a full day, hasn't it?'

'Yes – it has.' He tried to match the easy note that was in her voice. In the mirror beside the tub he watched himself as he spoke, saw the soapy lather oozing out from between his hands. 'Are you still tired?' he asked.

'No, not at all. Not now. Now I just feel – wonderfully relaxed.'

While Kester washed his face and arms Judith put the towel aside and began to brush the tangles out of her hair. Then she came towards him, her hair hanging damp and heavy about her shoulders. Her skin glowed. He thought he had never seen her look more beautiful. She smiled at him, showing her white, even teeth. 'Here – I'll wash your back for you.' She held out her hand and he put the cake of soap into it. He leaned forward a little and she sat on the edge of the tub. He felt the touch of her hand on his neck, soft and soothing, moving round and round, first with the soap and then without it, only the palm of her hand and her fingers on his tingling flesh, stirring up the lather. 'You have such a beautiful skin,' she murmured. 'So soft, so smooth.' Her hands went on moving, over his shoulders, beneath his arms, around the upper part of his ribcage, his chest, his neck. Then she took up the sponge and rinsed the suds away. Turning slightly to the right he watched the reflection in the mirror, seeing himself sitting there, Judith bending over him. He saw her lean forward; saw and felt the light kiss she planted on his left shoulder. He closed his eyes and lifted his face in the ecstasy of the moment. He could hear her breath close to his ear. A second later he opened his eyes and glanced down and saw that the soap had dispelled the suds and cleared the water. His member, red, stiff and tumescent, was clearly visible.

'Kneel up.'

At her words he was overcome by panic.

'. . . I can't,' he said.

'Come on, kneel up – so I can do your lower back.'

'I can't,' he said again. He didn't dare look at her. The next moment her hand had come down over his shoulder, was moving down his chest, over his stomach. He felt the tips of her fingers brush the sparse pubic hair, and then touch him – there – and hold him, her long, slim fingers encircling him with gentle tenderness. 'You're such a perfect, perfect boy,' she said.

Her hand left him, urging him to rise. He knelt, his genitals clear of the water, his penis standing out, proud, throbbing. She began to soap him again, this time his lower back, and then his buttocks, her fingers moving into the valley between them, the hole itself. She sponged him, and then her left hand moved around his thighs and began to soap his genitals. Her hands white with lather, she cupped the small sack and then closed her fingers again about the shaft. He gasped. 'Jude. Oh, Jude.'

'Darling. My darling.' She pressed her face against his wet, glistening body. 'You're *my* boy. *My* perfect, perfect boy.'

Her hand went on stroking for several moments, and then she sponged the soap away. Glancing down, he watched as her head bent to him, her mouth opening. He watched as her lips closed over the head of his penis. At the sensation, and the sight, he gasped and pressed himself deep into her mouth. The start of his orgasm seemed to rise up from some depth of his being that he never even knew was there. It surged within him like a spring long held in check, growing stronger as it rose up, flooding his body with exquisite sensations. His back arching, he felt Judith's working mouth tighten about him. He groaned, and the dam burst, and with a cry like an animal in pain he emptied himself into her loving mouth.

Much later he lay sleepless in bed. Beside him Michael slept soundly. Kester kept thinking of his mother.

After some time he slid quietly out of bed, crept from the room and crossed the small hall to his mother's room. Silently

74

he pushed open the door, as silently closing it behind him. He moved to the bed. As he did so he heard her voice.

'Kester,' she whispered in the stillness. 'Is that you?'

'Yes.'

'I knew you'd come.'

Seconds later he was in the bed beside her, hungry mouth upon her own, hungry hands exploring her body. He lay upon her, and then felt her hand reach down, guiding him into the warm wetness below. When it was over, so soon, they lay clasped in one another's arms.

In the morning Kester got up and went back to his own bed. Michael stirred, briefly waking as Kester got in beside him, then turned over and went back to sleep. For a minute or so Kester lay thinking of the night, and then he, too, slept again.

It was almost eleven before they sat around the breakfast table. They ate cornflakes, scrambled eggs and toast. From the cage the cockateel watched them with its round eyes. 'Yes, my pretty little love,' Judith said, looking over at the bird, 'as soon as we've had breakfast we're going to put you into your *proper* cage.'

When they had finished eating they left the breakfast dishes on the table and began to prepare the empty cage. When it was ready Judith moved to the smaller cage containing the bird. 'How do we go about this?' she said over her shoulder to the boys.

They eventually decided to open both cage doors and place the two cages together, the open doors face to face. It didn't work, though. 'The stupid bird won't move,' Michael said irritably. 'Look at it – it just sits there, watching us.'

In an effort to get the bird to go from one cage to the other they gently shook the cage it was in, rattled it, and in despair even gave the bird gentle little prods with a pencil. Growing increasingly nervous and agitated, the bird remained on its perch. His impatience growing, Kester shook the smaller cage again and slapped his hand against the side. As he did so he knocked the cage askew on the table, and the bird, suddenly

75

seeing the open door before it, darted towards it. Next moment, with a fluttering of wings, it was out in the room.

'Oh, shit,' Judith said. 'Stupid little bastard.'

They watched as the bird fluttered around the room a couple of times and came to rest on the horn of the old phonograph. Without hesitating, Judith leapt forward and snatched the bird up in her hands. A second later, as she turned triumphantly to the two boys, the bird dipped its head and sank its sharply curving beak into the soft flesh of her hand.

She screamed out in pain, letting the bird go and putting her hand to her mouth. 'Oh, God! Oh, Christ!'

'Jude . . . Jude . . . !' Kester moved quickly to her side, Michael following. When Judith took her hand away they saw that it was bleeding. Her eyes were screwed up in pain.

'That fucking bird!' Kester cried out and turned, glaring at the bird where it perched on a chair back.

Judith said pacifyingly: 'I'm all right, darling, I'm all right. Don't worry. Like you said, she's just a little nervous. And it's hardly surprising, is it? – not after what she's just been through.'

Kester hardly heard her words. With rage burning inside him, he snatched up one of Judith's sweaters from a nearby chair, moved forward, held the sweater high, aimed, and threw it. The bird, seeing it descending, tried too late to fly. A moment later bird and sweater had fallen to the carpet.

'That's good,' Judith said with a sigh of relief, and then: 'It's okay, she won't be hurt.'

On the carpet the sweater danced, bobbing up and down as the bird tried to escape. Then, a moment later, Kester was stepping forward and, his face contorted in fury, was raising his foot and bringing it down. For the space of a split second he could feel the resistance of the little moving body beneath the sole of his shoe. Then he felt and heard the bones crunch. He went on pounding the little heap beneath the sweater long after it held any vestige of life.

SIX

'Well, here we are. At last.'

For the last half-hour their route had taken them through the winding, undulating roads of the Devonshire countryside. Now, having reached their destination, Robert turned the Citroën right off the lane, drove it between the gate posts and parked it in front of the house on the forecourt. The time was just after four o'clock. He had picked up the house keys from the owners of the post office in the village of Reston, some three miles back. Now as he switched off the engine he turned to Netta and gave a sigh of relief and satisfaction at their arrival. Behind him the children began to pile out. He quickly followed them and for a few moments they all stood looking up at the house. Then, after Robert had unlocked the front door they began to unload the suitcases and bags and the boxes of provisions they had picked up on the way, and to carry them inside.

The house with its whitewashed stone walls and grey slate roof was surrounded by farmland. It stood secluded from the other dwellings in the area, the nearest, a group of farm cottages, standing some three hundred yards away. Once a farmhouse, the house was set on the side of a hill halfway between the villages of Reston and Moxham. The many acres of farmland that had once belonged to it had long since been sold off to neighbouring farmers, the only remaining land belonging being that immediately beside and behind the house – a flower garden, a wide lawn, a kitchen garden and an orchard.

When Robert, Netta and the children had carried most of the luggage inside they looked around the interior. The house had been built in the mid-nineteenth century, but had since undergone various modifications, and it looked very comfortable. The ground floor was comprised of the kitchen, a very large living room with a dining annexe and, on the right of the hall, a sitting room ('I suppose this is what they'd once called the parlour,' Netta observed), and a bathroom. Upstairs were four bedrooms and another bathroom. The furniture throughout the house, though plain, looked comfortable and well cared for.

When the children had been designated their rooms they were left to unpack while Netta and Robert concentrated on organizing the kitchen and preparing a meal.

Upstairs at a window of the bedroom given over to himself and Michael, Kester stood and looked out over the forecourt and front garden. Behind him his own case was open but unpacked, only the photograph of Judith out of it and standing on the small table beside the double bed. Before him, beyond the shrubs that hid the lane from view, the fields and moorland stretched out to the horizon. He gave a deep sigh and shook his head.

Michael, busy unpacking, turned and looked at him. 'What's up?'

Kester shook his head again. 'This place.'

Michael's face showed a flicker of disappointment. 'Don't you like it?'

'Do you?'

'Well . . .' Michael shrugged. 'It seems all right. It'll be okay.'

'Okay? You must be joking. Have you looked around you? There's going to be nothing to do. Fuck-all to do, and two weeks to do it in.'

Michael left his unpacking and joined Kester at the window. 'Two weeks isn't long,' he said. 'And it'll probably turn out to be all right.'

Kester's voice remained surly. 'Two whole weeks in this God-forsaken hole.' He shrugged. 'But I suppose the time will pass eventually, though. I suppose we'll find something to do.'

'Yes, we will. It'll be all right.'

'Be good if Jude were here with us. Be all right then.'

'Yes.'

'And it wouldn't be so bad if we were just here with Dad . . .'

As Kester spoke he saw Netta move into his view as she moved from the house to the car. He watched as she opened a rear door and leaned in.

'There's the fly in the ointment,' he said. Slowly he shook his head. 'Well, I don't care how the others feel about her, but I know I'll never be able to accept her. I know that now. Especially after what she's done.'

A little pause and Michael asked ingenuously, 'What *has* she done?'

Kester turned and gave him a withering glare. 'How can you ask that?'

Michael said nothing. Down below Netta closed the car door and, holding a box under one arm, turned and moved out of sight, back towards the house.

'Anyway,' Kester sighed, 'let's get this holiday over then we can go up to London and see Jude again.'

When he and Michael had finished their unpacking they went back downstairs and out into the rear garden. There they moved past the garage and the tool shed, up the path that cut through the lawn and the kitchen garden, past another shed, very old and ramshackle, and into the orchard. Beyond the orchard fence was a wild area, growing thick with weeds and brambles. Beyond that there was woodland and the spreading fields of the surrounding farmland.

Standing by the orchard fence, Kester gazed around him. 'Well,' he said grudgingly, 'perhaps it won't be *so* bad.'

Returning to the kitchen garden after a few minutes, they stopped and looked in the shed. It was full of garden implements and old junk – a battered old chest of drawers, boxes of ancient photographic plates, a strange, old-fashioned pram with huge wheels. As they poked around the dusty interior Kester turned and saw Ben standing in the doorway.

'What are you doing here?' he asked, 'You were following us, weren't you?'

Ben shook his head in protest. 'No, I wasn't. I came to tell you that Netta says tea will be ready in a few minutes.'

*

Netta had prepared a scratch meal of baked beans, sausages and bread-and-butter. They all ate hungrily. Afterwards, when the washing-up was done, they left the house to go for a walk.

After a rather overcast morning the afternoon had turned out warm and fine. From the gate they turned right onto the lane, heading for the narrow, winding road, where, careful of the occasional car that came by, they walked for a while in single file. After two or three minutes Robert, who led the way, pointed to a signpost indicating a footpath leading to the village of Moxham. 'This'll do,' he said. Turning off to the left, they clambered over a stile and began to make their way along a fairly wide path that ran beside a field where neat bales of straw lay looking like huge unwrapped toffees on the ochre-coloured stubble. Robert, Netta and Daisy walked together, with Ben some few yards before them, trailing in the footsteps of his elder brothers who kept some little distance ahead. He had wanted to walk with Kester and Michael but Kester had refused, sending him back to the others.

Robert, though aware of Ben's disappointment, refused to let it get to him, to ruffle the contentment and relief he felt at their arrival. The past few days had passed in a chaotic whirl of final preparations – and with four children to think of there had been a great many. Then, with everything ready he had driven to Gloucestershire, to Cirencester, to see his widowed mother in her small house on the outskirts of the town. And there he had found her in bed, suffering from a heavy cold, and his sister-in-law, Janet, wife of his brother Hal, ministering to her needs.

'Why didn't you tell me you weren't well?' he had said to his mother. 'You should have phoned me.'

She had dismissed his words with a wave of her hand. 'It's only a cold. I'll be all right soon. Besides, you've got enough to think about, getting ready for your holiday.'

In spite of her attempts to persuade him to the contrary, he realized that she was rather low in spirits. She seemed to be unusually conscious of her advancing years. She was eighty now, and, five years after a not very successful hip-joint-replacement operation, had become increasingly disabled over the past months. After he had sat with her for an hour or so she had insisted on getting up, and he had helped her downstairs where he had set a chair for her by the window. There, sighing, she had looked sadly out over the small front garden. Once for her a source of great pride and no small passion, the lawn and the herbaceous borders were clearly showing their increasing neglect.

'I just can't do it any more,' she said. 'I can't bend. I can't get down to it.' The stairs, too, he learned, were presenting problems, and Janet told him that they had talked about bringing her bed downstairs.

An added difficulty, he discovered, was the fact that his mother's eyesight was beginning to fade. Once an avid reader, she was finding such a relaxation more and more difficult, and was now relying increasingly on her radio and television for comfort.

When it was time to say goodbye he went to her side, bent and kissed her cheek. 'I'll see you soon.'

She smiled at him. 'Have a good holiday. And come and see me afterwards. And bring Netta with you.'

'I will.' He had introduced Netta to his mother a couple of months earlier. His mother, never having approved of Judith, but merely having tolerated her for Robert's sake, had taken to Netta at once.

When he left the house Janet walked with him to his car. 'She's growing so frail,' he said. 'I see such a change in her.'

Janet gave a nod, and a helpless little shrug. 'I know. But what can you do? What can anybody do? It's her age.' After a pause she added, 'Of course, we see her every day or two, but you don't see her nearly as often so you're bound to notice the change in her more easily.'

Robert wrote out the address of the house in Devonshire and gave it to Janet. 'In case you need me,' he said. 'There's no phone connected there, I'm afraid, but I can ring up from the village and see how she is.' Janet put the slip of paper into her apron pocket. 'Fine,' she said, 'but don't worry about her. She'll be okay. Take Netta and the children and go and relax. Go and have your holiday. I should think you need it.'

Now, walking beside the field in the light of the early evening sun, he turned to Netta and gave a little smile. She smiled back at him. His hand brushed hers, took it, held it. He bent his head to hers. 'I love you very much,' he murmured.

Her smile grew warmer. She pressed his hand. 'I love you, too.'

They reached the village of Moxham after some twenty-five minutes. Stopping at a pub there, The Crown, the children sat at a rustic table in the garden while Robert and Netta went inside and brought out to them Cokes, lemonade and, in spite of the fact that they hadn't long since eaten, crisps. Robert and Netta drank beer. They stayed there for almost an hour, talking of this and that, then made their way back towards the house.

By the time they reached the house it was almost eight-thirty and the sun was low on the horizon. Daisy was tired. She yawned as she sank down into a chair in the living room, and Robert said to her, 'You and Ben had better have your baths and go straight to bed.' There were no protests. It had been a long day. Soon after nine o'clock Ben and Daisy were tucked up in their beds in the room behind Robert and Netta's. Standing at the side of Daisy's bed Robert leaned over her and brushed a lock of dark hair back from her forehead. She gazed up at him sleepily and yawned, one hand grasping his own. 'My little Daisy,' he said, ' – she's so tired.'

She frowned. 'Daddy, can I come and sleep with you tonight? It's all so strange here.'

'Oh, you'll soon get used to it.'

'No, I don't think I'll be able to sleep – not in this strange bed.'

'You'll sleep all right, you'll see.'

'I don't think I will.'

She closed her eyes and he felt her small fingers tighten their grip around his own. She was already drifting off to sleep. Gently he eased his hand away, kissed her lightly on the cheek and got up from the bed. Moving quietly on the faintly creaking floor, he stepped across the small space of carpet to the other bed. Ben's eyes held him as he approached. Sitting down on the edge of the bed, Robert said softly, 'You should be sleeping.'

Ben smiled. 'I was waiting for you.'

'Well, I'm here now, so you can go to sleep.' Ben sometimes seemed so young for his years, Robert thought. 'D'you think you'll like it here?' he asked.

'Oh, yes.' Ben paused then added: 'I heard Kester talking about going up to London at half-term. To stay with Jude.'

Robert nodded. 'Yes, it's very likely.'

'Could I go too?'

'Well – would you like to?'

'And stay with Kester and Michael and Jude? Oh, yes.'

'Well – if you like I can talk to your mother about it. Would you like me to? I think perhaps you should spend a little more time with her occasionally. You know – get to know her a little better.'

Ben smiled. 'And go with Kester and Mike . . .'

'Yes.'

Ben's sleepy smile grew broader.

'Anyway,' Robert said, 'we'll think about it, okay?'

'Yes . . .'

Ben's eyelids flickered as sleep came nearer. Robert bent low over him and kissed his forehead. 'Goodnight, son.' Ben, already drifting into sleep, didn't stir. Softly, Robert eased himself up from the bed and crept out of the room.

Downstairs he found Kester and Michael sitting before the portable television set. Kester looked up as Robert came by. 'This screen – it's so *small*,' he said. Robert shrugged. 'Sorry about that – but you didn't come on holiday to watch television, did you?'

Later, when Kester and Michael had taken baths and gone up to bed, Robert put on the rear outside lights. Then he and Netta carried coffee and Drambuie and glasses out onto the small patio at the back of the house. There, in the warm glow

83

they sat on garden chairs facing out across the lawn. Robert lit a rare cigarette and blew the smoke up into the air of the mellow night. Briefly he closed his eyes, sighed.

'Oh, these moments are magic when all the children are in bed.' He kept his voice low so as not to disturb the children above. Into his mind came a picture of Ben as he had lain in his bed. 'Poor Ben,' he murmured, 'he doesn't know what he wants or where he belongs. I suppose he'll get it all sorted out eventually.'

'Of course he will.' Netta reached out and touched his arm. 'Come on, relax now . . .'

'Yes.' He nodded. Slowly they sipped at the coffee and the Drambuie. 'It's such a beautiful night,' Netta murmured.

'Are you warm enough?' he asked.

'Oh, yes.'

The waning moon shone brightly over the garden, lighting the smooth lawn before them with a silvery sheen. The stars were sparkling pin-points of light in the deep velvet of the sky. From somewhere above the garden beyond the lawn came the hoot of an owl. Over their heads a moth fluttered against one of the lights on the wall. Murmuring quietly together, Robert and Netta spoke of their gladness to be away from the town, away from the pressures of the classroom. They spoke of the things that they and the children might do during the holiday, the places they might visit. 'I just hope,' Netta said, 'that Kester and Michael won't find it all rather boring.'

Robert stubbed out his cigarette. 'No, of course they won't.'

She smiled. 'Kester didn't appear all that enthusiastic on our arrival.'

'They're fine. They're fine.' Robert reached out and laid his hand over her own. 'Listen, Netta, this holiday isn't only for Kester and Michael. It's for Ben and Daisy, too, and for you and me. Kester and Michael aren't the only ones to be considered.' Releasing her hand he picked up his glass and drank the last of the liqueur. 'Come on,' he said softly, 'let's you and me go for a little stroll.'

'At this time of night? Where to?'

He nodded towards the garden and the orchard beyond. 'Oh – around the estate.'

He got up from the seat and Netta set down her glass and stood up beside him. Hand in hand they set off across the grass.

Kester stood at the bathroom window, peering out around the edge of the curtain. 'They're walking over the lawn towards the garden,' he whispered to Michael at his side. 'They're holding hands.'

The night was so clear. Every leaf, fruit and branch stood out sharply in the bright, unhindered light of the moon. Robert and Netta had left the lawn and the kitchen garden behind them and now walked slowly in the orchard. Beside a bent and twisted apple tree Robert stopped, turned, and took Netta in his arms. Her own arms moved to wrap around him as he held her. He kissed her, gently at first, and then more urgently, passionately.

'Come – down here . . .' He lowered himself to the soft grass, took off his sweater and spread it out. Netta sat down beside him and then at his urging lay back. He leaned over her, kissing her again while his hands touched her breasts and then fumbled at the waistband of her jeans. When her jeans were off he rose, undid his belt, slipped off his own jeans and stood over her in his shirt and underpants. Netta got to her knees, grasped the waistband of his underpants and pulled them down. After looking up at him for a moment she bent her head towards him.

'Where have you been?' Michael said, sitting up in bed as Kester came into the room. The moonlight in the room was strong enough to see by. 'Have you been outside?'

'I followed them. They were in the orchard.' Kester sat on the edge of his bed and rubbed his hands over his bare feet. 'I watched them.' He held up a hand in a gesture for silence. 'Listen – they're coming back indoors.' From beneath them came the faint sound of a door closing.

'Did they see you?' Michael whispered.

'No, of course not.' Kester got into bed, turned and smiled at Michael. 'But I saw them.'

'And?'

'She was sucking him. The fly – she was down on her knees, sucking him.'

SEVEN

'Are you enjoying yourself?'

Robert, wearing only shorts, propped up on one elbow and lounging on a rug spread out on the soft grass on the bank of the lake, asked the words of Netta. She lay on her back beside him, her eyes closed against the bright afternoon sun. She wore shorts and a bikini top. After ten days she was almost as tanned as the children.

'Oh, yes.' She answered with her eyes still closed. 'It's wonderful. I don't think I ever had such peace before.'

He reached out a lazy hand and gently, lightly brushed his fingers through her thick, dark brown hair. From nearby came the voices of the children; Kester and Michael as they splashed and swam in the lake – their shouts, their laughter bouncing up from the water – and nearer, Ben and Daisy as they sat chattering together at the water's edge.

The days had passed pleasantly and peacefully. With only two or three occasions when the weather had been dull or wet, it had, for the most part, stayed bright and warm. Robert, Netta and the children had spent much of the time out in the open air, taking long walks, driving to the beach, and visiting unfamiliar towns where they had lunched and looked around the shops and the sights. Mostly, though, they had packed picnics and gone deep into the countryside, away from anyone else.

On this particular day, as on two or three other occasions, they had decided to spend some time at a lake that lay on the edge of Hazelton, one of the smaller villages on the borders of the moor. Enclosed by trees, the lake and its immediate surroundings had proved a favourite spot with the children, a place where they could amuse themselves for hours at a time.

With a sigh Robert lowered himself prone onto the rug,

stretching luxuriously in his contentment. Everything so far was going well. The news from Cirencester was good, too; he had called his mother the previous day and she was feeling a lot better. He sighed again, cupped his chin in his hands and looked across the lake. There were only a few other people about, two or three other families some distance away on the lake's far shore. Turning his head he gazed over to where Daisy sat on the bank. She was alone now; Ben had gone off. Robert watched her. In her concentration the upturned tip of her tongue showed between her lips. She was building something, a little construction of stones, humming to herself as she worked – 'The Ash Grove', it sounded like – in a high, piping little voice. The sun shone down on her dark hair, her tanned, naked limbs. As Robert gazed at her she glanced around and caught his eye. 'I'm building a house,' she said. Robert smiled and nodded in approval. 'So I see. How's it going?'

'Oh, all right. I've got a lot to do yet.'

'Keep at it.'

'I will.'

She went back to her task, her wordless song floating on the warm air. Looking further over to the left Robert saw Kester swim past, powerful arms and legs beating the water. A few seconds later Michael was there, following in his wake. A long pause, then Ben came into view, splashing clumsily along after his older brothers and keeping close to the bank, in the shallow water, as Robert had instructed him. Robert watched as Ben went thrashing past. It was a continuous fight for Ben, trying to keep up with the others.

'How – did I – do?'

Breathless, Ben floundered and splashed as he found a foothold in the soft bank of the lake. He pulled himself upright, gripping the grass on the bank, his head bent while he fought for his breath.

Kester and Michael had pulled themselves up out of the water and now sat on the bank. From where they sat their father and the others were distant shapes beyond the screen of trailing leaves of the weeping willows. Kester gave a little shake of his head.

'God, you were so *slow*.'

Ben gave a groan. 'Oh, Kester – I was faster than I ever was before.'

'Really?' There was amused doubt in Kester's voice.

'Yes, truly. I was much faster than at the baths.' Ben's feeling of achievement was draining off him like the water that ran from his body back into the lake. Somehow, whatever he managed to do, Kester had a way of making it all seem like nothing.

After a moment Kester got to his feet. 'Come on.' He jerked his head at Michael who got up beside him.

'Where are you going?' Ben asked as the two started off together.

They didn't answer. Michael looked back for a second but then Kester's hand was touching his shoulder, urging him on.

'Kester – Mike,' Ben called. 'Can I come with you?'

Still they didn't answer.

'Can I?' Ben stood there in the water, calling after their retreating backs. By the time he had scrambled out of the water and pulled himself up onto the bank his brothers had gone out of sight among the trees.

Sitting up, hugging her knees, Netta watched Kester and Michael walking away through the trees that bordered the lake. Then she saw Ben, moving tentatively after them. She turned, glancing across at Daisy who sang as she kept busy with her stones. Daisy was unlike Ben; she had an ability to be alone, always able to find amusement for herself. Not so Ben; he was far more dependent on others; particularly his older brothers; and Robert was right – Ben's anxiety to be at one with them was so apparent . . .

When Netta looked back towards the trees all three boys had gone out of sight. Lowering her glance, she looked down at Robert as he lay at her side. His eyes were closed but he was

89

not sleeping. She gazed at him in silence for some moments then asked quietly: 'Do you think it's been a success, Robert?'

He answered with his eyes still closed, his face on the rug. 'Do I think *what* has been a success?'

'The holiday, so far. You know what I'm talking about.'

He turned onto his back, opened his eyes, shaded them from the glare of the sun and looked at her. 'Oh, Netta, you're so full of doubt always. Can't you see for yourself that it's been a success?'

She smiled uncertainly. 'You really do think so?'

'I certainly do.'

She shrugged. 'I just can't be sure. How can I be sure?'

'Don't be so reluctant to recognize success when you see it. It's been a wonderful holiday, for everyone.' He smiled. 'Haven't you had a good time?'

'Oh, yes, you know I have.'

'Good.'

'But I'm not talking about me, you know that.'

'The children.'

'Kester – and Michael.'

'Kester and Michael. Of course.'

'Do you think it's worked for them all right?'

'Yes, I do. I really do. I wasn't so sure at the start, when we got here, but afterwards ... Oh, yes, they're having a great time.'

'I don't know – I feel so conscious of them, of what they say, what they do. All the time. In any way in which it affects me – I'm looking, looking all the time for any signs, any hints.'

'Signs? Hints? Of what?'

'Oh, don't be obtuse, Robert.' She sighed. 'It's so vital that I'm – accepted by them.'

'And have you seen any signs or hints that you're not?'

She didn't answer; in the silence she lay down at his side. *But Kester and Michael won't allow me close*, she wanted to say. *They keep their distance so.*

'Have you?' Robert persisted. 'Have you seen any signs?'

'No.' She shook her head. 'No.'

90

'I don't know why you're so conscious of it all the time. Why don't you just relax? Let things take their course. The children are relaxed and happy. All your worries are in your mind.'

She turned her head to him, opened her eyes and found him looking into her face. His hand came out and gently touched her cheek. 'This trip should have made it pretty clear to you that you need have no fears, no worries at all.'

Ben had followed his brothers at a distance, moving around the lake, going further and further away from his father, Netta and Daisy. Kester and Michael knew he was trailing them; they had only to look back and there he was, walking some twenty-five or thirty yards behind. At the beginning he had tried to conceal his presence, attempting to dodge out of sight behind the spindly silver birches or the shrubbery, but he was never successful and the boys had made it clear through their raised, laughing voices that they had seen him trying to hide. Moments later, humiliated, he had stepped from his inadequate conceal-ment to see them walking away from him even more quickly.

He lost sight of them altogether after a time, and knew a sense of panic as he searched for them, leaving the water's edge and moving into the little thicket on the lake's southern side, hurrying among the trees and brambles, no longer caring whether they saw him or not. But then, suddenly, on the edge of a little clearing, he came upon them again. They were bending, heads close together, beside the rotting trunk of a fallen tree. Crouching low, peering through the brambles, Ben watched and listened. Their voices were too low, though; he could hear nothing but the sound of the birdsong.

The seconds went by. Kester and Michael hardly moved; they seemed fixed there, leaning close together beside the tree-trunk. Kester was holding something in his hands. Ben won-dered what to do, whether to reveal his presence or wait a little longer. And then, suddenly, without looking up, Kester said in a voice just loud enough for Ben to hear: 'How long are you going to stay there, little fat boy? You going to stay there all day?'

91

Ben felt his heart thudding. He said nothing. After a moment Kester spoke again.

'Why d'you keep following us?'

After some moments of hesitation Ben got up and stepped out from behind his cover. As he did so Kester straightened and turned towards him, sighing and shaking his head. He was holding in his hand a rusty tin can. 'Did you think we didn't know you were there?' he said.

Ben said nothing.

'Of course we knew you were there,' Michael said. 'We knew all along.'

'Why d'you keep following us?' Kester asked again.

Ben took a step towards them, came to a stop. 'I don't know.'

'You don't know? You must know.'

Ben shrugged. 'I just – I just wanted to go with you. You wouldn't wait for me.'

'Correct.' Kester gave a nod. 'And why d'you reckon that was?'

Ben didn't answer.

'I should think it's obvious,' Kester said. 'We didn't want you with us. Well, I didn't, anyway.' He turned to Michael. 'Did you want him with us, Mike?'

'Me? No.' Michael shook his head.

'Quite. So there you are, little fat boy. You'd best go on back and join Daisy.'

Ben felt his lower lip quiver and desperately fought back the threatening tears. They must not see him cry. That was one thing he had learned over the years; any display of weakness brought immediate contempt.

'I don't want to join Daisy,' he said. 'I want to stay with you two.'

'Why?'

Ben shrugged. He had hoped that the holiday would bring him and his brothers closer, but it had not happened. He had remained apart from them; kept apart by them. Further, when he had repeated to them what their father had said about his joining them on their week-long visit to Jude his words had

92

been met with derision. Now, facing them in the thicket he said sulkily, 'You never let me go with you. You never let me join in anything.'

Kester shook his head in contempt. 'My God, you're pathetic,' he said. 'Listen to you whining. You're so bloody weak and useless. Don't be so bloody puerile. Is it any wonder we don't want you with us?'

'You – you don't give me a chance.'

'A chance? A chance for what?'

When Ben didn't answer, Michael said: 'Acceptance.'

'Is that it?' Kester said. 'Is that what you want?'

Ben shrugged. 'I just – just want to join in with you. Not to be left out all the time.'

'We've told you before,' Kester said, ' – it won't work. You're too hopeless, too useless. And while you show you're as useless as you are, well – you'll have to stay with Daisy.'

'Oh, please – Kester . . .' Unable to stem the tears, Ben felt them well up, overflow and run down his cheeks. He stood there for a second or two longer, then, with a sob, turned away.

As he did so Kester spoke again. 'Hey – wait a minute . . .' And now there was a new note in his voice. Ben turned back to him, looking at him through the screen of his tears. And for a moment he saw a different expression on Kester's face. He saw a softening there, a look that told him that for a second or two at least Kester had been touched by his, Ben's, unhappiness.

'You want to see what we've got here,' Kester said after a brief pause.

Joy leapt in Ben's heart.

'Well, do you?' Kester held up the tin can in both hands.

Ben grinned, feeling the wet of his tears cold in his crinkling eyes. 'Yes. Please. Can I?'

'Here. Come over here.'

At Kester's beckoning Ben stepped eagerly towards him.

After a moment Kester took his hand from the top of the tin can. 'Look.'

Ben looked into the tin and saw a frog.

The frog wasn't moving. 'Is it dead?' Ben asked.

'No, of course it's not dead.' Kester gave the can a little shake and the frog unhappily shifted on the rusty surface.

Watched closely by Ben, Kester put a hand into the can and carefully took out the frog. Tossing the can aside he held the frog cupped in his hands.

'Oh, can I hold him?' Ben asked.

'We'll see. In a minute perhaps.'

Ben moved closer, bending his head as Kester parted his cupped hands a fraction. Looking through the crack, Ben gazed at the frog. He grinned. 'Terrific! Oh, let me hold it, Kes. Let me go and show it to Dad, can I?'

'No.' Kester gazed at Ben with his head a little on one side, a slight frown of appraisal on his brow. 'You want another chance?' he said.

'Another chance?' Ben frowned.

'For acceptance,' Michael said with a little smile. 'That's what you mean, isn't it, Kes?'

Kester shrugged. 'Call it what you like.'

'Well – what d'you want me to do?' There was a faint note of anxiety beside the eagerness in Ben's voice.

Kester eyed him in silence for some moments, then he said casually, 'Go and find me a grass stem – hollow.'

'Hollow? You mean like a straw?'

'Yes. And not a word to anybody else.'

Ben nodded, then turned and dashed away, returning a few moments later with a dry grass stem. 'Here.' He held it out to Kester, but Kester shook his head. 'No, you hang on to it.'

Ben watched then as Kester moved his fingers, manoeuvring the frog between his hands.

'Right . . .' Kester nodded, ' – now stick it up his arse.'

'What . . . ?' Ben gaped. 'Do what?'

'You heard,' Michael said. 'Do what he says. Stick the end of the grass up the frog's arse.'

Ben stepped back a pace, his wide eyes and drawn mouth showing his horror. Kester gazed at him for a moment then turned to Michael. 'Here – you take it.' Carefully Michael took the struggling creature from Kester's hands and Kester reached out and took the grass stem from Ben. 'Hold the thing tight,' he instructed Michael, then put the stem to his mouth and blew through it into his palm, testing it. Nodding his satisfaction he bent towards the frog.

While Michael held the frog secure Kester inserted the end of the hollow stem into the frog's rectum, and then, the other end in his mouth, began to blow. The frog writhed and jerked in Michael's hands. Ben cried out, 'Oh, no, please! Don't! Oh, Kester, don't! *Please.* You're hurting it.' Before his eyes the frog was swelling, the smooth flesh distending. Held fast in Michael's grasp it jerked and writhed. Kester raised his head from the stem and smiled at Ben. 'Too much for you, is it?' He lowered his head and blew into the stem again.

Ben shook his head in distress. 'What will happen to it?'

'What will happen to it?' Michael said. 'It'll die, of course. What if somebody put a pump up your arse and pumped you up. What d'you think would happen to you?'

As Ben took a step away Kester said, raising his head, 'You'd better not leave. I want you to watch.' Putting his mouth back to the stem, he began to blow once more, this time more strongly, and the frog in Michael's hands writhed in agony. It was beginning to take on the appearance of some strange, grotesque, inflated rubber toy. Ben raised his hands as a shield for a moment, shutting out the sight of the bloated creature. And then suddenly he could stand it no longer. Afraid to look, and afraid of the sound that would surely come in another moment – the sound of the creature's body bursting like a balloon – he cried out, 'No! Oh, Kester, *no!*'

Turning from the sight, he dashed away into the cover of the trees.

Running from Kester and Michael, Ben had got a thorn in his foot. Sitting sobbing beneath a birch tree, he tried to pluck out the thorn, but it broke off. As he sat there he realized that the air had grown much cooler, and looking up through his tears he saw clouds gathering in the sky. After a while, when his crying had ceased, he got up and limped to the edge of the lake where Netta sat alone on the rug, pulling on a shirt over her bikini top.

'What's the matter, Ben?' she asked, looking around at his approach.

'Where's Daddy?'

'Gone for a walk round the lake.' She gestured off. 'With Daisy.' She turned back to him. 'What's the matter?'

'I – I got a thorn in my foot.'

She shook her head. 'Well, that's what you get when you run about the woodland in bare feet.' She beckoned him to her. 'Come on, let's have a look at it.'

He came to her and sat down on the rug at her side.

'Does it hurt much?' she asked as she lifted his foot.

'Yes, it does. I tried to pull it out but it broke.'

The thorn was embedded in Ben's heel. Netta studied it for a moment or two then reached over and pulled her bag towards her. From a little leather case inside she took a pair of tweezers. As she brought them towards Ben's foot he flinched and drew a little away. 'Now hold still,' she said. 'I won't hurt you. Don't be afraid.'

After a few moments she managed to extract the thorn. 'There!' She held it up for him to see. He looked at it for a moment then began to cry.

'Ben! My dear, what's the matter? It's out. There's nothing to cry about now.'

He couldn't tell her that he was crying not for the thorn, but for the horror of the frog. His crying continued. Netta put the tweezers aside and, leaning forward, wrapped him in her arms. He wept against her shoulder.

'Ben, what are you crying for?' she said. 'Is it that stupid old thorn?'

'No,' he sobbed. 'N-no.'

'Then what? Tell me.'

He raised his face to hers and shook his head. 'I – I can't.'

'Why not?'

No answer, though his tears were fading now.

'You can tell me. You can. You can tell me anything.'

'Oh, Netta!' His sobbing burst out again as he clutched at her. 'Oh, Netta, don't go away, will you? I want you to stay with us. Will you? Will you?'

She held him more tightly to her. 'Yes, my dear. Of course I will. Don't cry. Oh, don't cry.'

'For ever?'

'Yes, for ever.'

After a while when he was calm, quiet, Netta released him and delved into her bag again. She brought out some chocolate which she broke into two pieces. One piece she popped into Ben's mouth. The other she put into her own.

'Good?' she asked him, smiling.

'Yes, good.'

She hugged him to her. 'Everything's all right now, isn't it?'

'Yes.'

'Good.' She released him after a moment and looked up at the cloudy sky. 'I think it's time we were going,' she said. 'It looks as if the weather's on the change.'

A little later when they were all together again they got ready to leave. As the clearing-up got under way, Ben cast anxious glances at his brothers. They ignored him, while at the same time they dispensed their smiles and chatter between their father, Netta and Daisy.

'We saw so little of you two,' Netta said to Michael as they made their way to the car. 'Where were you all the time?'

'You weren't worried about us, were you?' he said.

'Oh, no, of course not. I just wondered.'

'We mooched about,' Kester said. 'Here and there. Exploring. Doing this and that.'

'No mischief, I trust,' Robert said.

'Mischief?' Kester looked at his father with a slightly pained expression. 'Oh, come on, Dad. We're not six years old, you know.'

'I was only joking,' Robert said.

As they settled themselves in the car Kester said, 'Oh, by the way, we found a frog.'

'A frog?' Daisy said. 'Oh, I wish I'd seen it.'

'No, you don't,' Kester said. 'It was horrible.'

'How? How was it horrible?'

Kester turned from Daisy and said in a low voice to Netta, 'Poor thing – it looked as if someone had blown it up.' He turned, glanced across at Ben who sat beside the window. 'Hadn't they, Ben? – blown it up till it burst.' Daisy gave a little squeal and pressed her face against Ben's shoulder. 'It was a real mess, wasn't it, Ben?' Kester said. His conspirator's eyes, catching Ben's, were opened wide. Ben hesitated for the briefest moment then nodded firmly.

'Oh, yes,' he said, ' – a real mess.'

EIGHT

On their return to the house Daisy, who had gone on ahead with Netta, came running back to Robert with an envelope she had taken up from the mat in the hall. It was a telegram from Janet, Robert's sister-in-law, asking him to telephone his mother as soon as possible.

'I'll come with you, Daddy,' Daisy said when he announced his intention of going to Reston to telephone, and with her sitting in a rear seat he drove into the village. Daisy insisted on going into the booth with him. There he dialled his mother's number and a few moments later heard Janet's voice on the line. He had received her telegram, he said, and then added: 'It's about Mother, I imagine – is it?'

'Yes, I'm afraid so.'

Janet went on then to say that Robert's mother had that morning had a fall in the sitting room and was now confined to her bed with concussion. 'She's feeling quite poorly,' she added. 'Hal's sitting with her now.'

'I'll come and see her,' Robert said. 'I'll leave as soon as I can.'

While Netta hurriedly prepared the dinner Robert went up to the bedroom to pack a few things into a bag. As he worked Netta came upstairs to tell him that they were ready to eat.

'Right.' He snapped the bag shut. 'Will you be all right?' he asked.

'Yes, of course. I'll phone you at your mother's in the morning, shall I?'

'Yes.' He paused. 'I hate to go off and leave you like this.'

'I told you – I shall be fine. Don't worry.'

He turned, looking out at the sky. 'It's grown so much cooler,' he said. 'I think we're in for some rain. If it gets cold, light a fire. There are plenty of logs and kindling. And if you need more Kester will cut it for you.' He shook his head. 'I'll have to take the car, I'm afraid, which means you'll have to go to the shops and anywhere else on foot.'

'Oh, dear, what a calamity.' She smiled. 'Oh, Robert, we'll be okay. We'll look after each other.'

'Yes, I'm sure you will.' He put his arms around her, held her to him and kissed her. 'Well,' he said as he released her, 'we'd better eat, then I can get going.' He moved to the door. As he reached it Netta called to him. He stopped, turning back to face her.

'Yes,' she said with a grave little smile.

'Yes? Yes, what?'

'Yes, I want to marry you. So much.'

He smiled. 'Truly? You will?'

'Oh, yes. *Yes*.'

They moved to one another, met, held. 'You're sure,' he said.

'Oh, yes, I'm sure.' She kissed him. 'I'm sorry to have taken so long to come to a decision – but I wanted to be sure.'

'And now you are.'

'Yes, yes. I told you, yes. Everything will work out fine, I'm certain.'

'We'll tell the children,' he said. He paused. 'But let's wait till I get back, okay?'

'Whatever you think is best.'

They went downstairs then where they joined the children at the table and ate the light dinner that Netta had prepared. Afterwards Robert picked up his bag, bade goodbye to the children and started out to the car. Netta was about to follow him when Kester moved quickly past her and out into the yard. She stayed there, watching from the kitchen window.

'Dad?'

Robert stopped beside the car as Kester moved towards him. 'Yes, son?' Kester was standing before him. He could see Judith in him, so clearly.

'I just . . .' Kester gave a shrug. 'Oh, I wish I could go with you, Dad. Can I?'

'Oh, but – don't you want to stay here?'

'I'd rather go with you.'

Robert hesitated. For a moment he was tempted to say yes. Then he shook his head. 'No, I think it would be better if you stayed here. If you come with me then Michael will want to also. And if Michael comes too, then Ben will want to as well. No, it'll be better if you stay. Okay?'

'Okay.' Kester gave a reluctant nod.

'I'm afraid you'll be somewhat limited as to where you can go – without the car, I mean,' Robert said. 'Still, you'll manage all right, won't you?'

'Yes, of course.'

'Good. And anyway, I'm relying on you to help Netta where you can.'

Kester said nothing.

'You'll do what you can to help her out, won't you?' Robert opened the door of the car and placed his bag on the passenger seat.

'Of course.'

'Thank you. I'm hoping Nanna will be well enough for me to leave again tomorrow. But I won't know that yet.' He looked into Kester's face. 'What's the matter?'

'Nothing.'

'Nothing? Yes, there is. Tell me.'

Kester paused. 'It's never going to be like it was, is it?'

'Like what was?'

'You know what I mean.'

'You mean – with your mother?'

'Yes.'

'Oh, Kester – son – what can I say? We were not happy together, your mother and I. You know that. And you know, too, that it would be a disaster for us – for both of us – for *all* of us – if we got back together again.'

'How can you be so sure of that?'

'Oh, I'm sure. Believe me, I'm sure.'

'But that was – well, all that was a long time ago.'

Robert smiled. 'It seems a long time – to you. But it's not that long.'

'Maybe not, but – well, people change. They change. If you and Mum tried again now it might all be different. It could be.'

'Oh, no, Kester.' Robert shook his head sadly. 'I don't think people change – not basically.'

Awkwardly, Kester turned his face away. 'I – I love Jude. And I love you, too, Dad. But Jude – she's so unhappy. And I want us all to be together again, the way it was.'

'The way it was?'

'Oh, Dad – ' Kester looked at Robert with pain in his eyes. 'Do you hate her so much?'

'No, no. I don't hate her. Of course I don't.'

'Then why – how did everything go wrong?'

'Oh, Kester . . .' Robert stood there, at a loss. How could he tell him the truth about Judith? Kester saw only her suffering, her unhappiness, and had no real idea of how she herself had caused so much of it. He was unaware of half the things she had done.

Before Robert could frame an answer, Kester said: 'So you don't think you ever will – get back with Jude.'

'I'm sorry . . .'

'There's no chance – at all?'

Robert said nothing. Kester gave a little groan. 'Oh, but – I want us all to be together. I want it so much.'

'I'm sorry.'

'Would there ever have been a chance?'

'What do you mean?'

'It's Netta, isn't it?'

A pause, then Robert said gently: 'I wasn't going to tell you just yet, but – we're going to be married.'

Long moments went by, then, sadly, Kester nodded. He gazed down at the ground for a moment or two, then his eyes flicked upward to meet Robert's. For a brief second their eyes were locked.

'Well, have a good trip, Dad. And give my love to Nanna.'

'I will.'

Turning, Kester started back towards the house. Robert stood watching him go.

A minute later Netta was coming from the house. Robert stood there, waiting for her to come to him. He took her in his arms. 'I told Kester,' he said after a moment, ' – that we're going to be married.'

'Oh . . .' She gave a little nod.

'I hadn't intended to. It just came out.'

She shrugged. 'Well, he had to know sometime.'

Smiling, he drew her more tightly to him. 'I'll be back soon,' he said. 'Just as soon as I can.'

'Good. Give my love to your mother.'

'I will.'

He kissed her. 'And you've got the number, so you know where to get hold of me if you need to.'

He kissed her again, got into the car and began to drive away. As he drew towards the end of the lane he looked into the driving mirror and saw her still standing there, waving. A moment later he saw the figures of Ben and Daisy as they came to her side and raised their arms. Another second and he was turning into the lane and they were all three out of sight.

A few minutes after Netta, Ben and Daisy returned to the house Kester and Michael went outside. Netta, in the kitchen as they passed her by, followed them to the door and called out after them. 'Kester . . . Michael . . .'

They stopped at the sound of her voice, turning back to her. It was Kester who answered. 'Yes?' His voice was cold.

'You won't go far, will you?' Netta said hesitantly. 'It's after seven.'

Kester gave a weary sigh. 'No, we won't.'

He turned then and, with Michael following, moved to the gate and out into the lane.

As they walked towards Reston Kester told Michael what their father had said about getting married.

'Jude will have to know,' Kester said. 'But let me tell her.'

When they reached the telephone booth outside the post office Kester dialled Judith's number. After it had rung a couple of times he hung up and dialled again. The signal having been relayed, he hung up and waited. A few seconds later the telephone in the booth rang out and he lifted the receiver.

'Hello?'

'Kester?'

'Yes, it's me.'

There was a smile in Judith's voice when she spoke again. 'Hello, my darling.' Kester and Michael had telephoned her frequently since arriving at the cottage and she had looked forward to their calls. Now, after they had exchanged greetings, Kester said: 'Dad's gone.'

'Gone? What do you mean, gone?'

'He's gone to Cirencester to see Nanna. She had a fall and knocked herself out. The doctor says she has concussion.'

'Oh, *dear*. How is she?'

'Not too well, I think. She's in bed.'

'Poor Nanna. When did your father leave?'

'This evening. Not long ago. He's hoping to be back tomorrow. Netta will phone him and find out. It's tough not being on the phone here.'

'Poor Nanna,' Judith said again, and then: 'And your father. He must be very worried.'

'I think he is.'

After a while it was Michael's turn to speak to Judith.

'So,' she said to him, 'Netta's looking after you, I suppose.'

'Yes.'

Judith sighed. 'Ah, well, never mind. Your father will soon be back. He'll have to be, won't he? You've only got a few days of your holiday left, haven't you?'

'Yes, another three days.'

A pause. 'I wish I were there with you.'

'I wish that too.'

Michael and Judith spoke for a minute more and then it was Kester's turn again.

104

'It makes me mad,' he said, 'that we'll miss seeing you this weekend.'

'Yes, me too,' Judith said. 'Still, I'll see you both the weekend after – and we'll have a whole week soon – the three of us. You wait till half-term.'

'Yes, Mike and I are looking forward to it – so much.' He wanted to add, *Dad told me we'll never again be together – all six of us.* Instead he said sadly, 'That's all we'll have, isn't it – you and me and Mike – the occasional week or weekend here and there?' He paused. 'That fucking Netta. I hate her. It's all her fucking fault.'

Later, when he had hung up, he had still said nothing about the marriage.

On their return to the house the boys had hardly got in the door when Daisy came running towards them, her obvious excitement clear in her face. 'Netta and Daddy are going to be married,' she said. 'And Netta says I shall be her bridesmaid.' She gave a little laugh. 'Netta says she's going to buy me a bridesmaid's dress!'

Later, after Ben and Daisy had gone to bed, Netta, Kester and Michael sat watching a film on television. Netta would have liked to watch a ballet programme that was showing, but Kester, looking in the newspaper, had exclaimed excitedly about a particular film that was on. Neither Netta nor Michael made any protest and so they watched *Madeleine*, the story of the young Madeleine Smith and her trial for the murder of her lover. 'Neat,' Kester said when it was over. 'You have to admire it, haven't you? – handing him poisoned cocoa through the railings. Boy, that takes some nerve.'

Netta gave a nod. 'Yes, but what a terrible, terrible thing to have done.'

After she had spoken she realized that Kester had asked the question of Michael and that her own response had been ignored. For a moment or two she continued to gaze at Kester. He didn't turn his head, though, and a moment later he and

Michael had begun to converse between themselves on the subject. Very much aware of the snub, Netta got up and went out to the kitchen. There she stood for some moments at the table. It was the first time that any of the children had overtly shown antagonism towards her. After a time she moved back to the door and opened it. The pictures on the television screen were still flickering, but now to an empty room. Kester and Michael had gone to bed.

Just after eleven the following morning Netta, accompanied by Daisy, walked into the village, to the phone booth. There Netta dialled the number of Robert's mother. Robert answered at once. He told her that his mother was making good progress. 'But she was badly shaken,' he said, 'and very bruised. Particularly her face. She looks a terrible sight. And she's in shock, of course. She's lucky, though, that she didn't break any bones. The doctor reckons she'll be in bed for a few days yet.'

'Poor thing,' Netta said. After they had talked for a while she asked him when he would be back.

'Probably tomorrow,' he replied. 'I'm not sure yet. Is everything all right at that end?'

'. . . Fine. Everything's fine.'

'Are the boys helping out?'

'. . . Oh, yes.'

'You sound a little hesitant,' he said. 'You sure everything's all right?'

'Yes, yes, it's fine. We're all fine.'

On leaving the telephone booth she and Daisy headed for the village grocery shop where Netta bought two or three items. 'We'll go for a picnic somewhere this afternoon, shall we?' she said, to which Daisy eagerly replied, 'Oh, yes, *yes*! Where shall we go?'

'I don't know,' Netta replied, 'but we'll find somewhere nice not too far from the house.'

After leaving the grocer's Netta and Daisy came across a shop selling secondhand books, and at Netta's suggestion they went inside. When they came out again some minutes later

Netta was carrying a book she had bought on the trial of Madeleine Smith.

Later, on their return to the house, they were moving to the back door when Netta heard the sound of raised, laughing voices coming from the rear garden. She felt herself tensing. Ever since arising that morning she had felt a growing estrangement between herself and the two older boys. Particularly Kester. He had not answered when she had said good morning, and he had continued to ignore her over breakfast. Michael, less sure of himself, but following Kester's lead, had also disregarded her presence. Ben and Daisy, unaware of their brothers' attitude, had filled up the silences with their chatter.

Once Netta had deposited the groceries in the kitchen she stood for some moments of hesitation then took up the book and went out into the garden. As she started up the path she was met by the sight of the three boys coming towards her from the direction of the rear shed. Ben, seeing her, came running towards her, while Kester and Michael followed, carrying between them some contraption with wheels. 'We've made a buggy,' Ben said excitedly to Netta. 'Well, Kester and Mike have. I helped them.'

'Oh, really? How clever you are!' As Netta spoke she was aware of the note of over-brightness in her voice. She wondered where the boys had found the wheels for the buggy – and then realized that they must have come from the old pram that had been hanging up in the shed. If that was so then she should reprimand them; the pram belonged to the owners of the house. She said nothing about it, though, but, as Kester and Michael drew closer, called to them: 'I came to see if you'd like to go for a picnic somewhere this afternoon – if the weather stays fine. I thought we could have a light lunch now, then pack something for tea and take it with us. We can easily find a nice spot within walking distance.'

At her words Ben made an awkward little jump. 'Oh, good!' he said. 'I thought with Dad having taken the car we wouldn't be able to go anywhere.'

The two older boys, with Kester leading, had drawn almost

level with her and she stepped aside on the path to allow them to go by. 'Kester?' she said, smiling at him.

'Mmm?' He turned his head to look at her as if until that moment he had not been aware of her presence. 'Yes? What is it?'

She felt a sinking feeling within her breast as she looked into the cold, aloof, slightly contemptuous gaze. 'A – a picnic,' she said.

'Picnic?' He frowned, as if the word were new to him. 'What *about* a picnic?'

Ben said quickly with a laugh, 'This afternoon. Are you deaf? Netta said that we can . . .' Under Kester's bleak glance his voice faltered and died away. Then Kester said with a faint, lukewarm little smile that didn't touch his eyes: 'No, I don't think so, thanks all the same. But you go ahead with Ben and Daisy if you like. Mike and I will be fine on our own.' Then, with a faint nod to Michael, he hitched the end of the buggy more securely under his arm and they started away again, Ben quickly following.

Feeling herself flushing with embarrassment, Netta stood for a moment watching as the three boys moved away from her, then, swallowing her pride and summoning her courage, she called Kester's name. The boys stopped and turned to her. She went towards them. When she stood before them she held the book out to Kester. With an attempt at lightness, at sounding casual, she said, 'I happened to see this when I was in the village this morning. I thought you might like it . . .'

For a moment Kester looked at the book in Netta's outstretched hand, then released a hand from the buggy and took the book from her.

Netta smiled uncertainly. 'I thought – seeing as we'd been watching a film about Madeleine Smith only last night . . .'

Kester nodded, turning the book over in his hand. Then his eyes raised to Netta's and his lips moved in the merest flicker of a smile.

'Thank you.'

108

Next moment he was turning and he and Michael were moving on along the path.

Ben stood watching his brothers for a second, then looked at Netta and gave an awkward little smile. Then, as the two older boys reached the yard there came the sound of Kester's laugh. Sharp and staccato on the air, it struck Netta like a blade, and she felt her cheeks burning again. Another moment and Kester's voice came as he called Ben's name. Ben shifted uncertainly on the path. 'I must go,' he said, avoiding her eyes. 'Excuse me.' Then he was turning, running away down the garden path.

'But are *we* going on a picnic?' Daisy asked.

She and Netta were in the kitchen preparing the lunch: cold meat, coleslaw, potato salad and green salad. 'I'm not sure any more,' Netta said as she put the bread on the bread board and set the whole thing down on the cloth.

'But you said we would,' Daisy said. 'You said we'd be going on a picnic. You said so when we went to the shop this morning. Why aren't you sure now?'

'I don't know, I don't know.' Netta's voice contained a note of irritation and Daisy shot a cautious look at her. 'Are you in a bad mood?' she asked.

'No, my dear, no.' Netta reached out and touched the top of Daisy's head. 'Don't take any notice of me.'

As Daisy smiled, Netta glanced at her watch. Almost quarter to one. She should go out and call the boys in to eat. She hesitated. She kept seeing Kester's expression as he had faced her on the garden path: the contempt in his eyes, in his voice.

It had been particularly shocking, she felt, as in the past there had been no overt sign of any hostility from any of the children – at least nothing that she had readily noticed. There had been a little coolness from Kester and Michael, but nothing very much. She had truly believed that she was coming to be accepted by them, by each one of them. And now, almost as soon as Robert had gone out of sight there had been these demonstrations, first at breakfast and, just now, out in the

109

garden. Had she been wrong in believing that they were accepting her? Did Kester feel that contempt for her that she had seen in his face? Had he always felt like that?

'What's the matter, Netta?'

'Mmm?' Turning, she saw Daisy looking up at her, concern in her wide brown eyes. 'Nothing, my dear.' Netta bent and kissed the top of Daisy's head. 'Why should you think anything's the matter?'

'You looked sad.'

'Did I? Oh, that won't do, will it?' Netta laughed, then: 'Look at the time,' she said. 'You stay here and finish setting the table, will you? I'll go and find the boys, and tell them it's time for lunch.'

Leaving Daisy in the kitchen, Netta left the house in search of the boys. Finding no sign or sound of them around the rear of the house she made her way to the front and onto the lane. And there she heard their voices. Moving towards the sounds, she same to a stop beside Michael and Ben and watched anxiously as Kester, riding the buggy, completed a run down the lane towards the main road. Afterwards he pulled the buggy back to the starting point near the gate. 'Oh, please, Kester,' Netta said to him, 'it's so dangerous. If you run out into the road you could be killed.'

Kester gave a deep sigh, as if her words were no more than he had expected, while at the same time he avoided looking at her. An awkward little silence followed, broken by Netta saying, 'Anyway – I came out to tell you that lunch is ready.' She gave an awkward little laugh. 'You boys must be starving.'

Addressing his words to Michael, Kester said with a shrug of his shoulders, 'Oh, I think we'll eat out here. All right, Mike?'

'Yes, if you like.'

'Fine.' Kester nodded. 'You want to go in and fetch it, then? Ben'll go with you.'

With his words Kester turned away, and after a moment's hesitation Michael and Ben started off towards the house. Netta watched them go for a moment then quickly called out: 'Don't

110

touch anything till I get there, Michael. Nor you, Ben. I'll be there in a moment.'

When they had gone from her sight she turned back to Kester. He was bending over the buggy, doing something to one of the wheels.

The silence hung between them like a curtain. After a moment Netta took a deep breath, hesitated and said, 'Kester . . .'

He said nothing, but continued to ignore her. She could feel her heart hammering in her chest. As none of the other children had, he somehow had the power to belittle her, to make her nervous, completely unsure of herself. He was like the child who sometimes appeared in a classroom; one of those who seemed able to pierce one's defences, to get behind one's mask and expose all one's uncertainties, doubts and pretences.

'Kester, please look at me when I'm speaking to you.'

'Yes?' His frown, deep, furrowing his brow, was no accident. He turned, looking up at her with a deep sigh. 'Yes, what is it?' He might have been addressing an irritating child.

Faced with his cold, contemptuous gaze, she faltered briefly and said: 'Why – why are you behaving in this way?'

'I don't know what you mean.' The frown was there again. 'What are you talking about?'

'You know what I'm talking about. I'm talking about your – your attitude.'

'What attitude?'

'To me. The way you're behaving towards me. Since your father went off yesterday you've been . . .' Her voice tailed off.

'I've been what?' Kester prompted her. 'How have I been?'

'Oh, Kester, please – stop doing this. Stop being so beastly to me. What have I done to you that you should suddenly start behaving like this? Is it – is it because of what your father told you – about our getting married?'

He straightened before her and gazed at her, his glance moving slowly down to her feet and up again. 'God, listen to you,' he said witheringly. He shook his head in distaste. 'Christ, you're really pathetic, you know that? You really make me sick.'

He turned away. Netta stared at him for some moments while

111

the tears welled, pricking at her eyelids. Then, stifling a sob, she turned and walked slowly back through the gateway and across the forecourt. Entering the back yard she came to a stop and stood leaning against the wall of the house. As she stood there, trying to control her emotions, there came a sudden gust of wind and she was vaguely aware of a piece of paper lifting, drifting, and coming to rest near her foot. She bent and picked it up. As she straightened she noticed the increasing force of the wind and the darkness of the sky. Sighing, she moved across the yard to where the dustbins stood behind the kitchen wall.

As she reached out to lift the lid of the dustbin she suddenly realized that the paper in her hand was a page from a book. She looked at it closely. It was from the book she had given to Kester.

Lifting the lid of the bin she saw there the rest of the book where, torn apart, it lay on top of the household rubbish. As she straightened, almost gasping from the shock, she heard her name called and, turning towards the house, she saw Michael standing in the back doorway.

'Can I take some food, Netta? What can I take for us?'

His image was distorted through the watery screen of her tears. A sob broke from her lips. 'Take what you want,' she cried. 'I don't care.' Letting fall the dustbin lid she turned and ran across the yard and down the garden path, past the kitchen garden and into the orchard. There she came to a stop and, sitting on the stump of an old apple tree, bent her head, putting her hands over her face.

NINE

'She seems to be a little better in herself this afternoon,' Robert said. 'She's such a terrible sight, though – what with her black eye and everything.'

His voice came to Netta over the telephone as she stood in the booth next to the village post office. It was just after five-thirty. Her call to him had taken him by surprise; he wasn't expecting her to call again until the following day, Thursday. She had had to call him, though. She had had a need to hear his voice, to find some reassurance.

Now at his words she murmured in sympathy, 'Poor dear. It must have been an awful shock. Still, as long as she's getting on all right – that's the main thing.'

After a further minute's conversation Netta asked him if he knew when he would be returning. *Please say you'll be back in the morning*, a voice pleaded in her head. 'Will it be tomorrow?' she asked.

'I don't know. I hope so. I'm not sure. But don't worry, I'll be back in time to help with the packing. Could you manage till Friday morning if necessary?'

'. . . Yes – of course.'

'Fine. It's just that my being here will give Janet a break. She's been so good and has worked so hard. So if I *can* stay till Friday . . .'

'Yes, of course.'

'Anyway, and how are things going with you?'

'Oh – okay.'

She could hear the lack of enthusiasm in her voice. Robert heard it too and said, 'Okay? Only okay?'

'Oh, it's fine. Really.'

'Good.' He sounded unconvinced, however. After a moment

he went on: 'I was telling Mother and Janet and Hal that we're going to be married.' He paused. 'I was thinking – early in September . . . What do you think? The sooner the better for me.'

'Oh, well,' Netta said quickly, uncertainty in her voice, 'we'll have to see.'

'Netta,' he said, 'what's the matter? And don't tell me I'm imagining things. I know damn well I'm not. Something's happened there, hasn't it? What is it?'

'Robert, it's nothing. Why do you – '

He cut in: 'Don't give me that. I mention our getting married and all of a sudden you start to sound very vague and evasive. What's happened?'

'Robert, what makes you think that anything – '

'Is it something to do with the children?' he broke in. 'Something to do with Kester or Michael? Have they said something?'

She didn't answer.

'Have they?' he insisted.

'Robert – oh, listen – we'll talk about it when you get back. This isn't the time to talk about it – not now.'

'Then it *is* something with the kids. Was it Kester? It has to be. Michael's never done anything off his own bat, and I can't imagine it could ever be Ben or Daisy. What has Kester said to you?'

'Robert – '

'What did he say? Tell me.'

'No, listen, please. I told you – this is no time for us to – '

'No, *you* listen, Netta. If you think I can just brush it aside until I get back you can forget it. Kester's said something to upset you and you must tell me what it is.'

'No, wait a minute . . .' Now she regretted making the call. She couldn't tell him what had happened. She just couldn't. 'It will be all right,' she said, not knowing whether she believed her own words. 'I'm sure it will. We just need to give him time to get used to the idea.'

'The idea of what?'

114

'Well – our getting married.'

'Ah, yes, that's it, of course.'

Robert tried again then to get her to tell him what had happened, but she would not. There was a little silence then he said, 'Well, anyway, get Kester to phone me when you get back to the house, will you?'

'Oh, Robert, no, please – don't make it worse. If he knows that I've come running to you, telling tales, it will only make it worse.'

'Okay,' he said reluctantly, ' – as you like . . . Anyway, you'll have to tell me when I get back.'

'Yes, yes, of course.' Playing the whole thing down now, she added, 'It's nothing much, anyway.'

He sighed. 'So you say now. But he's got to realize that he's not the only one to be considered. I won't have him upsetting you.' He paused. 'Maybe I should leave tomorrow after all.'

'No, no, it's all right,' she said quickly. 'You stay with your mother for a while longer. It'll be all right. I wish I hadn't mentioned it. Everything'll be fine, believe me.'

Robert said then: 'Yes, I'm sure it will. Trouble is, he's never stopped hoping – believing – that one day Judith and I would get back together. Now he knows we never shall. Well – he had to realize it at some time. Like you said, he just needs time to get used to the idea. We'll just have to be patient, I guess.'

'Yes . . .'

'Anyway,' he said, ' – listen: call me some time in the morning, okay? Let me know if he's still being difficult. If he is I'll leave at once.'

'Yes, all right.'

'You promise you will?'

'Yes, of course.'

And it was left at that. Robert told her he loved her and wished her a good night. 'And don't worry,' he added. 'Everything will be all right, you'll see.'

'She's coming out.'

Kester hissed the words to Michael while at the same time

115

he ducked back behind the cover of the pub wall. The Swan was situated some forty yards from the telephone booth, giving, from Kester's vantage point, a clear view of it. Now, after a few moments' wait, Kester peered cautiously around the corner again and watched as Netta moved away. Within a minute she had turned the corner and was gone from sight.

'She's gone now.' Kester stepped out from the cover of the wall, quickly followed by Michael, and together they walked towards the telephone booth.

'She'll go on back to the house,' Kester said.

'D'you think she'll have told Dad?'

'About me?'

'Yes.'

'Sure to have done.' Kester shrugged. 'I don't care.'

They entered the booth where Kester dialled Judith's number. A little while later, after the usual procedure, Judith's voice was on the line.

Kester spoke to her for a short while, then it was Michael's turn, after which Kester got back on the line again. He would have to tell her.

'Ah, well,' Jude was saying, 'your holiday's nearly over now. Are you sorry?'

'No, I'm glad. I wish we'd spent it with you.'

'Oh, but you've enjoyed being with your father, haven't you?'

'Oh, yes, but – well, it's *her* – Netta.' He paused. 'Jude, they're going to be married. Dad told me yesterday, just before he left.'

There was silence at the other end of the line. 'Are you there?' he said after a moment.

'Yes . . .'

Her voice sounded strange. Suddenly Kester said, 'Anyway, I let her know how I feel. She can't be in any doubt now.' He paused. 'I told her she made me sick – and she does.'

'Oh, Kester, my dear,' Judith said wearily, 'what did you hope to achieve by that?'

'Well . . .' He was a little taken aback at her question. 'Well – I've made it clear to her now how we feel, Mike and I, and

116

she'll go away. She won't marry Dad now, will she? How can she marry him, knowing how we feel about her?'

'Don't you think so? Oh, Kester, you're so young. Your father won't be stopped by that. I know him too well. He won't give up so easily. I know what he can be like. You won't make him change his mind about marrying Netta. And he won't let *her* change her mind, either. Don't you see? – he'll be drawn closer to her than ever.'

Kester was silent in his sudden pain. Judith went on: 'No, I'm afraid the damage has been done.' She gave a deep sigh. 'I'm afraid nothing will change now.'

'Oh, don't say that.'

'Don't you understand? We'll never be together again now, ever. All along I've been hoping, hoping – thinking that there was still a chance. But now – now he'll marry her, just as he said he plans to do. I'm afraid I've lost you and – ' Her voice broke in a sudden sob. 'It's finished. I've lost my boys for ever.'

'But why can't we walk *together*, Kes?'

Michael's voice was pleading but Kester was adamant. 'No, Mike. You go on back to the house. Now.'

As they stood at the edge of the road leading from the village there came to them the striking of the church clock. Six o'clock.

'But why?' Michael asked. Kester seemed to be avoiding his eyes. 'What are you going to do?'

'Nothing. I just want to be on my own for a minute or two.'

'What for?'

'To think, for Christ's sake! To think!' Kester's voice was suddenly shrill with anger. 'Now go on and leave me alone.'

Michael gazed at him for a moment with hurt in his eyes, then, reluctantly, he turned and started away along the road. Kester stood still, watching him go. At the bend in the road Michael stopped, turned and looked back, as if hopeful of some sign that Kester would relent. Kester said nothing, did nothing, just remained on the overgrown verge, watching. After a moment Michael turned back and walked on. A few seconds later he had gone out of sight.

Kester stayed there. A car drove past him, and another. He took no notice. Long seconds went by, and then, slowly, he started to walk in the direction taken by Michael.

After a few minutes, seeing a gap in the hedge on his left, he pushed through it into a field. There, next to the inner side of the hedge where blackberries were thick on the brambles he stood still for long seconds. Then, suddenly, with a groan, he sank down in the dry, sere grass.

'Oh, *Jude* . . .'

In his ears he could still hear her words: *We'll never be together again now, ever . . . It's finished. I've lost my boys for ever.*

'Oh, no. *No*! Oh, Jude, don't say that. Don't say that! Please.'

Slowly, his eyes shut tight, he let his body fall sideways, his face sinking into the sharp, prickling grasses.

'*Netta*!' he cried out. 'I hate you. Oh, Netta, Netta, you've ruined everything.'

He lay there for some time without moving while the midges hummed above his head and the birds sang. The air was humid. Turning his face to the sky he looked up. The clouds were gathering more darkly above. He would have to return to the house; they would all be wondering where he was.

He sat up in the grass. And what should he do when he got back to the house, he asked himself. The question kept going through his mind.

Although it was only six forty-five Netta, because of the darkness of the sky, had put on the light. She had prepared spaghetti with a bolognaise sauce – a favourite of the children, she knew – and in particular of Kester. Michael had returned to the house some little time past; Kester was following on his own, he had told her. She had waited a little while before serving the supper, in the hope that Kester would soon appear, but still there had been no sign of him.

And now Michael, Ben and Daisy had washed their hands and were coming to the table. When they were seated Netta served them and they began to eat. A few moments later there came the sound of footsteps on the gravel outside. Michael, cocking his head, gave a broad smile.

'Kester's back,' he said.

Netta felt her heartbeat speed up slightly, and reprimanded herself. Why should she allow this boy to have such an effect upon her, she angrily asked herself. It was ridiculous. Nevertheless she braced herself for his appearance.

Seconds later the door opened and Kester entered the kitchen. 'You're just in time,' Netta said, barely flicking a glance at him. She herself sat down at the table. As she put spaghetti onto her plate she was aware of Kester moving towards her. She concentrated on what she was doing. He came to a stop beside her.

'Netta?'

As she turned to him she was aware that his voice sounded awkward, a little embarrassed.

'Yes?' She managed to keep a coolness in her own voice.

He was holding out to her some flowers, purple heather.

'Here,' he said, 'I thought you might like these.'

'Oh . . .' She sat very still for a moment, then, without looking into his face she slowly took the flowers from his hand. 'Thank you . . .' As she held them before her she caught a glimpse of Michael's expression as he gazed in surprise at his elder brother. Her glance moved back and took in Kester's face as he looked down at her. His blue eyes were lowered. After a moment she smiled at him.

'Thank you, Kester. Thank you very much. They're lovely.'

Against the background of Daisy and Ben's chatter, Kester's glance lifted and his eyes met Netta's. 'I'm sorry. I'm sorry about everything.' He did little more than mouth the words, but it was enough. The feeling of relief in Netta's heart came surging up like a spring. It was going to be all right after all. Everything was going to be all right.

She gave a little nod as she smiled back at him. 'Oh, Kester – let's forget it. I have.' Lowering her face to the flowers she held them to her nostrils.

Kester quickly said: 'They haven't got any scent.'

'It doesn't matter. They're beautiful. Now,' she added softly, raising her eyes to him again, 'sit down and eat your supper.'

The meal progressed happily and it seemed to Netta that at last she and Kester were beginning, slowly, to come closer to one another. For the first time they actually talked together. They spoke of several things: of the beautiful countryside around them, the places they had visited, Kester's school work, Netta's teaching. And although the conversation was all a little awkward still, Netta felt, at least it was a start. And, further, in no time at all Michael had also begun to relax with her and, as usual following Kester's lead, was joining in the conversation. As they talked her happiness grew. She had no idea what had caused the transformation in Kester, but whatever it was she was glad of it. And, she said to herself, she was glad, too, that Robert was away. Perhaps, without his absence, this new closeness with Kester and Michael might not have come about.

After a time they rose and while Ben and Daisy went on into the sitting room, Kester and Michael helped Netta to clear the table. Afterwards, when they had washed up the dishes, the boys joined Ben and Daisy while Netta found a vase and arranged the heather in it. She set the vase on a small table near the window then sat down on the sofa next to Daisy and Ben.

'Well,' she said to Daisy, 'you and Ben have about half an hour before you go up to bed. What would you like to do?'

'Can we watch telly?' Ben asked.

'Oh, no, Ben,' Kester said quickly, 'you don't want to watch television, do you? Let's play some games or something.'

At the suggestion Ben's face lit up. 'Oh, yes!' he said eagerly. 'What shall we play?'

'Oh, no-o-o-o!' From Daisy the word was a long, drawn out wail. 'I don't want to play games. You never play games that I want to play.'

'Yes, we will,' Kester said. 'We'll play something you like.' At his solicitous tone Netta glanced at him in further surprise.

Kester got up from his chair and came over to stand before Daisy. 'What would you like to play?'

Daisy stared up at him for a moment or two, as if uncertain how to take this unusual display of brotherly concern and affection. Then she said, 'I Spy.'

Ben and Michael groaned, but Kester said quickly to them, 'Come on, now. I did ask her. Anyway, you'll have your turn.' He turned back to Daisy. 'All right, then. I Spy. Are you going to start?'

'Yes.' She smiled back at him then slowly turned her head, looking around her at the room. In her concentration her tongue came out and touched a couple of times at her upper lip. 'I spy with my little eye . . .'

They played Daisy's game for some minutes and then switched to Hunt the Thimble. This, Ben's choice, was suggested by Netta when he himself couldn't think of a game. Afterwards Kester said, 'Right, who's next? We must all have a go. Who's turn is it now to decide?' He smiled at Netta. 'What about you, Netta? You choose something. What would you like to play?'

She chuckled. 'Oh, well, since you ask, I think I should start getting Ben and Daisy to bed. It's ten past eight.'

'No!' Ben and Daisy protested loudly. 'Can't we stay up a bit longer?'

'Oh, yes, let them stay up a little longer,' Kester agreed. He laughed. 'And you're not going to duck out with an excuse like that, Netta. You've got to join in. What shall we play?'

'Oh, Kester.' With a nod of her head Netta said to Ben and Daisy, 'All right, you two can stay up for a little while longer.' Turning back to Kester she gave a laugh. 'But I can't think of anything right now.'

'Yes, you can. Of course you can.'

'No, I can't, I swear to you. My mind's gone blank.'

'All right, then, we'll come back to you later.'

'What about *you?*' Netta said. 'What would *you* like to play?'

'Yes,' Ben said. 'You choose something, Kes,' to which Michael added, 'Yes, go on, Kes.'

121

'Okay.' Kester gave a slow nod, remained for a moment in silence, then nodded again. 'Okay, then – I vote we play Trials.'

'*Trials*,' Michael said. 'There's no such game.'

'Well, we'll *make* one,' Kester said, and Ben quickly agreed: 'Yes, we'll *make* a game.'

'I don't know how to play Trials,' Daisy said, a little irritably, and Netta said softly to her: 'Never mind, you'll soon learn. I don't know how to play either, but Kester will tell us.' To Kester she said: 'What kind of trials d'you mean, Kester? D'you mean like horse trials or – '

'No, no,' Kester said quickly. 'I mean like a trial in a courtroom. Like in the film last night about Madeleine Smith.'

'Oh dear.' Netta grimaced slightly. 'You don't want us to play at murder trials, do you?'

'No, of course not.' Kester laughed. 'We'll be ourselves, not other people.'

'That sounds great,' Michael laughed. 'Who's going to be on trial first?'

'*You* are!' Kester swung about to face him, pointing at him, and the two boys laughed, joined at once by the others.

'What have I done wrong?' Michael demanded. 'Whatever it is, I haven't done anything wrong.'

Kester narrowed his eyes and put his head slightly on one side. 'How can you say such a thing?' he said. 'Everyone saw you at supper – making a pig of yourself.' Stepping closer to Michael he drew himself up before him and glared down at him.

'Stand up.'

Kester's voice had taken on a tone of quiet command, and at once Michael got to his feet and stood facing him, his arms at his sides.

'Now – Officer . . .' Kester turned to Ben, 'escort the prisoner into the dock.'

'Yes, sir.' Ben laughed, and then: 'Where is the dock?'

'Here.' Kester indicated the rug that lay before the empty fireplace. Then, stepping to a heavy, carved wooden grandfather chair that stood on the right he adjusted its position so that it

122

faced out into the room. 'And you don't address me as "Sir", you address me as "My Lord". I'm the judge. All right?'

'All right.' Ben got up from the sofa. 'My Lord.'

Daisy giggled and reached out for Netta's hand and they watched as Ben went over to Michael and took him by the arm.

'Don't be afraid of him,' Kester said. 'He's the prisoner. Never show you're afraid of him.'

Giggling, Ben escorted Michael to the chair and pushed him down into it. He turned then to Kester for further instructions.

'Now, tie him up,' Kester said.

From his pocket he took a length of cord. Netta gave a laugh. 'That was handy,' she said.

'Oh, yes, one has to be prepared when dealing with desperate characters,' Kester said. He handed the cord to Ben. 'After all, the prisoner's dangerous – and he might try to escape.'

While Ben inexpertly bound Michael to the chair – by looping the cord across his chest and behind the chair back – Kester turned to face Netta and Daisy, gave them a wink, then turned back to Michael.

'Prisoner at the bar,' he said solemnly, 'you are charged with – with . . .' He hesitated, as if unsure in his choice of words, and into the pause Daisy quickly piped up, giggling: 'With making a pig of himself – at supper.'

They all laughed, then Kester composed himself again and continued: 'You are charged with making a pig of yourself at supper. How say you, are you guilty or not guilty?'

Hesitating, Michael looked perplexed.

Quickly Kester said to him in an aside: 'You must plead not guilty – otherwise it's no fun.' Then in his judge's voice he repeated: 'How say you, are you guilty or not guilty?'

'Not guilty.' Michael set his lips and gave a firm shake of his head.

Kester looked around him for a moment and then moved to the small table on the side on which stood the vase of heather. After replacing the vase on the mantelpiece, he pulled the table out from the wall, set a chair behind it and sat down.

'Call the first witness,' he said. 'Call Daisy Farrell.'

Daisy gave a giggling little shriek and pressed close to Netta's side. 'Go on,' Netta said. 'You've been called as a witness.'

Still giggling, Daisy got up from the sofa. 'I don't know what to do,' she said.

'She must take the stand,' Kester said. Then, with a nod to Ben, he pointed to a spot near Michael's armchair, adding: 'She can stand there . . .'

Daisy moved to the spot indicated and stood giggling, shifting from one foot to the other and raising her eyes to the ceiling. 'Oh, Daisy,' Kester said with a note of impatience in his voice, 'stop being silly. Try to do it properly.'

Daisy gave a deep sigh and exchanged a glance with Netta.

Kester said: 'I shall have to be the prosecution as well as the judge. Does anybody object?'

No one did. Kester said then: 'But we shall need a counsel for the defence. Netta?' He smiled at her. 'How about you?'

'Oh – well – okay.' Netta grinned. 'Let me know when I'm needed.'

Kester nodded and went on – now in his new role of prosecuting counsel: 'Ladies and gentleman of the jury, I want you to look upon this creature, this glutton here – this – this pig who ate three helpings of spaghetti – and didn't leave any in the dish – even though his elder brother would have liked some more.'

There was laughter at this. Then, turning to Michael, Kester said, 'Have you anything to say to the charge made against you?'

'Yes,' Michael laughed. 'I'm guilty.'

'Guilty?'

'Yes, guilty. And I'll tell you something else. The spaghetti was delicious.'

Over the laughter Kester said a little irritably, 'Oh, Mike, you spoil it all. You've got to do it properly or not at all.'

'Well,' Michael said, 'choose somebody else to go on trial.'

'Me,' Ben said. 'Put *me* on trial. *I'll* do it properly.'

'No, you're too young,' Kester said. 'At the start we need somebody older, who'll know how to play. You can go on trial later. First we want somebody who knows what to do. Somebody like ...' He grinned and turned to Netta. 'Somebody like Netta.'

Netta laughingly frowned. 'Oh, dear, must I?'

'Yes, yes!' Daisy cried out. 'Oh, yes, put Netta on trial.'

'Oh, dear,' Netta said, 'this isn't fair.'

'Yes, it is,' Kester smiled. 'All's fair in love and war, as they say.'

'I don't know what love and war have to do with it,' Netta said. 'Anyway, what am I to be charged with?'

Michael, unwinding the cord and getting up from the chair, said, 'I know – she can be charged with not making enough spaghetti.'

'No,' Kester said witheringly, 'that's stupid.' He gestured to Daisy. 'You can go and sit down for now.'

'*I* know,' said Ben, as Daisy moved back to the sofa, 'Netta should be charged with wanting to send me and Daisy to bed too early.'

'No, that's no good either. We must think of something better than that.' Kester pointed to the chair. 'Anyway, in the meantime she can be put in the dock.'

'Oh, very nice,' Netta said as she got up from the sofa and moved across the room, ' – here I am going on trial and nobody's even thought up a charge. Some justice.'

'Don't worry,' said Michael, 'we'll think of something.'

'Yes, we'll think of something,' Daisy added gleefully. 'And something really *awful*.'

'Oh, dear me, not *too* awful, I hope,' Netta said. She giggled as she sat down in the grandfather chair. 'Just remember, I'm only a poor helpless woman.'

'Tie her up,' Kester said to Michael who stood holding the cord in his hand. 'And do it properly. She's not a poor helpless woman; she's a dangerous character.'

Netta laughed. 'Oh, very dangerous.' Michael began then to bind her to the chair, but Kester, watching, said, 'Oh, that's no good. She'd easily get out of that.' Moving from behind the table, he went to Netta and carefully and methodically bound her wrists to the chair's arms. 'Oh, Gawd,' Netta groaned, 'I don't think I'm *that* dangerous.' Kester, smiling, wagged a finger at her. 'You're more dangerous than you realize,' he said. Then, reaching into his pocket he brought out another length of cord. 'Her legs too,' he added.

'My *legs!*' Netta laughingly protested. 'Oh, is that really necessary?'

'Oh, yes, indeed.' Kester, crouching, head bent low, tied Netta's ankles to the chair legs. 'Well,' Netta said when he had finished, 'you've really got me now.'

'Yes.' Kester laughed lightly. 'We really have.' He winked at her, and she winked back. 'I'm trying to think,' she said, 'what I've done wrong to warrant this kind of top security.'

'Something very wicked,' Ben said, then added, 'and you'll soon find out what that is.'

'Yes,' Daisy echoed him, 'you'll soon find out what it is.'

'Silence in court!'

Kester's voice came ringing out over the voices of the others, and they stopped talking and turned to look at him where he stood behind the small table.

'This court,' he said gravely, 'is now in session.'

In the silence he sat down and cast his eyes around him. They lighted first on Michael, Ben and Daisy, who sat on the sofa, and then, his glance lingering a little, on Netta, where she sat bound to the chair.

'Listen,' Netta said as Kester's eyes met hers, 'just before we get started I'd better warn you that we won't be able to go on too long. Ben and Daisy will have to go to bed soon and – '

'Silence!' Kester snapped and Netta gave a little start and widened her eyes and made her mouth into an *O* in a little comic expression of fear. Daisy giggled.

'Silence!' Kester said again, glaring around him. 'Silence – or I'll find you in contempt of court.'

'What does that mean?' Daisy asked. 'What's contempt of court?' But Kester said sharply: 'Silence in court, I say.'

'Now . . .' Kester sighed. 'Now we get to the main case of the day.' He took from his pocket a pencil and a piece of notepaper. He wrote something on the paper, then, his eyes moving over the watching children, fixed his gaze on Netta. Netta's mouth twitched in a smile, but he made no sign of acknowledgement. His glance was cold, aloof. After clearing his throat he gazed at her for a moment longer in silence then took up the piece of notepaper and began to read aloud, solemnly:

'Prisoner at the bar, you are hereby charged with usurpation, with causing unnecessary suffering to Mrs Judith Farrell, and with enticing her husband Robert away from her. How say you, are you guilty or not guilty?'

TEN

Within the room there was a sudden silence. Even the breathing of its occupants seemed stilled. The atmosphere had become increasingly humid and the air was heavy. Into the stillness Ben gave an involuntary little laugh of nervousness and incomprehension. Daisy giggled while Michael let out his breath in a drawn out sigh. The eyes of all the children were fixed on Netta. A moth flew in through the open window and fluttered above the sofa. Daisy let out a shriek and covered her head with her hands. No one else moved. The moth fluttered about for a few moments and then settled on the shade of the lamp. There was silence again and Daisy raised her head and fixed her gaze on Netta once more. Netta, unaware of their glances, sat staring at Kester, her eyes wide, her mouth slightly open.

'What – what's happening here?' she said at last, frowning. 'What's – ?'

Kester's voice broke into her words.

'Silence!' he snapped, and rapped loudly on the table top with his knuckles. In the ensuing stillness he moved from the table over to the fireplace where he stooped and took up a small piece of wood – kindling that Robert had cut some days before when they had had a fire.

'Silence,' Kester said again, although there was not a sound in the room. Moving back behind the table he stood and coldly eyed Netta's horrified expression. 'You'll have a chance to speak in your defence,' he added. 'If you *have* any defence, that is.'

In the silence Netta could hear the sound of her own breathing. She could feel too the beating of her heart as it began to pound against her ribs. Under Kester's gaze she found herself wilting and, angry with herself, made an effort to thrust aside her weakness and face him squarely.

'Kester,' she said, forcing an awkward smile to her stiff lips, 'I'm afraid you're taking a joke a little too far. Come on now, I think it's time we stopped all this.' She gave a hollow little laugh. 'I don't think I like this particular game.'

As she finished speaking she made an effort to rise, but in the same instant realized that she was unable to move. She struggled futilely for some moments against the strength of the cords and then, momentarily giving up, said softly: 'Kester – untie me, please.'

Her words were met with silence, the three younger children looking from one to the other and then back to her, while Kester's gaze, unmoving, stayed fixed upon her helplessness. She laughed again, as if still intent on trying to make a joke of the whole thing. 'Hey, now,' she said, 'you tied these a bit too tightly.'

Kester still didn't move, but continued to look at her. There was a strange light in his eyes, and she found herself shrinking a little under his gaze. She laughed hollowly again, at the same time frowning, and then looked away, turning towards the other children. As she did so she saw Michael leaning forward as if he would rise, then halting in his move and looking at Kester, as if seeking some instruction or guidance. Kester ignored him. Then, uncertainly, Ben got up from the sofa. As he did so Kester said to him in a whisper as sharp as a knife: 'Don't you touch her.'

'But – ' Worriedly, Ben shook his head. 'But she wants to get free. She wants to be untied.'

'You heard me,' Kester said. 'Don't you dare touch her. Stay where you are.' Daisy stirred, as if she also would move to Netta. Quickly Kester turned his cold gaze upon her. 'That goes for you, too, Daisy. Stay where you are.' His eyes flicked to each of the children in turn. 'Don't any of you move.'

Silence again within the room. Then Netta raised her voice.

'Kester, let me go this instant. Untie me.' She paused. 'Listen, I'm perfectly happy to play games with you, but this isn't my idea of a game.'

129

Kester nodded. 'Quite so. I stopped playing games with you a long time ago. This isn't a game at all.'

'Kester!' Netta's voice rang out sharply in the room. Ignored, she turned her attention to Michael. 'Michael! Please, Michael, help me out of this.'

Michael gazed back at her for only a moment before, dropping his glance, he turned to take in Kester's continuing icy glare.

'Kester! *Kester!*' Netta shouted, a note of hysteria now ringing in her voice. 'Let me go. Untie me at once! If you don't untie me right now I'll . . .' As her words died away she made another vain effort to rise from the chair.

'Yes?' Kester said, raising an eyebrow while a quiet anger came into his voice. 'What will you do? You'll tell our father, will you? You'll go running to him the moment he gets back, will you?' His lip curled. 'Well, we could have guessed that. Tell us something to surprise us.' He paused. 'Is that it? Is that what you'll do?'

Netta gave a little sob of frustration and helplessness. 'Please,' she said, ' – just let me go. Just let me go and – and we'll say nothing more about it. We'll forget it ever happened.'

'Forget it ever happened?' Kester eyed her with a slight frown. 'You could forget? Is it easy for you to forget? Could you forget and forgive so easily?' He shook his head. '*I* couldn't. *I can't.*'

Netta's face crumpled and she hung her head. Then came Daisy's voice.

'Kester, you're being horrible! Stop it! Let Netta go!'

'Be quiet!' Kester rapped, and struck the table top with the piece of wood. 'You'll get your chance to talk. Till then just be quiet.'

'No, I won't!' Daisy stood up and stamped her foot. 'I *won't*! You've got to let Netta go. If you don't *I* shall tell Daddy – and he'll be very angry with you.'

Kester glared at Daisy for a moment then, stepping from behind the table, he moved across the room and thrust her

130

roughly back down onto the sofa. 'Be quiet!' he snapped. 'Or you'll be punished.'

'No, I won't be quiet!' Daisy spoke up bravely, though it was clear from the shine of tears that suddenly glinted in her eyes that she was afraid. 'Kester, you're being horrible!'

'Be quiet! Be quiet! Be quiet!' Kester shouted the words at her, then, raising his hand, he drew back his arm and slapped her sharply across the face.

Daisy cried out in pain and horror as she reeled from the blow, and then, turning her head, buried her face in her arms and wept.

Netta, giving a shake of her head, said, 'For God's sake, Kester, how can you be so cruel to Daisy.' To Daisy she said softly, 'Never mind, Daisy. Don't cry.'

Ignoring Netta's words, Kester continued to glare at Daisy for a moment longer and then his expression softened and he fell to his knees beside her.

'Daisy – don't cry. Don't cry.' He put his hand on her shoulder. 'But you mustn't defy me like that. You mustn't. It makes me angry.' He gave her arm a little pat. 'Just be a good girl – please.'

Daisy went on crying while Kester continued to make attempts to placate her. With a feeling of relief, Netta straightened in the chair. With Kester's words to Daisy she felt somehow that the whole episode was over and everything would be all right. After a while Kester straightened, turned and moved back to the table and once again took up his stance behind it. Netta looked at him for a moment and then said levelly: 'And now, perhaps, we can finish with all this nonsense. Perhaps now you'll untie me. The children have to get to bed – and I'm tired, too.'

In response he turned his head very slowly towards her, as if in disbelief and astonishment at her effrontery. Then, fixing her with a disdainful glance he said coldly: 'If the prisoner cannot keep quiet voluntarily she'll be *made* to keep quiet – or else she'll be tried in her absence.'

'Kester, this has gone far enough!' There was sharp anger in

131

Netta's voice. 'Stop being so ridiculous. Untie me right now –
or, I warn you, you're going to be very sorry.'

'*I'm* going to be very sorry?' Kester shook his head. 'No, Miss
Annetta, *you're* the one who's going to be very sorry.' He turned
away from her, directing his glance back to Daisy who lay
sniffing on the sofa. Ben, sitting at Daisy's side, was making
little murmuring words of comfort to her. Netta looked at
Kester in growing disbelief. She could hardly believe what was
happening. 'I don't understand you, Kester,' she said, a slightly
withering tone in her voice. 'I don't understand you at all.' She
paused, then added with dawning realization: 'You planned this,
didn't you?'

'Planned it?' He didn't look at her. 'Planned what?'

'This. This whole thing. You thought up this game just so
that you could – could humiliate me.'

The eyes he turned upon her now were the wide eyes of a
wronged, bewildered child; innocent, uncomprehending, a little
hurt. It was all too much, though, like an over-the-top perform-
ance from a bad actor. 'I don't know what you mean,' he said.
'How can you accuse me of such a thing?' He smiled.

'For God's sake, how did you learn to be like this?' Netta
said, the words erupting from her. 'And who did you learn it
from? Not from your father, that's for certain. If this is the way
your mother taught you to behave then I'm not surprised she's
not allowed to have control of you.'

The moment she had spoken she realized that she had gone
too far. She saw Kester's eyes blaze in fury as, his hands
gripping the edge of the table, he leaned across it towards her.
As his eyes burned into her own she thought for a moment that
he might come around the table and strike her. But he remained
where he was, speechless in his anger.

After a moment or two he said in a tight, steely voice: 'Don't
you ever speak of my mother again. You're not fit to clean her
shoes.' Then, turning to Michael, he rapped out: 'As she can't
be quiet on her own, then she'll have to be *kept* quiet. Get
something to shut her up. I won't listen to such things coming

132

from her mouth.' Michael looked vaguely about him for a second, then Kester added: 'Get her scarf. It's in the hall.'

Getting up from the sofa, Michael went into the hall and came back a moment later with Netta's blue silk scarf in his hand.

'That's it. Now gag her.' Kester gestured dismissively towards Netta, and Michael, after a brief hesitation, stepped towards her. As Michael approached Netta struggled and cried out, but very quickly the scarf was drawn tightly across her mouth and tied at the back of her head. At once her words of protest were reduced to impotent little muffled cries, while above the blue of the silk her eyes were wide in growing despair. She struggled, rocking back and forth in the chair while Daisy, her crying having ceased, gazed at her for a moment in fear and then buried her face in Ben's shoulder.

At last Netta's struggles ended and she sat without moving, her breast heaving, her nostrils dilated. Kester studied her. 'There, you see?' he said. 'If you don't do as you're told you're just going to regret it, that's all.' He paused. 'Well, now. Now that we've got a little peace perhaps we can get on with the proceedings. Perhaps we can continue with the trial.' Silence within the room again, and then he spoke once more.

'I shall present the case for the prosecution. Does anybody have any objection to that?'

No one spoke. Kester nodded and then stepped around the table. Standing with his back to Netta he faced the other three.

'Ladies and gentlemen of the jury, I want you to look upon the prisoner.' He turned briefly to fix his eyes on Netta, then looked back at the others. 'Look at her,' he said. 'But don't be taken in by her innocent expression. Don't allow yourselves to be moved by her present – anguish or discomfort.' He paused for effect. 'She is a homewrecker, ladies and gentlemen. A homewrecker. She has come into the lives of those in the Farrell family and caused havoc. And now, as if she hasn't done enough, she is now preparing to marry the father, Robert, and so separate the family for all time. She is a usurper – trying to take over, trying to take the place of Judith, the Farrell children's mother. She came into the Farrell home with her lies and her wiles, not caring at all about the trouble she caused, not caring one bit about the terrible pain – the agony – that she brought about. It doesn't matter to her what misery she has caused, and is causing – she has only one aim. And that aim, ladies and gentlemen of the jury, is to ensure that she herself is comfortable, that she gains for herself a husband, and a comfortable home.'

As Kester finished speaking Netta began to sway back and forth in the chair, her head jerking and twisting on her neck.

'She can't breathe,' Ben said.

Kester turned to her. 'Can't you? Can't you breathe?'

Netta wildly shook her head, her eyes rolling.

'No?' Kester asked. 'Or is this just a ruse? – to get the gag off?'

'Oh, please,' Daisy said, lifting her tearstained face and whirling to Kester. 'Take it off, Kester. She can't breathe.'

'All right.' Kester remained still for a moment then stepped towards Netta. 'Listen,' he said to her. 'If I take it off will you promise to be quiet? Will you behave yourself?'

Netta gave a nod.

'Okay, then.' Kester nodded. 'But if you start to make a fuss again it'll go back on. Is that clear?' He paused. 'Is it?'

Netta nodded again.

'Okay.' Kester snapped his fingers at Michael. 'Take off the gag. But leave it handy just in case.'

Michael moved to the chair and untied the knot at the back of Netta's head. As he removed the gag Netta opened her mouth and took in a great gulp of air. 'Thank you,' she said with a deep sigh of relief. 'I can't stand it. I go into a panic and I can't breathe.'

'All right,' Kester said, 'but remember – if you start kicking up a fuss again it goes back on. Understand?'

Netta opened her mouth to speak, but then closed it again and hung her head.

'Do you understand?' Kester said sharply.

'Yes, yes! I understand. Oh, for God's sake, Kester, what are you trying to do to me? Let me go, please. *Please* – let me go. What have I ever done to you that you should treat me in this way?'

Kester, appearing quite unmoved by her pleas, gave a little nod and said, '*That* we are about to find out.' He paused, gazing steadily at her. When he spoke again his voice had taken on the grave tones he adopted in his role as the judge.

'Prisoner at the bar,' he was moving back behind the table, 'you have heard the grave charge made against you. How do you plead? Are you guilty or not guilty?'

Silence. Daisy, looking at Netta, saw that there were tears in her eyes. 'Oh, Kester, please,' Daisy said entreatingly. 'Stop being so horrible to her. Can't you see you're making her cry!'

'D'you want more punishment?' Kester asked, and at once Michael echoed him, 'Yes, do you want more punishment? If not, be quiet.'

Kester turned his attention back to Netta. 'You heard the charge. I must insist on an answer. You are charged with usurpation, with breaking up the Farrell family, and causing pain and suffering to Mrs Judith Farrell. How say you, are you guilty or not guilty?'

Netta remained silent.

'I must have an answer,' Kester pressed her. 'Are you guilty or not guilty?'

'Oh, for God's sake,' Netta snapped, the tears running down her cheeks, 'of course I'm not guilty.'

'And is the court to take that as your plea?' Silence. Kester nodded to Michael. 'Let the plea be recorded.'

Michael, now sitting back on the sofa, looked at him in bewilderment. 'What d'you mean?' But Kester brushed aside the question with a wave of his hand. 'It's all right.' He turned back to Netta. 'Have you anything to say in your defence?'

Netta didn't answer. Kester nodded. 'Very well. You'll have a chance later on.' He rapped on the table with the wood, then moved from behind it and, standing with his back to Netta, faced the other three children. He was now the counsel for the prosecution again.

135

'I call the first witness,' he said. 'I call Benjamin Farrell.' He turned to Michael. 'Remember that for now you're the clerk of the court as well. You must say: "Call Benjamin Farrell."'

At the sound of his name a look of puzzled bewilderment had crossed Ben's anxious, uneasy features. Michael, getting to his feet, said, 'Call Benjamin Farrell.'

'There.' Kester pointed to the rug by the chair. 'The witness must take the stand.'

Without any further prompting, Ben left the sofa and took up a position on the rug. He looked enquiringly at Kester.

'State your name,' Kester said.

'You know my name,' Ben answered.

'You must say it anyway. You must state it to the court.'

'Ben. Benjamin Farrell.'

Kester nodded. 'And how old are you?'

'Nine. But I'm almost ten. I shall be ten on the ninth of September.'

Kester nodded again. 'Now, tell me, do you recognize the prisoner?'

'Yes, of course. It's Netta.'

'Right. Now – I want you to think back. Cast your mind back. Think carefully. Did the prisoner ever say anything to you about coming to live with us – with the Farrell family?'

'How d'you mean?' Ben frowned.

'You know what I mean,' Kester said. 'What about yesterday – when you got the thorn in your foot?'

'Oh – *then*.'

'Yes. Tell us what happened – what was said.'

'I told Michael all about it.'

'Yes, I know. And he told me. Now tell the court.'

'Well.' Ben giggled and shrugged, embarrassed at the sudden limelight. Kester frowned at him. 'What's so funny? This is a serious matter.'

Ben gave him an uncertain glance, nodded, cleared his throat, and said: 'Well – I got a thorn in my foot. In my heel.'

'Go on. Tell the court how she told you she would stay with us – with the Farrell family – for ever.'

'Well, I – I was crying,' Ben went on reluctantly. 'She – ' He turned his glanced to Netta. 'Netta – she took the thorn out with some tweezers. I said to her that I wanted her to stay with us always and to – '

Kester broke in quickly, 'Never mind about what *you* said to *her*. Tell us what *she* said to *you*.'

'Well – she said that she would stay with us. I just told you.'

'For always?'

'Yes.'

'For ever and ever?'

Ben didn't answer.

'For ever and ever?' Kester repeated.

'Yes. For ever and ever. Afterwards she gave me some chocolate.'

'Just a minute, now.' Netta's voice came in, a little shrill. 'He was crying. He'd hurt himself. He asked me if – '

She got no further. Kester whirled on her, snapping out as he did so: 'Silence. You'll have a chance to say your piece in a little while. Until then be quiet. If you can't be quiet we shall put the gag back on.'

'But – ' Netta began, shaking her head despairingly, 'I'm just trying to tell you what ha– '

'You want the gag, do you?' Kester said. He turned to Michael, sharply raising his hand as he did so. 'Michael, bring the gag.' Netta cried out, 'No, no, oh, please, no. I'll be quiet. I will. I promise I will. But please – don't put that thing on me again.'

Kester's hand rose again, bringing Michael to a halt as he got up from the sofa. 'Okay, it's all right. She's going to behave herself.' Michael sank back on the sofa and Kester turned once more to Ben. 'All right. The witness may step down.' He paused, waving the boy away. 'That means you can go back and sit down with the others.'

Turning briefly, Ben flicked a glance at Netta, then moved back to the sofa and took his seat once more between Daisy and Michael. Kester waited until Ben was settled then said to the three children: 'So, ladies and gentlemen of the jury, you've

137

heard from the witness the words the prisoner spoke. You've learned how she took advantage of the boy's tender age. Taking advantage of his pain, his discomfort, knowing how vulnerable he was. And afterwards she gives him chocolate. Chocolate to win him totally over to her side.' He paused, then slowly turned and looked at Netta. The eyes of the others moved and rested upon her also. For a moment she gazed back at them, a look of pain in her eyes, then hung her head. She became aware that rain was falling. She could hear the sound of it on the window pane.

'Right,' Kester said with a note of satisfaction in his voice. 'Call the next witness. Call Daisy Farrell.'

'No!'

Daisy's sharp little voice rang out in the silent room and she pressed back into the sofa cushions. 'No, I won't,' she said. 'I don't want to play this game. I don't like it.'

Kester said, 'It doesn't matter whether you like it or whether you don't. You'll have to do as you're ordered. Besides, I've made it clear, it's not a game.' He gestured towards her. 'The witness will take the stand at once.' He waited. Daisy didn't move but burrowed deeper.

'Come on,' he said. 'Come and stand over here.' He pointed to the spot recently vacated by Ben. 'And hurry up.'

'No, I won't.'

He eyed her with a steely glare. 'Do you want to be found in contempt of court?'

'I don't want to do anything,' she said, her voice breaking slightly. 'I want to go to bed. I want Daddy to come home.'

'You know what contempt of court means, don't you?' Kester said. 'It means you'll be punished.'

'No, Kester, no.' Daisy burst into tears.

'Then do as you're told.'

After a second Daisy slowly got up from the sofa and moved across to stand on the rug. As she did so Netta turned her head away, as if not wanting to see the hurt in the child's eyes.

'All right,' Kester said, watching Daisy. 'Now, tell the court:

138

did you ever receive any gifts from the prisoner? Did she ever give you any presents?'

'You know she did,' Daisy said, wiping her eyes, smearing the tears across her cheeks. 'She gave me my doll.'

'What else?'

'Some books.'

'What else?'

'All kinds of things. She gave you and Michael and Ben presents as well. Stamps and things, you know very well. She's always been so kind and nice to me. To all of us and – '

Kester raised a hand. 'Please confine yourself to answering the question. So – she gave you gifts. Did she also say anything about her marriage to your father?'

'Yes, she told us, Mike and Ben and me.' She paused. 'I'm going to be a bridesmaid. Netta said she's going to buy me my dress. A blue dress.'

'She asked you if you'd like to be a bridesmaid, did she? And she gave you numerous gifts?'

'What are *numerous* gifts?'

'*Many* gifts.'

'Yes.'

'Thank you. Now think back carefully. When your brothers Kester and Michael went to stay with their mother in London some weeks ago, did you stay at the prisoner's flat?'

'With Netta, d'you mean? In Netta's flat?'

'Yes, in Netta's flat. She's the prisoner. Did you go and stay with her?'

'You *know* we did. Ben and me, we both went.'

'Right. And is Netta's flat a big flat?'

'You know what it's like,' Daisy said. 'You've seen it.'

'Please, answer the question. Does it have many rooms?'

'No.'

'How many bedrooms does it have?'

'One.'

'I see. And where did you and Ben sleep?'

'On the sofa. You can make it into a bed. You know that. Daddy and Netta lift up the seat and make it into a bed.'

'And that's where you and your brother slept – on the sofa-bed.'

'Yes.'

'And do you remember where your father slept?'

'In the bedroom, of course.'

'In the bedroom. Was he with the accused?'

'He was with Netta.'

'In the same bed?'

'Yes, of course – it was *her bed*, wasn't it?'

'How do you know that your father slept in the same bed with Netta – with the prisoner?'

'I saw them.'

'In the bed?'

'Yes, I went into the bedroom in the night. I woke up, and it was strange – being in a different room. And I went into the bedroom.'

'You saw your father there?'

'He was asleep. I touched him on the shoulder and he woke up.'

'And then what?'

Daisy shrugged. 'He asked me what was the matter. Then he took me back to the other bed, the sofa-bed.' Another shrug. 'And I went back to sleep.'

'So you saw your father sleeping in the prisoner's bed. With the prisoner.'

'Yes. They were both asleep.'

'Thank you.' Kester turned his glanced towards Ben and Michael, a look of satisfaction in his eyes. He turned back to Daisy. 'Thank you. The witness may step down.' With his last words he gestured back to the sofa and Daisy scurried towards it, sat down and buried her face in the cushions.

Silence fell in the room again and the sound of the steadily falling rain could be heard. Kester looked around at the window, as if he had not been aware of the rain before. After a moment he moved to the window and closed it. He stood there unmoving, frowning slightly, as if in deep thought, then he said: 'Call the next witness. Call Michael Farrell.'

At the words a brief look of bewilderment flashed across Michael's face, as if he had forgotten what had gone before. But then he collected himself and, moving across the room, took up the position on the rug.

Daisy still crouched on the sofa, burrowing into the cushions, but at her side Ben straightened a little. His round face bore a little frown, while his mouth hung slightly open – it was as if he didn't want to watch, yet was at the same time compelled to, as a rabbit is hypnotized by a stoat.

'Tell the court your name,' Kester commanded.

'Michael Farrell.' Michael spoke clearly, without hesitation, as if determined, after the behaviour of the witnesses who had gone before, not to be found wanting.

'And you are the son of Mr Robert Farrell and Mrs Judith Farrell?'

'Yes, your honour.'

'No, you don't call me "Your honour",' Kester reprimanded him testily. 'I'm the prosecuting counsel.'

'What do I call you, then?'

'You don't call me anything at all.' Kester frowned and sucked in his breath, showing his displeasure at the interruption that took him out of his role. 'Now, please, pay attention and answer the questions.'

'Yes, sir.'

'When – and I'm sure you can remember – when did you last see your mother, Mrs Judith Farrell?'

'Early last month. In August. It was her birthday. We went up to see her for the weekend.'

'And would you say that she was happy at that time?'

'Happy? Well, no, sir.'

'Then would you say that she was *un*happy?'

'Well, yes, in a way.'

'I see. And can you tell the court what form this – unhappiness took? How it manifested itself?'

'Mm?' Michael blinked, not understanding.

'Manifested,' Kester repeated. 'How did it show itself – this unhappiness of your mother?'

'Oh, yes – well – she was just very unhappy. She cried.'

'She cried? Can you tell the court how this came about?'

'Yes.' Michael nodded. 'You and I were – My brother and I were in bed. It was the night before her birthday. She suddenly started to cry.'

'And do you know why she was crying?'

'When we asked her what was the matter she said it was because of Dad and Netta – the prisoner.'

'What about them?'

'Well . . .' Michael gave a shrug. 'She realized that if he married her, the prisoner, it would all be finished. We'd never all be together again, no matter how much she wanted it, and how hard she tried for it.'

'Did she say that to you?'

'Yes. Once she knew that Dad wanted to get married again she got very unhappy.'

'I see.' Kester paused. 'Do you love your mother?'

'Yes, sir. Very much.'

'Does she love you?'

'Oh, yes, very much.'

'She loves all her children?'

'Yes, sir, very much.'

'And does she want them with her?'

'Yes, sir. She can't have them, though. Only for a few times, now and then.'

'What about her husband – your father? Do you think she loved him?'

'Yes, sir, I'm sure she did.'

'And she hoped – believed – that one day she and her husband and children would all be together again, is that it?'

'Yes.'

'And that was the cause of her unhappiness, was it? The fact that she realized that she would never have her children – or her husband – with her again?'

'Yes.'

'Thank you.' Kester paused for a moment. 'Would you say,' he asked, 'that all Mrs Farrell's children love her?'

Michael hesitated before answering. 'Well – not all the same,' he said carefully. 'I don't think so.'

'What do you mean by that?'

Michael flicked a glance at Daisy and Ben where they sat on the sofa. Ben was sitting up watching the proceedings, frowning, while Daisy was nestled into his side, eyes closed, the marks of her tears still on her cheeks. She might have been asleep.

'Please answer the question,' Kester prompted him.

'Well . . .' Michael gave a little shrug, then said: 'I don't think the two younger ones love her as much as the other two.'

'That's not true!' Ben said sharply. 'We *do*.'

'Silence in court!' Kester said sternly. 'If the spectators can't be quiet they'll be removed.' He turned back to Michael. 'Please continue.'

'Yes, well – they didn't – don't – know her as well as we do. They don't care that much for staying with her when we go up to London.'

'I see. And when you and your brother go up to London the two younger children stay at home, do they?'

'Oh, no, not usually. Usually at those times they go out with Netta.'

'Can you explain that?'

'Well, I think sometimes she used to take them out. I know they went to the pictures a few times. And sometimes at night they'd stay at her flat. Or go there to have tea.'

'And did they enjoy these times, d'you think?'

'Yes, I think so. They used to tell us about it afterwards.'

'Tell *us* about it. Please.'

'Well – they were always full of it – what they'd done.'

'With Netta. The accused.'

'Yes.'

'Do you think it would be fair to say that the accused used to *attract* them to her at such times?'

'Well . . .' Michael looked hard at Kester for a second and then gave a positive nod. 'Yes, I would.'

'Thank you. No more questions. You may step down.'

As Michael moved back to the sofa and took his seat again

Kester stood in silence, unmoving, a faint touch of a smile on his lips. Then, addressing the room at large, he said clearly: 'Call the next witness. Call Annetta Robinson.'

In the silence the sound of the rain could be heard as it pattered against the pane. Netta looked at Kester with wide, hurt eyes.

'I'm not going to join in your games,' she said wearily.

Kester turned to her, frowning, looking for the first time a little thrown, a little at a loss. 'You wanted to speak,' he said after a moment. 'Well, now's your chance. Do you still want to speak? Or don't you have anything to say?'

She lowered her head, avoiding his eyes. 'Oh, I've got plenty I could say.'

'Then here's your opportunity.' He paused. 'All right?'

A brief silence as Netta thought on the matter, then she nodded. 'Yes – all right.'

At her words Michael got up from the sofa, stepped to the chair and bent towards Netta's bound ankles. Kester said quickly, 'What d'you think you're doing?'

'Well . . .' Michael straightened, looking at his elder brother. 'Well, if she's to take the stand then she'll have to be untied.'

'No, leave her where she is. She can speak from there.'

Netta broke in: 'Please, Kester, untie me, won't you? My hands and feet are – these cords are tied so tightly. It's so uncomfortable.'

Kester moved to the chair where he bent and tested the cords, first at her ankles and then at her wrists. 'They're not too tight,' he said shortly. 'They're fine.'

'Please. Please, Kester. Besides – I need to go to the loo.'

He waved her words away with a dismissing movement of his hand. 'We'll talk about that later,' he said. He turned to her. 'Do you swear to tell the truth, the whole truth, and nothing but the truth?'

Netta glared at him. 'I always tell the truth,' she said.

ELEVEN

Kester ignored her remark. 'Tell the court your name,' he said.
Netta said nothing.

'State your name for the court,' he insisted.

Still she remained silent.

As if he were accustomed to dealing with difficult witnesses
every day, Kester, refusing to be thrown any further, said to
her: 'Your name is Annetta Robinson, is it not?' He waited.

'Of course my name is Annetta Robinson,' Netta said. 'Let's
get on with this charade; I want to go to the loo . . .'

'All in good time. First you'll be required to answer a few
questions.' He paused. 'Will you please tell the court how old
you are?'

Netta didn't answer, merely gave him a contemptuous glance
then looked away. Kester eyed her angrily. 'You're twenty-nine,
aren't you?' She didn't answer. 'Yes,' he nodded, 'you're
twenty-nine.' He took a step towards her. 'You do realize what
you're charged with, don't you?'

She looked at him now. 'Usurpation? I never heard of such a
ridiculous thing.'

'But you do know what it means?'

'Of course I know what it means!' she snapped. 'For God's
sake!'

'Are you guilty of it?'

'Of course not!' After her sharp words a look of pleading
came into her eyes. 'Kester,' she said, 'are you aware how
humiliating this is for me? Are you really aware of what you're
doing to me? I don't think you can be, otherwise you wouldn't
put me through this awful misery.'

Unmoved, he said, 'We'll deal with the business of humilia-

tion a little later. And as for putting a person through misery –
well, that's something else we'll get round to.'

Clasping his hands he turned to face the other children.
'Now, ladies and gentlemen of the jury, I shall proceed to
question the witness.' He turned back to Netta.

'Have you ever met Mrs Judith Farrell, the mother of the
Farrell children?'

Netta looked sullenly away from him.

'Please answer the question,' he said. 'If you answer the
questions promptly and honestly then the whole trial will soon
be over. If you want to prolong it then that's up to you.'

'No,' Netta said, 'I never met Mrs Farrell.'

'So you only know about her from hearsay. From what you've
been told by others.'

'Yes.'

'And what do you think of her? – going by what you've heard
other people say?'

'What do I think of her?' Netta said scornfully. 'If you're
going to play at trials you should at least try to do it properly.
No judge would allow you to ask such a question in a real court
of law.'

Kester smiled. 'Ah, but in this court *I'm* the judge – as well
as the counsel for the prosecution. And I allow it. What I won't
allow, though, are your interruptions. Please confine yourself to
answering the questions as they're put to you.' He paused.
'Were you ever aware of the unhappiness you were causing Mrs
Judith Farrell?'

Netta sighed. 'No,' she said dully, 'I was not aware that I was
causing her any unhappiness at all.'

'You say you were not aware that you were causing her any
unhappiness?'

'No, I was not.'

'You can take another woman's husband and believe that it
can't make any difference to her? That it can't cause her any
unhappiness?'

'He was not her husband. Your father and mother were
divorced, you know that very well. This is ridiculous.'

'We'll see how ridiculous it is. You say that Robert and Judith Farrell were divorced. But in the sight of God there is no such thing as divorce, you know that. "He whom God hath joined together let no man put asunder." You have heard those words?'

'Yes.' A sigh.

'Do you think perhaps they're meaningless?'

'Oh, I don't know. For God's sake, haven't you humiliated me enough? Let me go. Please.'

'Would you agree that in some people's eyes Robert and Judith Farrell are still married to one another?'

She didn't answer.

'Would you?' Kester insisted. 'Would you agree that this is so?' He gave a deep sigh. 'Listen, we can wait here all night for your answer if you want it that way. I'll ask you again: do you think that in the eyes of some people Judith and Robert Farrell are still married to one another?'

'I suppose so. I suppose there are such people.'

'And just supposing one of those people was Judith Farrell herself, how d'you think she must feel about it all? About the divorce?'

'I don't know.'

'Oh, but I think you do. I think you must do. D'you think she would be unhappy about it?' He paused. 'Please answer the question.'

'Oh, God, I don't know,' Netta said wearily. 'Yes, I suppose so.' She raised her head. 'But that's not the case with your mother, and you know it. For one thing she was the one who sued for the divorce. Also, she's not a practising Catholic, and hasn't been for many years. She was – '

'Silence!' Kester snapped, but Netta went on:

'No, *you* listen to *me* for once! You know very well that your mother had finished with your father long before I came on the scene. She didn't want him. *You* know that, *I* know that, and *every*body knows that.'

'Silence, I said!'

'No, I *won't* be silent. I didn't steal your father away from your

147

mother. I didn't steal him away from *any*one. He came to me willingly, of his own accord. He was unhappy. He'd been badly hurt, and I think he was glad to find a little true affection, a little comfort and, more than anything, a little *sanity* in his li – '

She got no further. In one step Kester covered the distance between them and, raising his arm, struck her hard across the face with the flat of his palm. The sound of the blow rang out in the room. He stood glaring down at Netta while she hung her head, the mark of his hand appearing as if by magic on her cheek. Netta sucked in a great gulp of air, as if to stifle the sob that welled in her throat. After some moments had passed she said: 'You're very good at that, aren't you? – striking people who can't strike back.'

Briefly Kester's head turned, taking in the glances of the wide-eyed, watching children. He turned back to Netta again.

'Just be quiet,' he said evenly, fury still in his eyes. He stood for a moment in silence, as if collecting his thoughts, then he said: 'You heard the evidence of Daisy Farrell, didn't you?'

'Yes.'

'You heard how she found you and Mr Robert Farrell in your bed.'

Netta gave a nod. Her face was turned away from him.

'You admit it, then.'

'Of course I admit it. How could I deny it!'

'Thank you. And will you tell the court now how often you and Mr Farrell have – have had sex together?'

Netta turned to face him at this. 'This is disgraceful!' she said. 'I refuse to answer such a question. How dare you ask me such a thing!'

Kester smiled a thin little smile. 'Oh, we dare very much. But please, answer the question.'

'No, I won't answer the question. It's no damn business of yours. It concerns me and your father and nobody else.'

'Oh, you think so? I'm afraid you're wrong. It concerns other people too. Mrs Farrell and the Farrell children among them. Do you really think you can carry on as much as you want with a man and that it shouldn't have any effect on his wife and children?'

'He has no wife. Besides, whatever happened, d'you think it all depended on *my* actions? Your father has a mind of his own, you know.'

Kester considered this for a moment, then he said: 'You still haven't answered the question. How many times have you had sex with Robert Farrell?'

'I told you, I have no intention of answering such a question. Please, stop all this, and let me go. Besides, I told you, I want to go to the loo.'

'And *I* told *you*,' Kester rejoined sharply, 'that you'll have to wait.'

'Well, I can't wait much longer.'

'Would you say,' he said, ignoring her last remark, 'that you've had sex with him a hundred times?'

Netta turned her face away, setting her glance on the wall to her left.

'More than a hundred times?' Kester asked. He paused. 'Five hundred times?'

Netta looked around at this and gave him a brief, withering glance before she turned her eyes back to the wall.

'Less than five hundred?' Kester said. 'Less than a hundred?'

He got no response. Glaring at her averted head he asked, 'And was he willing each time?'

Netta hooted at this and, slowly turning her face towards him, gave him a look of such contempt that he momentarily faltered before it. His discomfiture didn't last long.

'Do you remember,' he asked her, 'the day of your arrival here at the house?'

She nodded. 'Yes.'

'And do you remember that same evening – that night – after the children had gone to bed?'

No answer. No flicker in her expression gave away her thoughts.

'Do you remember how the two of you went down the garden to the orchard?' he asked. 'Do you remember how you stopped

149

there and lay down on the grass together? Do you remember how you kissed him? Do you remember that? Do you remember kissing him? Yes, I think you do. And do you recall how you undid his trousers and took his – and *touched* him – there – down below? Do you recall how you *exposed* him? You remember all that, do you? I'm sure you do. Of course you do. You enjoyed it, didn't you? You enjoyed undoing his fly, touching him like that. And then touching him with your mouth. Kissing him – *there*. Taking him inside your mouth. Doing all those – '

Netta screamed, a high, piercing scream, and for a moment Kester's words were drowned, but then passionately he burst out, forgetting his role of prosecutor.

'Yes, you were seen that night. Everything you did. I saw you. *I*. I followed you down to the orchard, and I hid and I watched you. You were *disgusting*.'

'Stop it!' she cried out. 'Stop it! Stop it! Stop it!' Hanging her head, the tears ran down her cheeks. 'For God's sake leave me alone,' she added. 'Please, if you have any feeling of decency in you at all, please – stop it – stop it and let me go. I can't take any more of this.' She shook her head and a little thread of mucus swung from her nose and caught on her collar. Kester, watching her, pulled a face, said, 'Ulgh,' and beckoned to Michael. 'Bring a handkerchief or something, will you?' he said. 'Do something about her nose. It's revolting. I can't look at her when she's like that.'

As Michael got up from the sofa, Ben said, pointing: 'There's some Kleenex on the side.'

Michael took a piece of tissue and stepped towards Netta. When he stood at her side he looked up at Kester.

'Well, wipe her fucking nose,' Kester said sharply. 'Don't just stand there.'

'I'll do it.'

The words came from Daisy, as, with her own tears streaming down her cheeks, she got up from the sofa and stepped towards the two boys. As they stood there she snatched the tissue from Michael's hand and gently dabbed at Netta's nose and eyes.

150

'Okay,' Kester said to her. 'Now you can go and sit down again.'

'Oh, please – let me sit with her, can I?' Daisy was half leaning over the chair, a hand on Netta's shoulder moving in a gentle, ineffectual little stroking action.

Kester's lip curled as he gazed down at Daisy. 'Yes, you've always been on her side, haven't you? You're like Dad – totally taken in by her. Totally blinded by her. She's able to do that, it seems – take away a person's powers of judgement. Well, not everyone's like you, thank God.' He shook his head. 'No, go and sit down on the sofa.'

Daisy hovered for another moment or two and then reluctantly left Netta's chair and moved back to the sofa. There she laid her arms on the sofa's arm, laid her head on them and wept.

No one spoke for a long time. The only sounds in the room were of Daisy's crying and a rhythmic little sniffling sound from Netta. The rain had ceased but the rain-cooled atmosphere was swiftly growing warmer, humid again. Then, suddenly, startlingly, shattering the silence, there came a great crack of thunder. As Daisy raised her head and gave a little cry of fear a flash of lightning lit up the room and every eye turned to the window. Next moment the rain was falling again, this time in a fury, lashing the pane as it was driven by the rising wind.

The occupants in the room continued to remain silent. The children's attention seemed to be riveted on the storm as it raged on the horizon beyond the trees. Daisy hid her head under one of the cushions while Ben crouched beside her, hovering over her, one arm wrapped around her, though as much for his own comfort as for hers. Michael just sat there looking from the window to Kester and back to the window again, murmuring faint little scoffing sounds at Daisy and Ben while his eyes and tightly set lips betrayed his own dismay.

The storm came closer and the lightning lit the room even more brilliantly, terrifyingly, while the thunder clapped and growled. And through it all Kester stood there with a strange light in his blue eyes and a smile on his slightly parted lips.

At last, after some fifteen or twenty minutes the lightning and the thunder died away, the storm passed over and the only sound was the sound of the rain on the window pane.

'Well,' Kester said, pressing his hands together, 'we must get on.'

He gazed intently at Netta for a moment then quickly crossed the room to the kitchen door. Going into the kitchen he returned almost immediately holding in his hand a small mirror that he had taken down from the kitchen wall. 'I have just a few more questions,' he said, closing the door behind him, 'then I shall rest my case.' Putting the mirror down on the table, he took up a position not far from Netta and said to her: 'Will you please tell the court how many love affairs you've had over the past – say – eight or nine years.'

Netta ignored him.

'You might as well answer,' he said, ' – unless you want to *remain* in that chair.'

'One,' Netta said. 'And it didn't last, if that's what you're interested in.'

Kester nodded. 'One love affair – before your current association with Robert Farrell.'

'Yes. It was a long time ago. Years ago.'

'I see. But why only one? Weren't you interested in having a – a nice relationship with a nice man?'

She said wearily: 'It doesn't happen just like that.'

'What do you mean by that?'

'It just didn't happen. You can't just – go out and have a relationship. You'll learn one day.'

'But you would have *liked* a relationship, yes? A good, lasting relationship?'

'I suppose so.'

'I see. So you reached the age of twenty-nine without having had any real or – meaningful relationship in your life. Is that so?'

She shrugged. 'If you like.'

'No, not what *I* like. What did *you* like? Were you happy with that situation?'

'Oh, for God's sake!' she snapped out. 'Where is all this leading to? Isn't it time you stopped all this nonsense?'

He ignored her outburst. 'Why do you think you never had any real love affair?' he asked. 'Didn't anybody ask you out?'

She ignored the question.

He gave a little nod. 'I shall assume that the answer to that is no,' he said. He paused. 'And why d'you think no one asked you out? Can you think of any reason?'

She said sharply: 'Men *did* ask me out – sometimes.'

'Oh, I see. But not the *right* men.'

He crossed to the table and took up the mirror. Holding it before him he breathed on it and then rubbed it against the front of his shirt. Stepping back to Netta's side he held the mirror up in front of her face. 'What do you see?' he asked.

It was in that moment that she realized what he had been leading up to.

'What do you see?' he repeated.

'Myself, of course.'

'Thank you. And tell the court – are you pleased with what you see?'

The brief look she gave him was full of pleading. 'Don't, Kester,' she said. 'Please, don't.'

He still held the mirror in front of her face. 'Are you pleased with what you see?' he persisted. 'Tell the court.'

She didn't answer but lowered her eyes, refusing to look into the glass. Kester gave a nod.

'Quite so,' he said. 'You would not, I imagine, call yourself a beautiful woman, would you?' Pause. 'A pretty woman?' Pause. 'Attractive?' he nodded. 'Quite so.'

Kester moved back to the table, laid the mirror down on it and turned to face the children. Only Michael seemed to be giving his full attention to what was going on. Ben and Daisy, cowed by the storm and by the happenings in the room, crouched huddled together at Michael's side. Kester seemed unaware of their lack of attention.

'And that, ladies and gentlemen of the jury,' he said, 'concludes the case for the prosecution.' He stretched out his arm

153

towards Netta. 'And now, ladies and gentlemen, I want you to look upon the prisoner. Look upon this miserable creature before you and think upon the evidence you have heard.' He turned and looked at Netta as she sat slumped sideways in the chair, eyes closed, not appearing to be listening or taking any interest in the proceedings. Kester gazed at her for a moment or two then turned his attention back to the children.

'She pleads not guilty,' he said. 'Not guilty. But I must ask you to think how this could possibly be. Ladies and gentlemen, you have heard the evidence. You have heard the witnesses – children who have not the guile to lie. And they have not lied. They have spoken the truth. You have heard how the prisoner tried to win them to her side – the younger ones in particular. The boy Ben. When he hurt his foot she gave him chocolate – and told him that she would stay with him for ever. In other words, to be a mother to him. Taking advantage of a child's pain, his hurt, his discomfort. And the other child, Daisy Farrell. You have heard how she was given gifts by the accused. A doll, books, other presents. You have heard too how she would spend time with the accused when her brothers went to London to see their mother. Oh, yes, there's no question but that when this woman came into the lives of the Farrell family she caused total disruption. After her appearance on the scene nothing was ever quite the same again.'

Silence fell for a few seconds while Kester gazed at those on the sofa, as if looking for signs of the impact of his words. Michael gazed back at him, open-mouthed, while Daisy and Ben seemed oblivious of his words.

'You have heard, too, ladies and gentlemen,' Kester went on, 'how the prisoner used her wiles also on the husband. There is evidence of that, too. And you will remember, too, how the prisoner admitted that her love affair with him was her first relationship that had any meaning in her life. And this relationship was important to her. Very important. Remember – she is twenty-nine years old, and hardly what you would call attractive. Look closely at her, ladies and gentlemen. You don't need to take my word for it. You can see for yourselves.' He paused.

'And so, desperate to find a husband, and to move out of an ugly, rented little flat into a beautiful house, she sets her sights on a particular man – a man who is at a vulnerable stage in his life, a man looking for affection. And she does her best to snare him – and she succeeds. Yes, she succeeds, ladies and gentlemen, no matter the cost to whoever else might be involved.'

'Oh, God . . .'

The muttered words came from Netta, and Kester turned and looked at her as she sat with her head hanging low, her eyes shut tight, hands gripping the chair arms.

After a second he continued: 'And you have heard also how the true mother, Judith Farrell, was affected by such goings on, of her growing misery at her loss and the usurpation of her own rightful place in the Farrell household, in the Farrell family.' He gave a sorrowful shake of his head. 'And now, ladies and gentlemen, it is too late. It is too late for Mrs Judith Farrell. Her happiness was based in her family, in her husband and children. And from them she has for ever been cast out. And this – *this* is the caster.'

With the last word he turned, flung up his arm and pointed at Netta. 'She is guilty, ladies and gentlemen. You have heard the evidence and there cannot be any question in your minds. *She is guilty.*'

He remained standing there for a few seconds, his hand still outstretched, finger still pointing. Then, slowly lowering his arm he turned, standing straight, facing the children again.

'Ladies and gentlemen of the jury, I rest my case.'

TWELVE

After another moment Kester moved to take up his position behind the small table at the side. 'Now,' he said, 'in my role as the judge, I will sum up the case. After which the jury will retire to consider its verdict.' He paused, as if for dramatic effect, then continued, his voice taking on a more sonorous note.

'Ladies and gentlemen of the jury, you have – '

'Dear God, what a revolting little shit you are.'

Netta's voice, although not by any means loud, seemed to ring out and echo in the room. Daisy and Ben opened their eyes, raised their heads and, along with Kester and Michael, gazed at her.

Sitting upright in the chair once again, Netta's lip curled as she glared with blazing eyes across the room at Kester. He stared back at her, tensing, a little flicker of doubt suddenly in his eyes.

'You are one of the most disgusting creatures it's ever been my misfortune to meet,' Netta said, measuring her words. 'You're cruel, insensitive. You have no compassion in you whatsoever. You disgust me.' She shook her head. 'And I hope to God you're not planning to take up law as a profession. If so I pity the poor defendants.'

'Why?' Kester said, in control again. 'Why do you pity the defendants?'

'Dear God,' she said witheringly, 'it doesn't matter to you the other things I said to you, does it? – that you're cruel and insensitive? Your concern is that you're playing this charade in the right way. If it really matters, I was wondering whatever happened to the case for the defence. That never occurred to you, did it?' Then without waiting for an answer she added, 'But it doesn't matter. Just get it over with and let me go.'

Kester gazed at her for a moment. 'No,' he said, 'you shall have your defence. You shall have whatever you're entitled to.' He turned to the others. 'Would someone like to offer a defence of the prisoner?'

Silence in the room. He shrugged and turned to Netta again. 'You see? No one feels so inclined.' He smiled his thin little smile. 'Sorry about that.'

And then suddenly Daisy's piping little voice was heard.

'Yes – I do.'

The sound of her voice took everyone by surprise, not least Netta who turned to gaze at her with wide, surprised eyes. Kester, frowning, blinked at Daisy. 'You?' he said. 'What do you want to say?'

Daisy had got up from the sofa, was standing looking up at him. 'What does it mean,' she asked, 'defence of the prisoner?'

Kester laughed. 'God, how stupid you are. Go and sit down before I lose my temper again.'

'No, tell me. What does it mean?'

He sighed. 'It means to say something in her favour.'

'You mean to stick up for her?'

He sighed again. 'Yes – if you like.'

'To say something nice about her?'

'In a way, yes.'

'Yes – well, I want to say something nice about her – about Netta.'

Another sigh from Kester as he exchanged glances with Michael. He gave a nod and turned back to Daisy. 'Okay. Say what you have to say and get it over with. Don't be all night about it.' With his words he moved away and stood with his back to the small table.

Daisy hesitated for a moment, then stepped into the centre of the room. There she stood looking about her, taking in the glances of the others. She looked very small and insignificant.

'Well, go on,' Kester said impatiently. 'If you've got something to say, then say it.'

Daisy turned her face to him. 'You're not the way I thought

157

you were, Kester,' she said. 'I used to love you. I don't love you now. I don't think I'll ever love you again. I think you're hateful.'

'Oh – ' he said, 'just say what you want to say and shut up. Let's get on with it.'

Daisy stood there with her gaze upon him and in the brief silence Netta became vaguely aware that the rain had stopped. After a moment or two Daisy turned to Ben and Michael who sat looking at her with wonder in their wide eyes.

'Netta . . . is nice,' she said.

Hanging her head, Netta felt the tears well in her eyes and roll down her cheeks.

'Is that it?' Michael said.

Kester put up a hand, silencing him. Then to Daisy he said: 'Is it?'

'She *is*,' Daisy said. 'I like her so much. She's been so nice to me and Ben and – oh, Kester – ' she turned to him as he stood against the table, 'please don't be so horrible to her.' She stepped across the room towards him. 'Kester, *please*. Be nice to her.' The tears swam in her eyes. 'Let her go. I'll love you for ever if you will.' She reached out to him, clutching the sides of his shirt. 'I'll give you anything you want. Any of my books. I'll give you my best doll. Anything at all.'

He gave a short, scoffing laugh as he brushed her hands away. 'What the hell would I want with your stupid doll or any of your stupid books.' His eyes narrowed. 'But it doesn't surprise me – your talking like this. You've always been different from the rest of us. Apart. You're not one of us. You never have been. Still – you're very young. Perhaps you're too young to know any better. Now, go and sit down, so that we can get on with the rest of the business.'

Daisy still stood there, the tears running down her cheeks as she gazed entreatingly up at him. He looked away. 'Don't look at me like that,' he said. He glanced at his watch. 'It's after eleven. It's time you were in bed.'

'Oh, no, not yet. Please.'

'You heard me, it's time you were in bed. Off you go now.'

He glanced over at Michael. 'Mike – take her up to bed, please, and hurry back down here.'

At once Michael got up and came towards them. 'Come on, Daisy,' he said, not unkindly. 'Let's get you to bed.' He took her hand and began to pull her towards the door while she protested, struggling against his hold.

'No,' she cried. 'Oh, Mike, please. Let me stay. I'll be quiet, I promise I will. Let me stay with Netta.'

'Get her upstairs,' Kester snapped. 'She's getting on my nerves. Get her out of here.'

In a few moments Daisy, still protesting, was being led out of the room and up the stairs. Those in the room listened to the sound of her voice until it faded above them. No one spoke. Netta, in her chair, had a hurt, bruised look about her. Her face was set, her eyes closed. On the sofa Ben leaned back against the cushions, his eyes moving from Netta to Kester and back again, his mouth hanging open in his round, suntanned face. Kester stood without moving, looking at no one, waiting for Michael's return.

The minutes passed, and then Netta, shifting uncomfortably in the chair, said without opening her eyes: 'I have to go to the bathroom.'

Kester gave no sign that he had heard.

After a while Michael came back downstairs. 'She's quiet now,' he said as he entered the room and closed the door behind him. 'I talked to her for a while. I think she's settled all right now.' He moved to the sofa and sat down. Kester waited until he was settled, then, moving back behind the table, he rapped upon it with the piece of wood.

'The jury will now retire to consider its verdict,' he said. 'But before you go I must impress upon you the necessity to think very carefully on the evidence you have heard. Your verdict must be based upon it, and on nothing else. If you think that the case against the prisoner is proven then it is your duty to bring in a verdict of guilty. If you think that the case is not proven against her – if you have doubt – then you must give the prisoner the benefit of that doubt and give your verdict accord-

159

ingly, which is in a verdict of not guilty.' He nodded gravely. 'Thank you for your patience. You may now retire to consider your verdict.'

Michael and Ben looked at him blankly.

'We'll go into the other sitting room,' he said, 'the parlour – where the prisoner can't hear us.' He moved out from behind the table and walked out of the room, across the hall and into the room beyond. After a moment Michael and Ben got up and followed him.

From her chair, Netta watched the door close behind them, heard the fading sound of their footsteps and then found herself in silence again. From outside in the night an owl hooted, the sound eerie in the stillness. Minutes passed and then a short, sharp little cry rang out in the night, the sound coming from somewhere in the fields beyond the lane. Some small animal, a part of her mind acknowledged. Perhaps the owl had found its prey.

She tried to move her hands but the cords about her wrists were tighter than ever, pressing more deeply into her flesh; with the constant friction against her bonds, in her efforts to free herself, her wrists had become inflamed and slightly swollen. Her ankles were the same. The discomfort of her bonds apart, she was increasingly aware of the fullness of her bladder. They would have to let her go soon. She couldn't hold out for much longer.

She could still hardly believe that she was in such a situation. Dear God, how could it have happened to her? How could Kester be so unutterably cruel? Well, she had always thought that she had never really known him, and now she knew that it was the truth. Who could have supposed that his brain could conceive of such horror, of inflicting such torment on another human being? Yet he had done it. What was more, he had planned it, that much was clear. God, how he must hate her. That alone was terrifying. She shuddered. She had never imagined that she could ever be the focal point of such unadulterated, unwavering hatred.

160

Soon, though, it would be over. Soon he would let her go.

Suddenly the tears were spilling down her cheeks again. It was over. It was over between herself and Robert. She knew that now. She could never marry him now. There had been many times when she had had doubts about the wisdom of such a course and now she knew that she had been right to have those doubts. She could never marry him now – not knowing how much she was loathed, hated, by some of his children. She wept silently, the tears running down her chin and dripping onto her blouse. When this dreadful time was over she would go away. She would leave the school, too. She would have to. 'Oh, God,' she whispered. 'Kester, please come back. Say what you have to say to me and get it over with. Get the rest of it over with and let me go.'

The time went on, the minutes ticking by. She had no idea how long she sat there. As she waited she became aware again of the increasing discomfort of her full bladder. It was so acute now that there was no pushing her need from her mind any longer.

A sound from the hall. The door opened and Kester appeared, followed by Michael and Ben. While Kester moved to take his position behind the table the other two boys went to the sofa and sat down. No one looked at Netta. When everyone in the room was still Kester looked across at the two on the sofa.

'Gentlemen of the jury,' he said, 'have you agreed upon your verdict.'

Michael stood up. 'We have, my Lord.'

'And what is your verdict? Do you find the prisoner guilty or not guilty?'

'Guilty, my Lord.'

'And is that the verdict of you all?'

Michael flicked a swift glance at Ben, then said stoutly, 'It is, my Lord.'

Netta, her glance moving from one to the other, felt a sense of relief. The verdict was exactly as she had expected. And now, she said to herself, it was almost done. Their humiliation of her now was almost complete.

161

THIRTEEN

Perhaps now they would let her go, she said to herself. They couldn't keep her tied up like this for much longer.

She was aware that there was silence in the room and looking at Kester she saw that he was standing with his eyes upon her. Even when her glance met his he didn't look away, but remained quite still, fixing her with an unseeing stare. Then at last, as if coming out of a trance, he moved, his head lowering, his hands coming down and resting on the table top.

'And now,' he said, 'there will be a brief adjournment while the court decides upon the sentence.'

Next moment, followed by the other two boys, Kester was moving away again, across the room and out into the hall.

'Kester . . . !'

At Netta's cry Kester stopped, looking back at her over Michael's shoulder.

'Yes? What is it?'

'Please. I have to go to the bathroom. I *must*.'

He hesitated. 'In a moment. You'll have to wait.'

'I *can't*.'

He shrugged. 'You've got no choice.' He turned again. Seconds later the door was closing and Netta was alone once more.

In the parlour Kester turned to Michael and Ben as they entered from the hall.

'What's going to happen now, Kester?' Ben asked, a worried frown on his brow.

'Yes,' Michael said, 'what's the sentence going to be?'

'I don't like it,' Ben said. 'I don't like this game any more.'

Kester stood for a moment without answering, then he said,

nodding towards Ben: 'Well, you've got to go to bed, that's the first thing.'

'Oh, I don't want to go to bed yet,' Ben protested.

'You've got to. Daisy went up ages ago. It's time you went too.'

'But I'm older than Daisy.'

'I know that, but it's way after eleven and long past your bedtime. Go on now.'

After a few more words of protest Ben turned to the door. 'And,' Kester said after him, 'don't wake Daisy when you go up.'

As Ben left the room Kester followed him and stood watching while he started up the stairs. Ben was tired; he moved wearily. 'I'll be up in a minute,' Kester whispered after him, 'to see that you're in bed all right. And once you're there don't come down again.'

When Ben had turned the corner onto the landing, out of sight, Kester went back into the parlour. 'Now,' he said, 'the sentence.'

'Yes, what are we going to do?' Michael said. 'What's it going to be? Though we'll have to let her go soon, won't we?'

Kester didn't answer, just looked at him.

'Won't we?' Michael said.

Kester was standing very still, tension in every line of his body; his shoulders were hunched, his hands clenched, his lips pressed into a thin line.

'She should die,' he said at last. 'For all the sorrow she's caused this family.'

'Die?'

'Yes.'

There was a long silence, then Michael said softly: 'We can't go that far, Kes. We can't. We'll have to let her go.'

Kester made no response.

'We'll have to, Kes,' Michael said. 'We'll have to let her go. We'll send her away – so that she'll never have a chance to cause any more harm.'

Long, long, silent moments went by, then Kester's shoulders drooped and he gave a deep sigh.

'All right,' he murmured, reluctant resignation in his words. 'Have it your way.'

Sitting in the chair Netta closed her eyes tightly in an effort to dispel her discomfort. Her need to urinate was becoming more and more desperate, the pressure of the fullness of her bladder almost a pain. She gritted her teeth and waited, willing the time to pass.

The seconds, the minutes, went by. And then at last the hall door was opening again and Kester was standing on the threshold. He gazed appraisingly at her for some moments then stepped into the room, closed the door quietly behind him and came towards her. Coming to a stop in front of the chair he looked down at her.

'Kester,' she said, 'untie me, please. If only for a moment. Just so that I can go to the bathroom. That's all. You can tie me up again afterwards, but please, just let me go to the loo.'

He said nothing.

'Please, Kester.'

Ignoring her pleas, he said: 'You've been found guilty. You know that.'

'Yes, yes, I know that. Please – untie me.'

'And you have to be sentenced.'

'Kester, please – '

'Be *quiet*. I told you, you'll have to wait.' He paused. 'Tell me – if the sentence of the court was – banishment – what would you do?'

'What?' She felt her head swimming slightly, and insanely the thought of Romeo came into her head. Banished from Verona. Banish-ed. 'Banishment?' she said.

'Yes.' Kester's voice was so cold. 'If that was the sentence of the court – what would you do?'

'Oh – listen – I'll go away. Of course. I'll do anything you want. Just let me go. Please, let me go.'

'It isn't what *I* want,' Kester said quickly. 'I might as well tell you that now. *I* think your sentence should be more severe, *far* more severe – but I've listened to – ' He broke off, paused, then said: 'Well – would you?'

'What? Would I what?'

He sighed with exasperation. 'Go away. Away from my father. Give up all ideas of marrying him.'

'Yes, yes, of course I would.'

'You'll have to leave the school, too.'

'Of course. I know that. Oh, yes, of course I'll go away. I would do it anyway – without your demanding it. How could I stay with your father after this – knowing how much you hate me? I could never marry him now.'

He frowned, a little taken aback. 'So banishment wouldn't really be a punishment for you. You'd go anyway. Perhaps banishment isn't enough.'

'Oh, for God's sake, Kester,' she cried out, 'haven't you done enough? You think I *want* to go away? I love your father. I wouldn't *want* to leave him. I have no choice now, though. Oh, please – haven't you put me through enough misery and humiliation already? You can't want to do more!'

'Keep your voice down,' he said sharply. 'And don't you talk to me about being put through misery and humiliation.' He bent his head to her. 'Start on that and I'll ignore what Michael says. Start on that and you'll get what you really deserve.'

She shrank from his words and the naked hate in his face. 'Oh, God,' she muttered, 'I never dreamed I could be the cause of so much hatred.'

'Well, you know now, don't you?' He almost spat the words at her. '*I* hate you. I hate you more than I've ever hated anyone in my life before. More than I ever thought it possible to hate anyone. I hate everything about you: your manner, the way you've totally beguiled my father; I hate you for all the misery you've caused; I hate your stupid, ugly face and your bright, understanding, dependable ways. I hate everything you are.' He paused. 'I don't think *any* punishment would be too terrible for you.' He continued to glare at her for a moment then took a step back. 'You'll have to write to him – my father,' he said. 'A

165

letter. We've got to have a letter to give him. If you just go off without a word he'll be bound to try to find you. We can't have that.'

He turned and left the room and Netta heard the soft sound of his footsteps on the stairs. Two minutes later he was back, carrying in his hand a writing pad, an envelope and a ball-point pen. After going on past her into the kitchen he returned with a tea tray. He stopped before her, set the tray on her lap and laid the writing pad, envelope and pen upon it.

'Think carefully about what you're going to write,' he said. His fingers moved to the cords that bound her right wrist. He raised his eyes to hers. 'And don't try anything,' he warned.

He untied the knot and Netta felt the cord loosen about her swollen wrist. As the blood surged through the veins again she almost wept with relief. He took the cord away and she raised her hand and shook it, shaking the life into it again. 'Thank you,' she breathed. 'Thank you.'

'I don't want your thanks. Just get on with it.'

'Just give me a moment, please. My hand – it's so stiff.'

'A minute or two, that's all.'

She continued to shake her hand and flex her wrist and fingers, then as the impatience grew on Kester's face she drew the opened pad nearer and took up the pen.

'I don't know what to write,' she said.

'Oh, Jesus,' he sighed. 'Just tell him that you're going. You made a mistake. You don't love him. Get on with it, for Christ's sake.'

Netta remained in silence, without moving, then after a moment she began to write:

Dear Robert,

I have had time with your absence to think things over, and I have come to the realization that we have no future together. I thought I loved you, but I was mistaken; I know that now. I have decided to go away, to leave you and the children to live your own lives. I'm sorry this letter is so brief, and I know it will come as a shock to you. It is the only way, however. Please don't try to find me or make contact with me. I shan't change my mind. I wish you good luck, always.

Yours,
Netta.

When the letter was finished Kester took it up and read it. He studied it closely for some moments then finally gave a nod. 'Okay. Now write his name on the envelope.'

She wrote on the envelope: *Robert*, and Kester took it, folded the letter, put it inside and slipped it into his shirt pocket.

'I'll give this to him when he comes back,' he said. Reaching down he picked up the cord, then took her wrist and put it back on the chair arm. 'Oh, wait – please,' Netta said. 'I thought you were going to untie me.'

He shook his head. 'Not yet. You're not getting off that easily.' Holding her wrist tightly to the chair arm he began to bind it once more. 'Besides, we haven't yet pronounced sentence on you. It has to be done properly. No, I'm afraid you'll have to wait a little while yet.'

He finished tying the knot then turned and started off across the room.

'Wait, please,' Netta said. 'Oh, please – just let me go to the bathroom.'

Without answering or even acknowledging that he had heard, Kester opened the door to the hall and left the room.

Michael was standing waiting when Kester entered the parlour.

'God,' Kester said with a shake of his head, 'she makes me want to throw up. I can't stand being in the same room with her.'

'Did she write the letter?' Michael asked.

Kester nodded, slipped the envelope from his pocket, took out the letter and handed it to Michael. Michael unfolded it and began to read.

*

167

Upstairs in the rear bedroom Daisy slowly sat up in bed and gazed across at Ben. In the dim light that filtered in she could just make out the shape of him. He didn't move. He was sleeping. She sat there for another moment or two, making up her mind, then softly and carefully crept out of bed and crossed to the door. The handle turned silently under her hand, and the next moment she was slipping through onto the landing and silently closing the door behind her.

When she reached the head of the stairs she stood quite still, listening. She could make out the occasional faint murmur of voices coming from down below, from the parlour on the left of the hall. Almost afraid to breathe, she began to make her way down the stairs, one careful step at a time.

The murmured voices grew a little louder the lower she climbed. When she at last got to the hall she put her head close to the parlour door. She could just hear the words that Kester spoke. 'For *your* sake,' she heard him say. 'That's all – for *your* sake.'

Turning from the sound she reached out to the living room door and grasped the handle.

In her chair Netta still sat with closed eyes and clenched teeth, trying to deny the pain in her bladder. The room, the house was so quiet that she could hear the creaks of the settling woodwork. To take her mind from her discomfort she had begun, in her head, to sing a song. She sang 'The Ash Grove', the song she had heard Daisy singing.

> *Down yonder green valley where streamlets meander,*
> *When twilight is fading I pensively rove,*
> *Or at the bright noontide in solitude wander*
> *Amid the dark shades of the lonely ash grove.*
> *'Twas there while the blackbird was cheerfully singing . . .*

She had come to a stop, unable to think of the next line. *'Twas there while the blackbird was cheerfully singing . . . was cheerfully singing* . . . The words wouldn't come. *'Twas there while the bla–*

As she opened her eyes the voice in her head broke off. The door was opening, and swiftly and silently Daisy was slipping into the room.

Closing the door behind her, Daisy turned, briefly put a warning finger to her lips then hurried across the room to Netta's chair.

'Daisy,' Netta breathed. 'You've come to help me, have you? Oh, you dear, wonderful child.'

'We must be very quiet,' Daisy whispered. 'Kester'll be so angry when he finds out.' She was bending to the cords that secured Netta's feet, and Netta quickly said, 'No – my hands. Free my hands first. Then I can help untie my feet.'

Quickly Daisy straightened and gave her attention to the cords at Netta's right wrist, Netta watching impatiently as the small fingers plucked ineffectually at the knot.

'Oh, hurry, hurry, please,' Netta whispered. 'Do hurry.'

'I'm trying, but it's so hard,' Daisy breathed. Her fingers were making no headway.

'Try the other wrist,' Netta said, a little sob of desperation in her voice. 'It might be easier.'

Daisy's hands moved to Netta's left wrist and began to work at the knot there. Lifting her head slightly, Netta could see the concentration in the child's face, the way her tongue protruded between her teeth and touched at her upper lip.

'Ah . . .' Daisy breathed the sound, and Netta saw that part of the knot had loosened.

'Good girl, good girl,' Netta whispered. 'Oh, Daisy, you're such a clever girl.'

And all at once a cry, part groan, part scream, rang out in the room, so sharply and so abruptly that Netta and Daisy started, gasping in sudden fright. Then as Daisy whirled about to face the door Kester launched himself across the room at her.

'You bitch! You bitch!' he screamed, his hands grabbing at her shoulders. 'You'd let her go! After all she's done, you'd let her go!'

169

As Daisy shrieked out in fear, Netta saw beyond the struggling figures the face of Michael as he appeared in the doorway and stood there, eyes wide as saucers.

'I knew you couldn't be trusted!' Kester was screaming out. 'You little Judas. You'd betray us all!' Violently he began to shake Daisy, and Netta shrieked at him, 'Stop it, Kester! Stop it! Leave her alone, for God's sake! It's not her fault. It's mine. *Mine*! Don't hurt her! Oh, *please* don't hurt her!'

And briefly her words penetrated his fury, got through to him. He froze, turning to Netta, glaring at her – and in that moment Daisy, sobbing, twisted out of his grasp and dashed across the room. A second later she was scrambling past Michael, through the hall and into the parlour.

Gesturing towards Netta, Kester rapped out to Michael, 'See to *her*! See that she's still tied up properly!' With his words he hurried across the room and into the hall.

Daisy had slammed the parlour door, but there was no way of locking it and a second later she was screaming out in terror as Kester came bursting through. She ran from him, but there was nowhere to hide.

She had never in her life been so afraid; never in her life seen him in such a fury, and in a desperate bid to shield herself she ran behind the old sofa, her cries coming from her in loud pulsing shrieks, her arms flailing to ward off his reaching, grasping hands. There was nothing she could do, though, in the face of his anger and determination, and in moments he was seizing her and dragging her out into the centre of the room.

'Bitch! Bitch! Bitch!' he screamed as he shook her, her head snapping back and forth on her slender neck. 'I'll kill you! I'll kill you for what you've done tonight!'

A few moments later Michael appeared in the doorway and stood there aghast, watching as Kester draw Daisy towards him and, with all his strength, hurled her from him across the room.

In a blur of windmill-flailing limbs, Daisy was thrown violently backwards, crashing over a small table and coming to

170

a thudding halt against the corner of a dresser. Kester, as if blind to everything, lunged after her, snatched her up and began to shake her again. '*Stop it*!' Michael shouted at him, seeing the red of the blood that smeared Daisy's cheek. 'You're hurting her!' As he spoke he felt a warm touch on his bare arm and looking down saw spots of blood there. 'You're killing her!' he yelled. 'For God's sake, Kester, you're killing her!'

And all at once Kester's movements ceased and he was standing stock still, Daisy clutched by her upper arms in his strong suntanned hands, her head lolling on her shoulders while from her open mouth a trickle of blood ran down her chin and onto the front of her nightdress. Neither of the boys spoke; the only sound in the room came from Kester's harsh breathing as he stood gasping from his exertions.

After long, long moments he spoke.

'Daisy?' His voice was gruff.

She didn't react. He spoke again.

'Daisy? *Daisy* . . .' This time there was fear in his tone. He gave her a slight shake. 'Daisy – answer me.'

She made no sound, no move. Kester lifted her higher so that her legs swung clear of the ground. She hung like a rag doll in his grasp. Then, slowly, lowering his arms, he allowed her to sink gently back onto the floor. She lay there unmoving, eyes closed. Kester looked down at her for a second then fell to his knees at her side.

'Daisy?' His hands began to move over her body, touching at her face, her limbs. He bent his head, putting his ear to her breast, listening, eyes screwed up in concentration. Then, lifting his head he gave a deep sigh of relief. 'She's all right,' he said chokingly. 'She's all right.'

He bent to her again, murmuring to her. 'Daisy . . . Oh, my darling little Daisy . . .' He lifted her to him, one hand supporting her head, holding her to his chest. Then, suddenly releasing his hand from the back of her head he held up his palm and stared with wide eyes at the blood that covered it and trickled down his arm.

'Oh, Kester,' Michael said with terrible dread in his voice, the tears springing in his eyes as he came forward, 'you've hurt her. You've hurt her badly.'

Netta, sitting in the living room, had heard clearly through the open doors Daisy's screaming, the sounds of the violence.

Now, in the silent seconds that followed, she leaned forward in the chair, breath gasping, straining to hear, her mouth wide open, tears streaming down her cheeks. Then at last she heard Michael speak, his voice trembling, 'Oh, Kester, you've hurt her. You've hurt her badly.'

A little whimpering cry sounded in the room; another, and another, and through the sounds Netta dully realized that the cries were coming from her own throat. And as the cries went on she felt the last thread of her control snap and the next moment the warm wetness of her urine was seeping down, saturating the underside of her thighs and the chair's cushion.

FOURTEEN

The two boys faced one another across Daisy's inert body. Michael had placed a cushion beneath her head, but she remained still, no movement, no merest flicker of her eyelids showing that she was coming out of her unconsciousness.

'What's happening?'

It was Ben's voice, plaintive and bewildered, and Michael looked around to see him standing in the doorway, dressed in his pyjamas, clutching the door handle and leaning into the room. 'What's happening?' Ben said again. 'I heard a lot of screaming. There was so much noise. I didn't know what was going on.'

'Go back to bed!' Snapping out the words, Kester got quickly to his feet. 'Go back upstairs this minute.'

'B-but what's happening. Daisy wasn't in her bed and I had to see what – ' Ben's words broke off as he suddenly realized that the shape on the floor, almost hidden by Michael's kneeling body, was Daisy. '*Daisy!*' he cried out, starting forward into the room.

He didn't get far. In just a moment Kester was in his path, grabbing at his shoulders, holding him. 'It's all right,' he said, softening his voice and putting a note of reassurance into his tone. 'Everything's all right.'

'But Daisy – '

'Don't worry.' Kester held him tighter. 'There's been a – an accident. A little accident. We – we were playing a game and – '

'She's hurt!' Ben cried out. 'Oh, let me see her!'

'No, no, not now. You go on to bed like a good boy. And don't worry. She'll be all right.'

Ben stood there uncertainly for a second or two, Kester's

173

hands still on his shoulders. Then he said, 'Will you bring her up to bed soon?'

'We – we'll see. I think probably she'll sleep down here tonight. But don't worry, I'll stay with her.'

After a few moments Ben allowed himself to be backed up towards the door. 'Are you sure she'll be okay?' he asked, turning, looking up into Kester's pale face.

'Yes, of course. Go on to bed now.'

Reluctantly Ben moved into the hall, followed by Kester. Ben was still looking back.

'Off you go now – quickly,' Kester's firm tone pressed him, and Ben flung one last glance at him and started up the stairs.

When Ben had turned the corner at the top of the stairs Kester turned back to the parlour door. As he did so he heard Netta's voice call his name. He stood for a moment then turned to the living room door and opened it.

'What are you yelling about?' he said.

'Daisy – ' Netta said anxiously, 'what's happened to her? She's been hurt.'

He moved towards her, glaring. 'Oh, you're giving a thought to somebody else for once in your life, are you?'

Biting back a retort she said, 'What's happened to her? She's been hurt.'

'It's nothing you need worry about.'

'Well, I *am* worried. What's happened to her?'

'She's all right.'

'If you've hurt that child, well – '

'Yes?' he said contemptuously. 'You'd do something about it, would you?' His lip curled. 'You're not in a position to do anything about anything.' He began to turn away.

'Wait, please,' Netta said. 'I heard Michael say she'd been hurt – badly hurt. Has she? I want to know.'

He turned to face her once more. 'I told you, she's *all right*. She had a little fall. She bumped her head. It's nothing. And if you yell out again you'll get the gag back on.' He raised his head, sniffing the air. 'God, this room stinks. It smells like some fucking public lavatory.' Realization came into his eyes and he

174

lowered his gaze to hers. 'Christ,' he said, 'you really are disgusting.'

He went from the living room then, back into the parlour. Michael, kneeling at Daisy's side, looked up as he entered. 'Her head,' he said, ' – it's still bleeding.'

Quickly Kester knelt down and leaned over her. 'Oh, my God,' he breathed. The pink cushion beneath her head was turning crimson with her blood. 'We must find some bandages,' he said. 'We'll have to bandage her head.'

Michael nodded. 'Yes – and we must get a doctor.'

Kester didn't answer. He got to his feet and moved back to the door. 'I'll see if I can find some bandages. She'll be all right then.'

Out in the hall Kester turned right into the ground-floor bathroom and moved at once to the medicine chest that hung on the wall. It was almost empty; a few sticking plasters and other odd things, but no bandages. Leaving the bathroom he went up the stairs to the bathroom on the first floor. No bandages there either. Turning to a cupboard he opened it and found inside some clean sheets. He put one under his arm then went into the bedroom he shared with Michael and took one of the spare blankets from the bottom of the wardrobe.

Downstairs he and Michael tore up the sheet, made a pad of a part of it, placed it at the back of Daisy's head and then wrapped it around with a bandage made from a strip of the sheet. As Kester gently moved her head Daisy gave a moan and her eyelids fluttered. Michael, watching, felt his breath catch in his throat and tears springing in his eyes again. When Kester had secured the bandage he gently picked Daisy up in his arms and laid her on the sofa while Michael took a clean cushion and placed it beneath her head. That done, Kester covered her with the blanket.

'What do we do now?' Michael asked.

Ignoring the question, Kester said, 'I didn't mean to hurt her.' He stood beside the sofa looking down at Daisy. 'She just – got me so mad. I didn't mean to hurt her. I didn't know what I was doing.'

'No – I know.' Michael paused then said: 'What are we going to do?'

Kester didn't answer.

'We must get a doctor,' Michael said.

Kester didn't look at him.

'We must,' Michael said. 'We've got to. Get a doctor.'

'We don't know any doctors round here,' Kester said.

'No, I know, but – well, we can find one all right. Netta will know how.'

Kester quickly turned to him. 'You think we're going running to her for help? You must be joking.'

'Well, we've got to do *something*.' Michael's hands were tight fists. 'We can't just leave Daisy like this.'

'She'll be all right.' Kester, tight-lipped, avoided his eyes. 'She'll come round soon. She'll be all right soon.'

'But what – what if she *doesn't* – come round?'

'She will!' Kester whispered harshly. 'For Christ's sake, of course she will! It's nothing serious. She'll be all right after a while.'

'But her head – she's been bleeding so and – '

'Yes, but that'll stop now that we've put the bandage on.' Kester suddenly raised his hands and shook them violently, distractedly, while he screwed up his eyes. 'For Christ's sake,' he said, 'don't keep on! She's going to be all right. She *will*, I tell you. Just shut up about it.'

Michael gave a little nod and sat very still, eyes fixed on Daisy.

After a moment Kester said: 'Look – you go on to bed. I'll stay down here with her. I'll look after her. It doesn't need both of us.'

'No, that's all right. I'll stay.'

'No, please – I'd rather you went to bed and left me alone with her.' Kester's tone had become softer now. 'Please . . .'

'Okay.' Michael nodded then reached out and gently touched a fingertip to Daisy's pale cheek. He turned and moved reluctantly to the door. 'You will come and get me if you need me?' he said.

176

'Yes of course.'

When Michael had gone from the room, closing the door behind him, Kester pulled one of the easy chairs nearer to the sofa. A glance at his watch told him it was almost one o'clock. He sat down in the chair, gazing at Daisy's still form.

In the still-lighted living room Netta prayed for the morning to come. It would be all right then, she kept saying to herself. It would be. Things were always different in the mornings.

And in the meantime were they going to keep her tied up? No one had been into the room for a long, long time. They seemed to have forgotten all about her. But they couldn't keep her there all night. Surely they couldn't. Kester would have to come and release her soon. There had been no sign of him for so long, though; nor any of the others.

Thoughts of Daisy preyed on her mind. What had happened to her? Was she still in the parlour? Going by the words she had overheard, the child had been hurt. She thrust the thought from her mind. Daisy would be all right. She would be. Hanging her head, Netta closed her eyes and prayed for the morning to come soon. When morning came and Kester released her she would be free to leave. And she *would* leave. Immediately. She would go at once. She didn't care how. She could find a bus that would take her to the nearest railway station or the nearest town, and if not a bus then she would hitch a lift. It didn't matter. She would walk if necessary. The only thing that mattered was to get away.

Thoughts of Daisy came back again, pressing on her mind. If Daisy was hurt? Badly hurt? But what could she do about it? Nothing. Nothing as long as she was tied up, unable to move a muscle. Once she was free, though, she could do something. She could report it to the police and they would send someone to the house with a doctor. Anyway, Robert would be returning soon. He would take everything in hand. Daisy would be all right once he was back. Robert ... Robert ... She herself would be gone by the time he returned ...

Her head ached, her limbs were stiff and sore and her mouth

177

was dry; her urine-soaked clothing and the cushion beneath her were wet and clammy. She was tempted for a moment to call out, to call Kester's name. But she couldn't summon the courage, and with her failure she suddenly realized that there would be no respite for her that night. She would remain in the chair. She dare not ask Kester for anything. She was in his hands, totally. She could do nothing but wait for the light.

After a long, long time sleep came to her, but only very fitfully, so that it seemed to her that she was for ever waking and being faced with the shock of finding herself in her situation. And when she slept she dreamed vivid dreams, like the dreams of the sick, with ever-changing shapes moving swiftly and jerkily across the screen of her unconscious mind. Sometimes in her misery she wept.

Kester sat hunched up in the chair. He didn't sleep. Most of the time he sat with his head buried in his hands; at other times he sat looking at Daisy. She didn't stir and many times he left the chair to bend over her and listen to the faint sound of her breathing. Hearing it, the relief would sweep over him like a wave and bring out the sweat on his brow.

He kept thinking of Michael's insistent words: 'We must get a doctor.' They couldn't, though. Too much had happened in the house that night to allow strangers in. And anyway, he said to himself for the hundredth time, it wasn't necessary; Daisy was going to be all right.

A long, long time went by before Daisy eventually moved. Kester was sitting with his eyes closed, head hanging low, when he heard a sound. He sat upright, his breath indrawn, and leaned towards her.

She was turning her bandaged head on the cushion, faint little moans, little mewing sounds issuing from her dry, parted lips. At once he was out of the chair and kneeling at her side. '*Daisy – Daisy* . . .' At the sound of his voice she opened her eyes and looked at him. For a moment or two there was no recognition there but then he saw it dawn, followed at once by a look of fear as memory came back.

'I'm sorry, I'm sorry,' he said quickly. 'I'm sorry, Daisy. Forgive me. I didn't mean to hurt you. Forgive me.' The tears ran down his cheeks and his voice broke on a sob. He put his arm around her, held her and laid his cheek against her own. 'Forgive me, Daisy.'

'Kester . . .'

At the breathy murmur of his name he raised his head and looked into her face. 'Yes, yes . . .'

'I – I'm cold. I'm so cold.'

Lifting up the blanket he folded it and laid its double thickness back upon her small body, tucking in the edges. 'There – you'll be warmer now. You want some water or anything?'

'No.' A pause. 'My head hurts.'

'Oh – yes, I know, baby. But you'll be all right soon. Would you like an aspirin?'

'No.'

Silence. Kester remained there on his knees, leaning over her.

After a moment she said, 'Will Daddy be back soon?'

'Yes, soon.'

'I want him to come back.'

'Don't worry; he'll be here soon.'

'I don't like this place any more. I want to go home again.'

'Yes, we shall be going soon.'

'Is it still night-time?'

'Yes, it's very late.'

'Why aren't I in bed?'

He didn't answer for a moment, then he said, 'You're all right down here for now. I shall stay with you.'

She gave a faint nod and then winced as pain shot through her head. She began to cry, the tears streaming down her cheeks and onto the pillow, her mouth gaping wide. He held her closer, his cheek next to hers once more. 'Don't cry, oh, don't cry.'

After a time her crying ceased. When he raised his head he saw that her eyes were closed and he realized that she was

179

sleeping. Slowly, slowly he released her, got up off his knees and sat back in the chair. She would be all right now.

Dawn came at last, creeping over the moor, slipping into the parlour past the undrawn curtains and slowly eclipsing the light of the single lamp that burned. In the chair Kester slept, his head on his chest.

Silently, silent as the house, the door handle turned and Michael gently eased open the door. He stood for a moment taking in the picture of Kester asleep in the chair and then came on into the room. At the sofa he bent and looked into Daisy's face.

Kester was dreaming. He was in London with Jude. They were walking along a London street and she was talking of Marie Antoinette. And suddenly he realized that the busy street was populated not with people but with wax figures. He laughed and Jude laughed with him. They were alone. She began to call his name and he turned his head from the insistent sound of her voice.

'Kester . . . Kester . . .'

And it was not Jude's voice but Michael's, and he opened his eyes to find Michael leaning over him, hands on his shoulders.

'Kester, wake up.'

'W-what's up?' He was still half asleep.

'It's Daisy.' Michael's face was deathly pale; his lips were trembling. 'Look at Daisy.'

At the words sudden remembrance flooded Kester's brain and he thrust Michael aside and leapt to his feet. Bending over the sofa he looked into Daisy's still face and then clutched at her hand as it lay curled like some tender newborn creature beside her cheek. Her fingers were cold.

Netta's head jerked up, and as she gazed through red-rimmed eyes at the brightening room around her she realized that she had been dozing. She was still there, tied to the chair; it hadn't been a dream; it was real; it was still happening. Now, though, now, it was morning. The end of it all must be very near. Kester would let her go soon.

A sound came to her, and she realized that it was some noise that had awakened her in the first place. It came again. A cry. She could hear it through the door; it came from the parlour. The cry sounded once more, louder, and a great surge of fear and horror swept over her and she closed her eyes in dread. The cry came again, again, and again, growing in volume. Kester. The cries came closer, then ceased, and then the door was opening and Kester was standing framed in the doorway, wide-eyed, wild-eyed in his distraction, tears on his cheeks.

'She's dead,' he said, his voice very low. 'Daisy – she's dead.' As he advanced into the room Michael appeared in the doorway behind him, weeping.

'No!' Netta cried. 'She can't be. No, it's not true!' The tears sprang to her eyes and ran down her cheeks. 'Daisy . . . Daisy . . . Daisy . . .' She stared at Kester. 'What did you do to her?' she cried.

'I?' Kester said harshly, incredulously, fixing Netta with piercing eyes. 'It was *you*. *You* did it. *You*. It's because of you.' He stepped closer and Netta shrank back in the chair. '*You*. You came into our lives and destroyed everything you touched. *Everything*. You destroyed every chance of my mother and father getting back together again; you poisoned for ever all our family's hopes for happiness. You've killed my mother's contentment; every hope she had remaining.' He choked on a sob. 'And now you've killed Daisy.'

He came closer still, looming over her, and Netta cowered, closing her tear-filled eyes, tense, waiting for the blow she felt must surely come. But the moment passed and she opened her eyes to see him suddenly whirl and fling himself about the room. Terror-stricken she watched as he struck out at everything that came in his path. Under the sweep of his arm the small table went flying. She saw him reach out and snatch up a book; saw it fall from his rending fingers in a shower of torn pages; saw him sweep from the mantelpiece the flowers that he had brought from the fields, heard the crash of the china vase as it struck the wall. She watched as with one single violent movement of his arm he pushed from the top of the dresser a number of books, an ashtray, a mug, the pile of pebbles that Daisy had collected on a trip to the seaside.

The rampaging destruction went on, and then, just as abruptly as it had begun, it ceased, leaving in the room only the sounds of his gasping, sobbing breaths, and Michael's weeping as he stood there, hands clenched before him.

For some moments the three occupants of the room remained like statues, and then all at once Kester moved. Slowly but very definitely, as if he had assumed the mantle of some other personality, he squared his shoulders, turned and walked towards the small table. With icy precision he lifted it and set it back on its feet. Through her tear-wet lashes Netta watched as he stepped behind it and turned to face her.

When he spoke his own tears had gone from his voice which, though trembling, was grave and measured; it was the voice she had heard during the trial – the voice of the judge.

'Prisoner at the bar,' he said, 'you have been found guilty of a most heinous crime.'

At his words Michael took a small step forward, frowning in bewilderment through his tears.

'Prisoner at the bar,' Kester repeated, 'you have been found guilty of the crime of which you have been charged. It only remains now for the court to pass sentence upon you.' His eyes were burning into hers. 'The sentence of the court is that you shall suffer the extreme penalty of the law, that you be taken to a place of execution and that there – '

'Wait a minute,' Michael said, starting forward, 'that's not what we agreed.'

'Silence!'

Kester barked out the word and Michael came to a halt. Kester turned back to Netta.

'You shall be taken to a place of execution,' he went on, 'and there you shall be put to death. And after your body be dead you shall be buried in the earth.' He paused. 'And may God have mercy upon your soul.'

At his words Netta felt a terrible chill drench her body and she screamed out at him, '*No! No!*' She shrieked out the word over and over. '*No! No! No! No! No!*' She was still screaming as Kester turned away from her, moving towards the kitchen.

FIFTEEN

In the kitchen doorway Kester turned to look back at Michael who stood, mouth agape, gazing after him.

'Go on upstairs and see that Ben is all right,' Kester said. He frowned at the piercing sound of Netta's continuing shrieking cries. 'I don't want him coming down here, is that clear?' He paused, waiting. 'Well, don't just stand there. And don't mention anything about Daisy or – anything else. I'll tell him later.'

Michael gave a hesitant nod, hovered for a moment then moved towards the hall.

Netta's loud cries faded as Michael got to the top of the stairs. In the bedroom Ben awakened to find Michael slipping into the room. 'What's happening?' Ben said. 'There's been so much screaming – so much noise. What's going on?'

'Don't worry about it,' Michael said.

'Where's Daisy?' Ben asked. 'Is she still downstairs?'

'Yes.'

Ben started out of bed.

'Where are you going?' Michael asked.

'To see her.'

'No – no, you stay where you are.'

'Oh, but – '

'No, stay here. Kester says you're to stay here.'

'But – why? I want to see Daisy.'

'Don't you go upsetting Kester. You stay where you are. You're not to come downstairs at all till Kester says you can. Now – lie down again and go back to sleep for a while. It's still early.'

Reluctantly Ben got back into bed and pulled up the covers. After a moment Michael sat on the edge of the bed. He didn't look at Ben. Ben, lying there watching Michael, thought there was something different about him. He didn't know what the difference was, but it was there. Michael just sat staring ahead of him, hands clenched in his lap.

While Michael had gone upstairs Kester had gone into the kitchen. Netta, numb, sat unmoving in the room while her sobbing faded to a faint, dry little catching of her breath.

After while there came from behind the kitchen door the chink of china and the clink of cooking utensils. A little later the smell of frying bacon drifted into the room. A few minutes afterwards the door opened and Kester came in carrying a tray which he placed on the small table. Picking up the table he set it down beside Netta's chair. Dully she noticed on the tray a plate holding bacon and two fried eggs. Beside it another plate held buttered toast. There was also a mug of coffee with milk in it. The sudden relief she felt was like a wave; she was about to be released. Yes! *Yes*! a voice in her head cried out. Everything now was going to be all right. Now her humiliation was complete; her ordeal was about to be over.

Straightening before her, Kester looked down at her and said: 'I'm going to untie your left hand so that you can eat your breakfast. But only for that purpose. If you make any attempt to free yourself you'll be tied up again – at once. Do you understand?'

Netta opened her mouth to protest. 'Oh, but I – ' She got no further.

'Do you understand?' Kester repeated. 'Do you?' In his voice and his eyes there was a terrible coldness. She had seen him in so many different moods over the past hours but his manner now was quite unfamiliar to her.

She nodded. 'Yes. Yes, I – I understand.'

He nodded in turn, then bent and deftly loosened the knot that held the cords about her left wrist. When her arm was free he gazed down at her with further warning in his eyes then turned to the tray. As she lifted her stiff, aching arm and shook the blood back into her hand she saw him take up the knife and fork and neatly cut the bacon into bite-sized pieces. That done he laid the knife down on the table and placed the tray on her lap. When it tilted slightly he took a small cushion from the sofa and inserted it beneath the tray.

'All right – now you can eat.'

He stepped away from her a few paces, seated himself on the arm of the sofa and sat watching her, waiting. After a moment or two, feeling his eyes burning into her, she took up the fork, cut into the egg and put a small portion of it into her mouth. After that she took up a slice of the toast and bit off a small piece. As she chewed, the morsel seemed to fill her mouth and she had to swallow hard to get it down. She took up the mug and sipped at the coffee. As she set the mug down her hand shook. She took up the fork again, hesitated for a second and then laid it back on the tray. If she tried to eat anything else she would choke. Making no further effort to eat, she sat there while the tears filled her eyes and spilled down her cheeks.

'Have you had enough?' Kester asked. He was rising from his seat on the sofa arm.

She couldn't answer, and as her body shook with her sobs the cushion became dislodged and slipped onto the floor. Next moment she felt the tray slipping away. She made no effort to stop it and a second later it had crashed onto the floor in a mess of spilled coffee, toast, eggs and bacon. 'I guess you've finished,' Kester said. He came to her side and took her left hand. She made no effort to struggle as he tied it to the chair arm once more. Bending, he picked up in his hands what he could of the spilt breakfast, then carried the tray out to the kitchen. A moment later he came back with a wet cloth and cleaned up the rest of the mess. Throughout it all Netta wept.

When Kester came back from the kitchen he crossed the room into the hall and she heard the sound of his footsteps as he climbed the stairs.

Ben looked around as Kester entered the bedroom. 'Can I get up now, Kes?' he asked.

Kester curtly shook his head. 'No, you stay where you are.'

Ben was about to argue the point but there was something in Kester's voice, in his face, that stopped any further word of protest.

'Okay, Mike?' Kester had crossed to Michael and stood looking down at him. 'All right?'

Michael's face was pale as he looked up. For a moment he didn't speak, then he said: '*Is* it the right thing, Kes?'

'Of course it is. You know it is.' Kester's voice was calm. 'It's the *only* thing, now.' He stretched out a hand and touched Mike's shoulder. 'Come on – brother.'

After a second Michael got up from the bed while Kester turned and started towards the door. Michael followed.

Turning in the doorway, Kester faced Ben over Michael's shoulder. 'Mikie and I have some work to do,' he said. 'And I don't want you coming downstairs until I tell you that you can.' He glanced down at the keyhole in the door. 'No key,' he murmured to Michael. Looking back at Ben again he said, 'Stay where you are until I call you, okay?'

Ben frowned. 'Can't – can't I come with you?'

'You heard me – stay where you are.'

And then they were gone, closing the door behind them, leaving him alone.

He remained in bed for a few minutes and then got out and left the bedroom to go to the bathroom. After he had urinated he opened the window and looked out. The warm sun struck at his face; the morning was bright after last night's storm. He was just about to close the window when a movement caught his eye. Leaning out he saw Kester and Michael emerge from the shed behind the garage. Kester was carrying something in his hand – the axe their father had used to split the firewood. For a brief moment Ben was about to call out, but remembering Kester's words he closed his mouth again and drew back. He watched then as his brothers started up the garden path towards the orchard. When they had gone out of sight he went back to the bedroom. Kester and Michael were planning something, as usual. And as usual he was being excluded.

He stood for several minutes of indecision and then, return-

187

ing to the bedroom, began to dress. A little while later he was creeping from the room and down the stairs.

He was aware of sounds coming from the living room as he reached the foot of the stairs. Kester and Michael were back in the house; he could hear their voices. Kester's voice had in it a tone of command; Michael's was a faint echo of it. He could hear no sound from Netta.

Slowly, silently, Ben turned the door handle, eased the door open a crack and peered into the room.

Before him, and entirely oblivious of his watching eye and listening ears, Netta and his brothers seemed to be almost motionless, like figures in a waxworks tableau. Netta, with her feet unbound and the blue scarf gagging her mouth, was bending forward in the chair. Kester, standing at her side, was reaching down behind her back. Michael stood on the other side of the chair, one restraining hand on Netta's shoulder. Through the gag Netta was making faint little crying sounds. Ben noticed that her hands were no longer tied to the arms of the chair but were behind her. The three figures remained still for further moments and then suddenly Kester moved, withdrawing his hands and straightening up.

'Okay,' he said to Netta. 'Stand up.'

Protesting with her body, Netta pressed herself back into the chair.

'Get up,' Kester said to her. *'Get up.'* When she still didn't move he put his hands on her upper arm, gripping tightly. At the same time Michael, following Kester's lead, put his hands on Netta's other arm. A few moments later she was standing between them and then was being led away across the room towards the kitchen. Her hands, Ben now saw, were bound behind her back.

Ben remained standing there for some seconds then opened the door fully and moved out into the room. Now, able to see clearly, he saw the chaos all around him. The heather was lying scattered, as were Daisy's pebbles. There were pages of a book littering the place and bits of broken china. And on the wall there were splashes of a dark red colour. Blood?

188

Crossing the room he went into the kitchen. The back kitchen door was open and peering around it he saw the three moving across the yard towards the garden path. When he thought it was safe to move, he slipped out from behind the door and crept silently along in their wake.

At a distance he followed them up the garden path and into the orchard, now, after the storm, strewn with twigs, leaves and small green apples. Neither Kester nor Michael looked behind them. Netta didn't have the opportunity. Held tightly between the two boys she was led quickly over the grass; she struggled but their hold on her was firm and she was given no chance to escape. At the far end of the orchard there was a gap in the fence, and with Kester leading the way the three of them went through into the wild, overgrown area beyond where the brambles grew thickly and the bracken stood as tall as a man. Swiftly and silently Ben scurried after them.

He came upon them again when, crawling in among the bracken, he peered out between the tall stems and saw the three of them gathered together in the centre of a small clearing. Kester was holding Netta while Michael was applying to her eyes a blindfold of some white material. Netta, faint little mewing noises issuing from behind the gag, was struggling like a person demented. Her strength was not enough, however; she could do nothing to help herself. On the rough grass in the centre of the clearing Ben saw a rough block of wood. A moment later he watched as Kester and Michael led Netta towards it. It was then that Ben saw the axe lying in the grass. Stifling a little cry of fear he clenched his eyes tightly shut and turned his head away.

This is no mere humiliation; Netta is almost sure of it now; though in her heart she continues to hope that she is wrong. In her head, however, she somehow knows that humiliation is not the purpose of her ordeal; the realization has been crystallizing in her brain ever since Kester brought her the breakfast tray. That, following his death sentence upon her, had set the new alarm bells ringing; quietly, so quietly at first, that she had

189

hardly heard them, but then growing in volume so that their sound was deafening. And now she is afraid – terribly, terribly afraid, and her fear seems to drag at her legs, her feet, and pull down her jaw. *No*! she tries to scream out, *please, please don't hurt me. Don't hurt me! Please! Please! Pleeeeeeease* . . . But she is forced down and there is the feel of sharp, spiky grass rough under her knees. She struggles but the hands that hold her are too strong for her and she is powerless against them. *Don't hurt me, don't hurt me, don't hurt me* . . . As she wildly throws her head from side to side she hears Kester's voice, cool detached: 'She's a Madame DuBarry, I'm afraid, she's no Marie Antoinette, that's for sure.' And then his hands are on her back, roughly pushing her forward, down. *No! No-no-no-no-no-no-no! Pleeeeeeeeease*! His voice comes again: 'All right, let's get it over with.' Suddenly there are hands on her hair; she can feel as it is moved from the nape of her neck; she can feel the sun upon her skin. *No-no-no-no*! The hand fumbles then at her collar, reaches over it to the front, unfastens the buttons. *Don't hurt me. Please don't hurt me. Please, please, please, please, please* . . . In her brain she continues to scream out but only muffled sounds come from her throat, and then the hands are on the back of her skull, forcing her head down. *Please, please* . . . Beneath her throat suddenly there is rough wood; now her chin hangs over the other side of it. *Please, please* . . . This can't be happening, a voice in her brain keeps repeating. *It can't*. But it is all so real. Then it is all just a continuation of their humiliation of her. It must be. In another moment the awful charade will end, must end; they will let her go and it will all be over.

There is a silence suddenly, when it seems that even the sound of the birdsong is stilled. Then comes Kester's voice, a whisper across her bent body.

'What about our clothes?'

'Our clothes? Oh, you mean . . .'

'We'd better get out of them.' Kester laid down the axe and gestured towards Netta. 'Make sure she doesn't move . . .'

As Michael placed a restraining hand on Netta's shoulders

Kester got out of his clothes, bundled them up, moved to the edge of the clearing and tossed them down in a heap. Naked, he walked back to Netta and bent over her body, placing his hands on her shoulders. 'Now you,' he said to Michael.

When Michael too was stripped bare he faced Kester across Netta's body while Kester bent and took up the axe again. Kester held the axe over Netta's neck for a second or two, fixing his aim, and then raised the axe high above his head. As he brought it down again in a swift, flashing arc, Michael closed his eyes. A split second later there came the sound of the impact, the blade biting deep into Netta's neck and cutting off abruptly the sounds of her moaning. In the same moment Michael felt the warm wetness of her blood as it sprang from her, drenching his naked skin.

SIXTEEN

When they had showered and dressed again, Kester and Michael went into the woodland behind the rear garden of the house to search for a suitable spot for the grave. Eventually Kester chose an area among the trees where the ground – still wet from last night's rainfall – was soft and didn't present too many problems. Then he and Michael went back to the garden shed and collected shovels and spades. Returning to the wood, they pulled aside the brambles, pulled up a number of plants that were in the way – bracken and rosebay willowherb – and began to dig. It took them a long time and on several occasions they stopped to rest on their spades, but at last the grave – deep, at Kester's insistence – was dug.

As they returned to the little clearing in the wild patch near the orchard fence they could hear the buzzing of the swarms of flies that had gathered. As Kester stopped beside the grotesque, bloody thing on the ground the flies rose up in a cloud.

While Michael hovered on the edge of the clearing, looking the other way, Kester gazed down at Netta's body. 'We must get something to carry it in,' he said. 'I'll get a blanket or something from the house. Stay here.' With his words he turned and headed for the house. When he returned a few minutes later with a blanket under his arm he found Michael just as he had left him, standing on the edge of the little clearing, his back to the dreadful thing lying in the grass.

'I looked in on Ben,' Kester said. 'He's still asleep. He must be tired after staying up so late last night.'

Michael said nothing.

Kester laid the blanket on the grass, called Michael to him and together they lifted Netta's body, Michael taking it by the ankles and Kester by the shoulders. As they laid it on the blanket Michael still kept his eyes averted as best he could, as he did when Kester lifted the bloody head and placed it on the body. After a moment Kester's voice came.

'Okay, lift your end of the blanket.'

When Michael turned to look he saw that the body was covered, wrapped in the blanket. Obediently he stooped to the blanket and took up one end of it.

Carefully they carried the body into the wood and laid it in the grave. Afterwards they took up their shovels and began to fill in the grave with the loose earth. When the pressed-down earth was at a level with the surrounding ground they spread the spare soil about them, scattering it among the shrubs and the trees. Afterwards Kester pulled the brambles and other plants back over the grave. He stood surveying the results of their labours. They had done their work carefully and there was no obvious sign that the ground had been disturbed. He gave a slow nod of satisfaction. 'No one will ever know,' he said. 'The weeds will grow and no one will ever discover what's underneath.'

When they had cleaned the implements and replaced them in the shed they returned to the place of execution where the flies still buzzed over the blood-soaked grass. There they did what they could to cover up the signs of what had taken place there. When they had finished Kester looked around him. 'It'll be okay,' he said. 'And I doubt if anyone ever comes here.' He looked up at the sky. 'And if there's any more rain that'll do it. There won't be a sign left after that.'

He moved then to the block, picked up the axe, took aim, swung down and split the block cleanly down the middle. He handed the axe to Michael. 'Wipe this and put it back in the shed.' He bent and picked up the wood, started off towards the gap in the orchard fence. 'I'll take this into the house. It's not all that warm. Maybe we'll have a fire.'

Michael didn't move. He was just standing there. Kester stopped, looked at him for a moment and then moved back to him.

'It's done,' he said.

Michael stared ahead of him.

'It's too late for any second thoughts,' Kester added. 'And it was the right thing to do. You know that.' He paused. 'You do, don't you?'

After a moment Michael gave a slow nod. Kester nodded his satisfaction. 'Yes, of course you do.' After a moment he said: 'And we must never, never tell.'

'No – no, of course not.' Michael breathed the words while he shrank from the thought.

'You must swear to it. We must both swear to it. We're in this together.'

'Yes . . .'

Kester let fall the wood into the grass at his feet and held out his hand. Taking Michael's free hand in his he said: 'I swear that I shall never tell a living soul.'

'Yes,' Michael said. 'Yes.'

'You must say it. Say you swear.'

'I swear it. I swear that I shall never tell a living soul.'

Ben lay beneath the bedcovers. But for his shoes he was fully dressed. 'Dad,' he murmured. He couldn't seem to stop shaking. 'Dad . . . Daddy . . .' He wanted his father to come back. Only then could everything be all right. He knew, though, that after those terrible happenings even his father's presence couldn't put it back to how it had been before. Perhaps nothing would ever be the same again.

He didn't know how long he had been lying there. It seemed like a very long time. When his brothers had done what they had done to Netta they had left her there, lying in the grass, and then gone off into the woods beyond. That was when he had come back to the house; not creeping carefully, as he had done on the outward journey, but quickly, running blindly, gasping for breath in his horror and his fear, not caring whether Kester and Michael heard or saw him.

Entering the house he had suddenly thought of Daisy; the dreadful happening with Netta had driven all thought of her from his mind. Still gasping, he ran into the hall, to the parlour

194

door. It wouldn't open; it was locked. He called out: 'Daisy. Daisy, are you in there?' There was no answer. After a while he had gone upstairs, back into the bedroom.

A little later he had heard the door open and then Kester's voice softly calling his name. He hadn't answered. After a moment Kester had closed the door and gone away again. That was a long time ago.

Now, pushing the sheet and blankets from his chin he sat up and got out of bed. Sitting on the edge of it he remained still for long moments, staring off into space. After a while he heard the sounds of voices coming from downstairs. Kester and Michael, they were back. He continued to sit there for some time and then, bending, picked up his shoes and put them on. He was tying the laces when the door opened and Kester appeared in the doorway. Ben concentrated on his shoelaces.

'Hello, Benny boy,' Kester said. 'Had a good sleep?'

'Yes, thanks.'

'You must have been tired. Well, I'm not surprised; you went to bed so late last night.'

'Yes – I know.'

Kester came a step nearer. 'Is there anything the matter?'

'No, nothing.'

'You can come on downstairs now – and I'll get you some breakfast. I'll bet you're hungry, are you?'

Ben shrugged, then nodded. 'Do you know when Dad's coming home?' he asked.

'No, I don't. We're going to phone him up and ask him after breakfast. You can come down to the post office with us if you like.'

'Okay.' Ben's fingers trembled so; he had difficulty tying the lace in his right shoe. A moment later Kester was bending before him. 'Come on, let me do it.' Kester was smiling into his face. 'What's up with you, Benny boy? Suddenly you can't tie your own shoelaces. You sure you're all right?'

Ben raised his head as Kester tied the lace. Now Kester's head was bent; Ben couldn't see his eyes.

'There you go.' Kester finished tying the lace and straightened again. He stood looking down at Ben for a moment or two, then he said: 'We've got a couple of things to tell you . . .'

'Oh . . .' Ben waited. Was it going to be about Netta?

'First of all,' Kester said, 'Netta's gone.'

'Netta? Gone?' Ben forced himself to keep looking into Kester's face. There was nothing there that he could read; Kester's eyes gazed back into his with no hint of his guilt or dishonesty.

'Yes, gone,' Kester said. 'She went late last night, while you were asleep. She left a letter for Dad.' He gave a shrug. 'Well, it was probably the best thing, don't you think?'

Ben didn't answer.

'After all,' Kester added, 'we didn't really want her with us – not for always, did we?'

Ben obediently shook his head.

'No,' Kester said, 'of course not. So – last night she decided to leave.' He put out his hand, ran his fingers through Ben's untidy hair. 'And – the other thing,' he said.

'Yes . . .?

'It's – Daisy.'

Ben stared.

'She – she's dead.'

Solemnly then, Kester told his story: they had been playing. Oh, it was late, very late, long after Ben was asleep. Daisy had come downstairs and they had played a game. And she had tripped and fallen. Ben began to cry.

'Where is she now?' he asked.

'Downstairs in the parlour.' Kester's hand fell onto Ben's shoulder. His lip quivered. 'We shall get over it in time,' he said huskily.

When Ben came downstairs he found that the room had been tidied and cleaned. There was no sign that anything untoward had ever taken place there. While Ben sat crouched on the sofa Kester and Michael went into the kitchen where they fried bacon and eggs and toasted some bread. When it was ready the three of them sat around the table. Kester and Michael ate well, but Ben, after a few mouthfuls, just picked at the food and pushed it around on his plate. 'You're not getting ill, are you?' Kester asked him.

'No, no, I'm all right. I'm fine.' To prove it, Ben forced more of the food down.

When breakfast was finished, Michael and Kester cleared away the dishes. Then, with Ben between them, they left the house, heading towards the village.

When they got to the post office they had to wait a minute or so for a woman who was using the telephone. When she came out she smiled at them and went away up the street. Followed by Michael and Ben, Kester went into the booth and dialled.

'Hello?' It was Aunt Janet's voice. Kester greeted her then asked for his father.

'He's not here right now,' his aunt said. 'But I can tell you that your grandmother's making good progress and your father will be leaving here right after lunch. He should be back with you late this afternoon.'

Kester thanked her, hung up and turned to his brothers. 'Dad's leaving after lunch,' he said. 'He'll be with us this afternoon.' He directed his gaze to Ben. 'Don't say anything to him about what's happened when he arrives. I'll find the right time to tell him.'

It was just after five when Robert drove the car into the drive and parked it near the back door of the house. Moments later as he got out he saw Kester, Michael and Ben appear from the back door. Ben ran towards him while the older boys stood still, smiling gravely. He grinned at them, 'Hello, boys,' then bent to Ben and hugged him.

With his jacket over his arm, carrying his overnight case in one hand, and with Ben clinging to the other, he moved across the yard. As he drew near them Kester and Michael turned and went on into the house. Releasing his hand from Ben's firm grasp he followed them in.

In the living room he tossed his jacket on the sofa, put down his case, sat down and let out a long, deep sigh. 'Thank God that drive's over,' he said. He smiled at the boys. 'You'll be glad to know that Nanna is doing all right. The doctor's very pleased with her, and it looks as if she's going to be okay. I shall go and see her again as soon as I get you all home.' He patted Ben's shoulder as the boy sat beside him, pressing close, then asked, looking around him, 'Where's Daisy and Netta? Are they out?'

'Yes,' Kester quickly replied.

'Ah, well,' Robert said, 'I'll make myself some tea. Unless one of you boys would like to do it for me.'

'I will.' The offer, made very swiftly, came from Michael, and he at once turned and went into the kitchen.

Robert watched him go then turned back to see Kester standing looking at him. Uncertainly, Robert smiled at him. Kester didn't smile back.

'What's going on here?' Robert asked after a moment. 'Is there something the matter?' His voice became suddenly grave. 'There is, isn't there?' He paused. 'There's something wrong. I could tell the moment I got here.'

Kester continued to gaze at him for a second or two longer, then turned to Ben. 'Ben – why don't you go outside for a while. I want to talk to Dad.'

Ben hesitated then gave a nod, rose and left the room. As the door closed behind him Robert frowned. 'What's all this about, Kester? What's happened?'

Slowly Kester moved to the other end of the sofa, sat down, then said gravely: 'Dad . . .' Suddenly there were tears in his eyes. 'You must prepare yourself for – for a terrible shock. You see – Netta's gone – and Dai– '

'*Gone*. What do you mean, Netta's *gone?*'

'She's – gone. She left. Last night.' A pause. 'She left a letter for you.'

Robert stared at him, frowning, speechless. After long moments he said, 'I see.' Then he shook his head. 'No, I don't. I don't see at all. I don't get it.' Kester took from his pocket the letter and handed it to him. Robert was about to open it, when he said suddenly: 'And Daisy? What was that about Daisy? Where is she?'

198

There was a short, hushed silence, then Kester said: 'Dad – our Daisy's dead.'

In the bathroom Robert bent over the washbasin, turned on the cold tap and splashed water over his face. Straightening, he stared at himself in the glass. His eyes were bloodshot from his weeping, the lids pink and swollen. He bent his head again, gripping the sides of the basin. He felt he would never be able to take it in. After a while he lifted his pounding head and went back into the bedroom.

He lay down on the bed. It had to be a dream, he kept saying to himself, though of course he knew that it was not. Kester had given him the key to the parlour and he had opened the door and gone in. Daisy, completely covered with the blanket, lay on the sofa. Lifting the blanket he had looked into her still face, had held her cold lifeless hand . . .

Kester had told him then how it had happened. They had been playing a game, Kester said. Daisy had fallen, tripping backwards over the rug and striking her head on the corner of the dresser. 'But why didn't you call a doctor?' Robert had asked through his tears. 'For God's sake, you could have got some help!'

'I don't know why I didn't,' Kester answered. 'I guess I panicked. And besides, it was too late. It was just too late for her; I knew that.'

Afterwards Robert had questioned Ben. 'Where were you when Daisy had her accident?' Robert had asked him, and Ben had tearfully answered that he had been upstairs in bed. 'I didn't see what happened,' he added. 'I didn't see anything, anything at all.'

Robert remained on the bed for a long time. The boys were downstairs; occasionally he could hear the murmur of their voices. Earlier Kester had brought him up a cup of tea. He had taken a few sips of it, mechanically, and then put it back on the bedside table. It stood there now, cold and forgotten.

He realized through his numbing grief that he would have to call a doctor. And then, of course, the police must be informed as well. There would have to be an inquest. *Oh, Netta*, a voice inside his head cried out, *why did you choose to go away at a time like this!*

He realized that he had kept forgetting Netta in his grief over Daisy's death, and at other times when the thought of her came to him he would thrust it aside. The letter Kester had given him he had brought upstairs where he had sat on the edge of the bed and read its contents, only half aware of the words she had written. Now, remembering it, the letter, he turned and took it up from the bedside table.

Dear Robert,

I have had time with your absence to think things over, and I have come to the realization that we have no future together. I thought I loved you, but I was mistaken; I know that now. I have decided to go away, to leave you and the children to live your own lives. I'm sorry this letter is so brief, and I know it will come as a shock to you. It is the only way, however. Please don't try to find me or make contact with me. I shan't change my mind. I wish you good luck, always.

Yours,
Netta.

He stared at her familiar handwriting for some moments and then let the letter fall from his hand. It drifted onto the floor. The letter didn't make sense. Nothing made sense any more.

After a while he picked up the letter and read it again. No, it made no sense at all. Netta just going off like that, without even waiting to see him – and leaving the children alone to fend for themselves. It was totally uncharacteristic of her behaviour and there was no accounting for it. Unless – unless the older boys had been unkind to her in some way. It was very possible. And after what she had told him over the phone . . . He thrust the worrying thoughts aside. No, no – later there would be a time to think about all that. And anyway, whatever had happened with Netta it wasn't over with her, he knew that. He would see her and everything would be all right again. It would. But he wanted her here now. *Oh, Netta, I need you.* He turned and buried his face in the pillow while the tears that he was sure had been all cried out welled up and spilled over onto the linen. *Daisy is dead, and I need you now, Netta. I need you.*

After a while, when his tears were dry once more, he sat up on the bed and looked at his watch. After seven. He had been lying there for so long. The boys would be hungry. He must do something about getting them some supper. Life had to go on. And then? After supper? Yes, the doctor had to be called. The police too . . . He shrank from the thought.

When he got downstairs he found that Kester and Michael were already preparing a meal. They had opened a tin of corned beef and a tin of beans. While the food was heating they were making toast and preparing a salad. Ben was sorting out the cutlery ready to take to the dining table. Robert stood in the kitchen for a few moments, feeling useless, till Kester said gently: 'It's all right, Dad, we can manage. You go and sit down.'

Robert left them then and went back into the living room, glad to relinquish the responsibility. After a moment or two Ben came into the dining annexe and selfconsciously set out the knives, forks and spoons. As he moved around the table Robert was vaguely aware that the boy didn't once look at him.

When they had eaten – for the most part without speaking, the occasional words pointing up the silence – Robert pushed back his chair and got to his feet.

'I have to go out,' he said. 'I have to find a doctor – and go to the police. Daisy . . . I have to report what – happened. I should have done it the moment I got in.' He moved towards the hall. 'I'll just go and have a quick wash.' In the doorway he turned back. 'Kester, I'd be glad if you and Michael could wash the dishes and see that Ben gets to bed, will you?'

Kester nodded. 'Of course, Dad. Don't worry, we'll take care of it all.'

'Thank you.'

In the bathroom Robert washed, then went into the bedroom

to change his shirt. As he stood buttoning it there came a knock and Kester opened the door and hesitantly came into the room.

'Yes?' Robert said gently. 'What is it, Kester?'

Kester crossed the room and stopped before him. 'Oh, Dad . . .' Kester sadly shook his head; the misery was clear in his eyes. 'Oh, Dad, I'm so sorry about everything. I wish – I wish I could make it all be all right again. I'd do anything if only I could – bring Daisy back.'

Robert shrugged. 'There's nothing anyone can do now. We – we've just got to – to live with it, that's all.' He stood there looking at Kester, feeling the tears pricking at his eyes again. He felt he could cry for ever. And then suddenly Kester was stepping towards him, was in his arms, and they were standing there holding one another. While his own tears flowed Robert could feel the wet of Kester's tears against his neck. 'I need you so much,' Robert said brokenly. 'I need you all more than ever now.' He kissed Kester's cheek. 'And I shall depend on you, for a while yet. I know I shall.' He drew back his head and looked down into Kester's blue, blue eyes. 'You won't let me down, will you?' He shook his head. 'No, I don't need to ask you that. I know you won't.' They stood there for some seconds longer, then, briefly tightening his hold on the boy, Robert said, 'Anyway, you go on back down and look after your brothers. I shan't be gone long.'

Kester nodded, turned away and stepped towards the door. Robert said: 'Did anything happen with Netta before she left?'

Kester turned back to face him. 'Happen? What do you mean?'

Robert shook his head. 'I just can't understand why she'd just – leave like that. With only that brief note as explanation. It's not like her. It's all so – strange.'

Kester gave a helpless shrug. 'I'm sorry. I don't know of anything.'

'When Netta phoned me yesterday she hinted at some kind of – disagreement with you. Well, more than hinted. She seemed quite upset about it.'

Kester was avoiding his eyes. 'What, exactly?'

'Well, nothing specific. But she was upset at your behaviour towards her. In fact she was so upset that she was clearly having doubts about our getting married.'

'Oh, Dad,' Kester said sorrowfully, 'it was just a little – bust-up, that's all. They happen in all families, don't they? You know that as well as I do.'

'Yes, but – '

'Believe me, it wasn't anything. Nothing for anybody to get excited about.'

Robert gave a slow nod. 'Okay. Well . . .' He shrugged. 'I guess there's nothing anybody can do about it right now, anyway. We'll sort it out later.'

When Kester had gone away Robert finished dressing and then made his way downstairs. Murmuring quietly, 'I'll be back soon,' to the boys as he passed through the kitchen, he made his way outside and across the yard to the car.

Ben came running from the house as Robert opened the car door. Stopping in his action Robert waited for Ben to come to him. Sadly he smiled down at him. 'And what does my Ben want?' he asked.

'Oh, Daddy . . .' Ben stood there, awkwardly moving from one foot to the other. 'Can I come with you?'

'Come with me?' Robert shook his head. 'Oh, I'm sorry, son, but I don't think it would be the best thing. You stay here with Kester and Michael.'

'Oh, please, let me go with you. I'll stay outside in the car. I'll sit quietly. I won't be any trouble.'

'I'm sorry, Ben.' Frowning, Robert gazed at the boy. 'Ben – what's the matter?'

Ben shook his head. 'Nothing.'

'Yes, there is. Tell me what it is.'

'No, Daddy, it's nothing.' Ben turned his head, he was avoiding Robert's eyes.

Robert said: 'What was Netta like yesterday? In the evening, do you remember?'

'Netta?'

203

'Yes. I'd like to know what happened to make her go off like that the way she did. Can you tell me?'

Again Ben shook his head, still avoiding Robert's eyes.

'Look at me, Ben.'

Ben didn't raise his head.

'Ben – look at me, please.'

Slowly Ben lifted his head, raised his tormented eyes to Robert's steady, penetrating gaze.

'Now,' Robert said, 'tell me what happened.'

Ben continued to gaze at him for a second or two, his eyes wide, then with a little cry he whirled and ran away across the yard. Robert stared after him for a few moments and then hurried in pursuit.

Ben ran up the garden path. He ran fast, but Robert caught up with him at the entrance to the orchard. Reaching out, he grasped Ben's shoulder and turned the child to face him. Ben began to cry, the tears bursting from him in great gasping sobs. 'Don't make me!' he cried out. 'Don't make me. Oh, Daddy, don't make me say! Don't! Don't!'

Robert crouched before him, put his hands gently on Ben's shoulders and drew him into his arms. 'It's all right,' he said. 'It's all right, It's all right. There's nothing to cry about. I'm here. Everything's all right. Don't cry. Don't cry.' Taking his handkerchief from his pocket he dabbed at Ben's tears while Ben clung to him, desperation in his small, plump, white-knuckled hands. After a time the boy grew calmer and just stood there, holding on to Robert while from his throat came little rhythmic sobbing sounds as he caught at his breath.

'Now,' Robert said softly, 'tell me.'

SEVENTEEN

Robert opened his eyes to find that he was lying on the grass, looking up at the sky through the twisted branches of an old apple tree. He became dully aware that around him birds were singing. Turning his head he saw a blackbird pecking about, overturning last autumn's fallen leaves. He sat up. His shirt was damp from the grass. Questions teemed in his mind – What was he doing there? How long had he been lying there? What had happened? – and even as the questions formed, the answers came as the nightmare returned.

And it was all true.

Daisy.

Netta.

It was true. It was all true.

When Ben had told him he had thought at first that the boy must be mischievously lying, or that the whole thing was some insane, macabre joke. But then realization had dawned; it was no lie; it was no cruel joke. It was true; it had really happened.

Afterwards Ben had led him through the orchard into the wild area beyond the fence and to the edge of the little clearing in its centre. There while Ben had cowered back among the bracken and the brambles Robert had stepped into the clearing and seen for himself the blood stains on the grass. Then, as full realization had come swamping him with its horror, he had fallen to his knees and, lifting his head, had cried out his protests to the grey, scurrying clouds: *No, no, no, no* . . .

A little later, when he had risen unsteadily to his feet again he saw that Ben had gone. He had made no attempt to go after him but had begun to make his own way back to the house. He had got as far as the orchard. There, coming to a stop beneath the apple tree he had staggered, his head reeling, while the clouds had descended, enclosing his mind. In an effort to save himself he had clutched at the twisted branches of the tree but his hands, without strength, had slipped off the rough bark and he had fallen in the grass.

Now, sitting in the grass, his head was pounding; there was pain, and he put up a hand and touched the bruise that had appeared there. He must have struck his head in the fall. It didn't matter. He remained sitting there for some minutes longer and then got unsteadily to his feet and walked stiffly towards the house.

Entering the living room he found Kester and Michael sitting watching television. There was no sign of Ben. Looking at the two older boys he could see at once that they knew that he knew. He stood there looking down at them as they sat side by side on the sofa, avoiding his eyes. Stepping over to the set he switched it off. Neither of the boys made any protest. He stood before them in the room's sullen silence.

'Where's Ben?' he asked. His voice was hoarse.

Michael gestured upwards. 'Upstairs. He came in and went upstairs.'

Robert nodded, then: 'I know what happened.'

The boys didn't speak.

'I know,' he said again. 'Ben told me. He saw it happen. He was in the garden. He was watching.'

They sat like stone before him. Long, long moments went by.

'Why?' he said at last. 'Oh, dear God, why? *Why?*' He hung his head. After a moment Kester spoke.

'It just – happened. I don't know how.'

Silence.

'Will you forgive us?' Michael said.

'Forgive you?' Robert stared at him, eyed wide. 'Oh, God, how can you talk about forgiveness? Don't you realize what you've done?'

'She was spoiling everything,' Kester said.

Robert blinked, wondering for a moment whether he had heard correctly. 'Spoiling? *Spoiling?*'

'She came into our lives and destroyed all our happiness. Everything was okay till she came.'

'Everything was *okay*? Do you know what you're saying?'

'Well – maybe not exactly *okay*, but we had – hope.'

'Hope? Hope of what?'

'Of being all together again. You and Jude – and us.'

'Are you serious? Did you really think that could ever happen?'

'Yes. And it could have. It *would* have. But then you met *her*. Netta. She spoiled it all. She caused so much unhappiness.'

Robert shook his head in horror and disbelief. 'So – you killed her.'

Silence. The seconds ticked by. Then Robert spoke again.

'Show me.'

'What?'

'Where she is. I – I want to see.'

After a moment the boys got up and moved past Robert towards the door. He followed them into the yard and up the garden path. From the orchard they moved through the wild, overgrown area into the wood. There Kester came to a stop.

'Here. She's here.' Briefly he pointed down at the patch of newly turned earth among the rosebay willowherb and brambles. Robert looked down and saw the signs of their digging. He stood there for a moment then slowly turned and began to walk away. His legs were heavy; he moved stiffly; he felt as if in the past hour he had aged years.

As he walked through the orchard he became aware that Kester and Michael were following a few yards behind, and suddenly, coming to a stop, he whirled to face them.

'How could you do it?' he cried out. 'How could you do it?'

They stopped, looking at him.

'You've taken away life!' he said. 'You've committed murder.' Briefly he closed his eyes in anguish as the realization struck him anew. Then he went on: 'You said Netta came into our lives and destroyed our happiness. But it wasn't Netta. It was you. Daisy is dead – and Netta is dead. And *you took their lives*.' The boys stared back at him, silent. 'You've ruined all our lives,' Robert said. 'Yours as well. And mine. Not that I care about mine any more. But it's all finished now. Nothing will ever be the way it was. Nothing. It's finished. For all of us. It's finished.'

And then Kester spoke, cried out.

'No, Dad, no, it's not!'

With his words he rushed forward and clutched at Robert's arms. 'It's not over,' he cried. 'It's not! No one has to know. No one will find out. I won't tell, and neither will Michael. And we can tell Ben too that he must never speak of it to anyone – never, for the rest of his life. And he'll be all right. He'll keep quiet. He will. It'll be all right. It *will*.'

Robert shook his arms free of Kester's grasp. He stared at him. 'Do you really think so?'

'Yes! Oh, yes!'

Michael came forward and stood at Kester's side. 'Yes, Dad,' he said. 'We can forget it. We can put it all behind us in time.'

'You could do that?' Robert continued to stare at them. 'Oh, dear God . . .'

'Dad,' Kester said, 'people make mistakes. But once they're made, then you have to go on from there. There's nothing else to do.'

'And you could do that, could you? Just go on with your lives as if nothing had happened?'

Kester shook his head. 'Dad – we've got no choice.'

'No?' Robert shook his head. 'Well, perhaps you two could go on with your lives and forget what you've done. I can't. I never will be able to. My life is finished.' They were looking at him blankly, not understanding. 'Don't you realize?' he said, 'I've lost my daughter, I've lost Netta – whom I loved – and I've lost two of my sons as well.'

'No,' Kester cried, 'you haven't lost us.'

'Of course I have. You don't think our lives can just go on as before, do you? You don't think we can continue to stay together, do you?'

Kester frowned. 'I see. You don't want us any more. I thought you loved us.'

208

'Oh, Kester!' Robert felt the tears springing to his eyes. 'It doesn't matter what *I* want, or whether I love you or not. You're my sons, and I helped make you what you are – so I must bear some of the responsibility. But that won't come into it – what I feel, what I want. I won't have any say in your futures. Don't you realize that? It won't be up to me.'

'You mean – we'll be taken away?'

Robert turned from them, hanging his head as he wept.

'Is that it?' Kester said. 'You mean we'll be taken away?'

'Yes.' Robert almost choked on the word.

'We'll go to prison – is that what you're saying?'

'Oh, God . . .' Robert lifted his hands, burying his face in them. For some moments there was only the sound of his weeping, then Kester said: 'But Dad, no one has to know. *We* won't say anything, and if *you* don't – then no one will ever know.'

Robert raised his head and turned to face them again. 'Do you really think it'll be as easy as that? Oh, Kester, how can you be so blind? For God's sake, you've read enough books on crime over the past few months. You must have learned that no one who commits a – does such a thing – gets to live happily ever after. It doesn't happen.'

'But if we all keep quiet . . .'

'Kester, people don't just – disappear. Enquiries will be made. It doesn't matter what you want, what you intend. Netta has family. Friends. They'll want to know what's happened to her. And they'll find out. They will. Believe me, they will. You think people will be content with the thought that she's just vanished from the face of the earth? Oh, Kester.'

Robert stared at them for a moment longer then turned and made his way on through the orchard, through the garden and back to the house.

Entering the living room he saw Ben standing at the window. Ben turned, looking at him with great sadness and confusion in his eyes, but saying nothing. Robert went past him towards the hall. In the doorway he turned.

'I have to be on my own for a while. I need – time to think.

Be a good boy, Ben – get yourself up to bed, will you? And tell the others the same, please. All right?'

'Yes, Daddy.'

'I'll have to go out soon, but till then – I don't want to be disturbed.'

Robert closed the door behind him and went upstairs to the bedroom. There without taking off his shoes he lay down on the bed and closed his eyes while the images tumbled over and over in his brain. In the front parlour Daisy lay dead; out in the wood, Netta.

'Where's Dad?'

Ben turned from the window at Kester's question.

'Upstairs. He said he wanted to think. He said he'll be going out soon.'

'For the doctor, I suppose,' said Michael.

'Yes,' Kester said. 'And the police.' Turning to Ben he said, 'You told him.'

'Oh, Kester, I – I had to.'

'You *had* to?'

Nervously Ben shrugged. 'I – I couldn't – couldn't help myself.'

'Yes, and now you've spoilt everything.'

Ben bent his head, the tears near the surface. 'I'm sorry. I'm sorry.'

'Sorry. What good does it do being sorry? That's not going to help anything. For Christ's sake why didn't you stay upstairs like I told you to?'

'I'm sorry.'

Kester moved away, threw himself down on the sofa. After a moment Michael sat down beside him. Ben remained standing by the window. It was almost nine, and the light was fading. Kester sighed, leaned forward and laid his head in his hands. 'I just don't know what to do,' he said miserably.

'It'll be all right,' Ben said with a trace of eagerness in his voice. 'Dad's home now. He'll make everything all right again.'

'God, listen to him,' Kester said witheringly. He raised his head and looked at Ben. 'You told,' he said, 'and nothing can make it all right now.'

'Oh, but – but he'll forgive you. You know he will.'

'Forgive us? Forgiveness has nothing to do with it. It's too late. And what we did we did partly for you.'

'For me?' Ben frowned. 'What you did – to Netta, you mean?'

'Yes.'

'Did you?' Ben's eyes opened wider. 'Why?'

'So that we could all be together, for always. You always wanted to be with Mike and me, didn't you?'

'Oh, you know I did. I *do*.'

'That's why we did it. You were always on about how we never let you join in anything. How you were always kept on the outside. And I thought you were ready to – to join us. But then you went and told.' Kester shook his head. 'I was wrong about you. I should have realized that.'

'No, no, Kester, you weren't wrong. I *am* ready. I'm sorry for what I did. I'm so sorry, truly I am. I'm sorry. I'm sorry.' Ben sat down on a chair and bent his head, fighting back the tears.

After a while Kester said to him: 'I think you'd better go on up to bed.'

'Oh, no, please. Let me stay down here with you two.'

'I told you, you're not ready. You never will be. Besides, we've got things to discuss.'

'Please – let me discuss them with you. I won't do anything wrong again.'

'No.' Kester shook his head. 'It's too late. We've got to decide what to do – and you've already proved that you're a liability.'

'I'm not. I won't be any more.' Ben moved to Kester, stood before him, hands clenched. 'I promise you. Oh, please, Kester.'

'Oh, let him stay,' Michael said. 'He's already done so much harm, what does it matter what he does now?'

Kester shrugged, turned to Michael, shutting Ben out. Ben stood there awkwardly for a moment then moved to the grandfather chair. He was about to sit down on it, when,

211

suddenly recalling its recent occupant, he moved away and sat in the overstuffed chair on the other side of the fireplace.

'Kes,' Michael said, 'what are we going to do?'

'I don't know.'

'We've got to do something.'

'I'm well aware of that.'

'What – what will happen if we do nothing?'

A shrug. 'We'll be locked away. For years.'

'Oh, God . . . Would Dad tell on us, you reckon?'

Hopelessly, Kester sighed. 'Probably. I don't think he feels he has any choice. He thinks that whatever we say the police will find out anyway.'

'Listen,' Michael said quickly, 'we could run away. We could go to London. To Jude's.'

Kester gave a disparaging nod. 'Oh, great. That's the first place they'd look. Use your head, for Christ's sake, can't you?'

'You really think he would tell on us?' Michael said after a little silence.

Kester gave a slow nod. 'Yes, I do – the more I think about it. I don't think he's strong enough *not* to – what*ever* he intends.'

'And so then – we'll go to prison.'

Kester didn't answer.

'Would it be for a long time?'

Kester nodded. 'Years. And the best years of our lives. You were there; you heard him, for Christ's sake; he told us – our lives are finished.' He sat staring ahead for a moment then said: 'And once they start investigating Netta's death they might start looking into Daisy's death as well. We've got to think of that, too.'

Ben, who had been listening intently, frowned at this. He said nothing, though, and they took no notice of him.

'But I don't believe it,' Kester went on. 'I don't believe the police would be bound to catch us. I don't think they're that smart. Look at Constance Kent, in that book I read – when she killed her stepbrother the police couldn't pin anything on her. Her father didn't give her away, yet he knew. She beat them all, the best brains of Scotland Yard. And she was a girl.'

'So it – it depends on Dad, you reckon,' Michael said.

'Yes.'

'Oh, if only we could persuade him not to say anything. It would all be okay then.'

'Yes. But I doubt very much that we can.'

Neither spoke for a long time, then Kester stood up and said, 'I'm going up to see him. Talk to him. Ask him again.' He looked across at Ben, as if suddenly remembering his presence. 'It's time you were in bed, Ben. Come on upstairs.'

'Will you see me into bed?' Ben asked, getting up from the chair.

'Yes, if you want.'

With Kester and Michael following, Ben went upstairs. When he had been to the bathroom he put on his pyjamas and got into bed. Kester and Michael stood close by. 'Now, you go to sleep,' Kester said.

'Yes.' Ben nodded, then looked at him beseechingly. 'I am sorry, Kester. For telling.'

Kester gave a little shake of his head then reached out and touched his forehead. 'It's done now, Ben. Forget it.'

Kester and Michael left him then, and moved into their own bedroom. There they sat side by side on the bed. 'I'm so tired,' Kester said. 'I was up all night.' He paused. 'I can't sleep yet, though.' He got up and walked to the door.

'Are you going to see Dad now?' Michael asked.

'Yes. I won't be long.'

As the door closed behind Kester, Michael kicked off his shoes and lay back, his head on the pillow.

Lying in the darkened room Robert heard the door open and soft footsteps entering. Kester? Yes, Kester; it sounded like Kester. He kept his eyes closed, tense, waiting. After a moment came Kester's whispered voice.

'Dad . . . ?' Pause. 'Dad . . . ?'

Robert didn't stir. He felt he never wanted to open his eyes again. He had lain there with his thoughts going over and over in his mind. Soon he would have to get up and go for the doctor

213

to report Daisy's death. He couldn't put it off much longer. He should have done it hours ago, as soon as he returned to the house. But then he had learned about Netta . . .

And that was the dilemma. What should he do about Netta's death? . . . He didn't know. He just didn't know. No matter how he wrestled with the problem, no matter how often he turned the question over in his mind he never seemed to be any nearer to a solution.

After a little while he heard Kester's footsteps receding, the door quietly closing again.

'What did he say?' Michael asked, sitting up as Kester came back into the room.

'He's asleep,' Kester said. 'I called to him a few times but he didn't answer.' He crossed the room and sat on the edge of the bed. Leaning forward he put his head in his hands. 'It wouldn't do any good anyway, I realized, even if he agrees not to say anything. I'm afraid he's too weak.' He sighed. 'We've got to do something, though. Any moment he'll be going off out. Then it'll be too late.'

'What are we going to do?'

When Kester raised his head again his mouth was pressed into a thin, straight line. His face was pale. He sat there for a few moments and then purposefully got to his feet. Another few seconds and he was at the door. As he reached out to the doorhandle his hand shook.

'Where are you going?' Michael asked.

Without answering Kester took a deep breath and stepped through the doorway, onto the landing.

Several minutes went by and then the door opened again. Michael, sitting up on the double bed, expected to see Kester appear, but instead it was Ben who slipped quietly into the room.

'What are you doing here?' Michael whispered.

'Oh, Mike, can I come and sleep with you and Kester tonight?'

'Why? Don't you like being on your own?'

214

'No.'

'God, Ben, you're such a baby.'

'No, I'm not. I'm not a baby.'

'All right, you're not.'

'Can I? Sleep here tonight?'

'Yes, okay.' Michael gave a weary nod. 'I doubt Kester'll care one way or the other.' He pulled the bedclothes aside and Ben crawled in beside him.

While Ben put his head on the pillow and closed his eyes Michael sat waiting, his eyes on the door.

Several minutes passed before Kester returned. Michael had heard no sound of his approach; he was just suddenly there, coming slowly into the room and standing there in the soft glow of the lamp. Closing the door behind him Kester leaned back against it. In his right hand he was carrying the axe. Michael looked at the axe and said in a hoarse whisper: 'What are you doing with that?'

Kester didn't answer. Then all at once his shoulders heaved and he burst into sobs. Ben opened his eyes, sat up and stared at him, aghast. *Kester – crying.* Kester's sobs, muffled in the crook of his raised left arm, continued for some time before he gradually grew calmer. When at last he spoke his voice was a pale broken whisper in the stillness of the room.

'I – I couldn't do it,' he said.

Michael stared at him.

'I tried,' Kester said. 'And it would have been so easy. He didn't hear me go in. He's lying there asleep. It would have been so easy. But – I just couldn't do it.'

Slowly, Kester moved to the bed, sat down on the edge of it and sat staring out from his stricken eyes. 'I even thought up an alibi for us,' he said. 'I thought – well, we could go away afterwards – and we could ransack the place before we leave. You know – make it look as if somebody broke in here after we'd gone. Some tramp or somebody. It happens. I've read about it in the papers, that kind of thing. And the police would think that he – he killed Dad – and Daisy, too. The tramp. They'd believe us, I know they would.' He shook his head, shrugged. 'But I couldn't bring myself to do it. I watched him lying there and I – I just couldn't do it.'

He looked down at the axe in his hand as if only just becoming aware of its existence. Carefully, he leaned it against the bedside table. 'I told myself how unhappy he had made Jude,' he said dully, 'but I still couldn't do it.' He lay back on the bed, the tears swimming in his eyes. Michael and Ben gazed down at him. 'He was right,' Kester said. 'Our lives *are* finished.' He turned his face to Michael. 'They *are*. Finished.'

'No, Kester, don't say that!' Michael clutched at Kester's arm. 'You mustn't say that.'

'It's the truth. We'll probably never see each other again after tonight. Not as we were before, anyway.' Kester's tone was resigned now. 'There'll be a trial, and then they'll put us in prison. Separate prisons.'

'No-o-o-o-o!'

Kester seemed unaware of Michael's cry. He lay looking up at the ceiling, the tears running down past his ears onto the pillow. 'It's finished. It's all finished.' Turning, he buried his face in the pillow.

Michael continued to gaze down at Kester in his anguish and then with a sob bent over him, clutching at him. Ben, on the other side of Michael, watched while the tears rose in his own eyes and spilled onto his cheeks. Their lives were ruined. Kester had said so. And it was because he, Ben, had told . . . He sat there watching his brothers as they lay together, Kester clasped in Michael's arms.

Robert was not sleeping. Still in his jeans and sweater he lay on the bed with his back to the door. He had not moved for a long time; he lay in the same position as when Kester had first come into the room. Kester had come back again since that earlier time, his feet moving so softly, as before coming to a stop beside the bed. This time, though, Kester had not spoken. Robert hadn't turned his head, hadn't opened his eyes. After long, long moments Kester had crept away again.

And now the door was opening once more. Someone coming

in. Kester again? No – Michael. Michael? No. Robert couldn't
tell; the footfalls were soft, making hardly a sound. Who was it?
Not that he cared, anyway. He didn't want to talk to anyone;
didn't want to see anyone. He didn't move. He waited for
whoever it was to call his name, but it didn't happen. There was
only the continuing silence in the room; a silence broken only
by the faint sound of breathing.

The moments went by. What was he doing – whoever it was –
just standing there, waiting? And waiting for what?

Robert sighed, hesitated another moment then opened his
eyes and turned his body towards the door.

'Ben . . .'

There was a second when the two faced one another in
complete immobility, Robert's swiftly widening eyes against
Ben's staring gaze and gaping mouth. High, high above Ben's
head the axe head hovered at the apex of its swing. Robert
made a little sound, a soft *Oh*, part shock, part hurt and, in
its fading breath, part resignation. And then the axe, with all
its weight, and all Ben's strength behind it, was swinging
down.

As the sharp corner of the blade cut deep into Robert's
temple, sending his blood up in a slashing spray, his head was
rising up off the pillow, as if he was eager to meet his end. His
head thumped back onto the pillow while his whole body
shuddered. He cried out, one sharp, rasping cry. His back
arched, his eyes, popping, feet drumming a tattoo on the
counterpane. The axe rose up again, swung down again, this
time its blade biting into Robert's cheek as his bloody head
turned on the scarlet pillow. Ben, feeling the blood splash again
on his hands, his face, lifted the axe once more.

Lying together on the bed, Michael and Kester had not even
been aware of Ben's departure. Hearing the one faint cry
coming from the direction of their father's room they had
sat up, listening. Kester had seen then that the axe was
gone.

When they went out onto the landing they met Ben emerging

217

from their father's room, the bloody axe hanging from his hand. Walking slowly, like a somnambulist, he came to a stop before them, looking up at them and offered up the axe. Kester took it from his hand.

'We *can* be together now,' Ben said. 'We shall be all right now, for always.'

When the boys were dressed they packed their belongings in cases and bags. Afterwards, while Ben sat and watched, Kester and Michael took what money they could find and then went through the house pulling out the drawers and cupboards and scattering the contents. After that Kester went around the furniture smearing the surfaces – so no one could tell whose fingers had been there, he said. The last thing he did was to go outside and smash the kitchen window.

They left the house then and walked into the village, to the telephone booth. There Kester dialled Jude's number. When she answered she sounded sleepy. 'Kester,' she said, 'you woke me up. It's almost one o'clock. Why are you calling at this hour? Is anything the matter?'

'No, nothing's the matter,' Kester said. 'Everything's all right. It's just that – we're coming home.'

'What do you mean, you're coming home?'

'We're coming home – to you.'

'Here? You're coming here? Who? You and Michael?'

'Ben as well. Dad and Daisy are – are staying on. It'll just be us, the boys.' He smiled. 'Your boys. We'll be with you this weekend after all.'

There was a little silence then Judith said with a trace of a sigh, 'Oh, dear – I'm not quite prepared.'

'What d'you mean?'

'I mean, it'll be a bit – difficult right now, I mean. Does your father know about this? Whose idea was this, anyway?'

Kester didn't answer. After a moment he slowly replaced the receiver in its rest.

'What did she say?' Ben asked him.

Kester was pushing past them, thrusting open the door. He

didn't look into their eyes. 'She's glad,' he said. 'She's very happy about it. She can't wait to see us.'

When they had left the booth the three young boys set off on the journey to London.